PRAISE FOR LICENSE TO THRILL
LILY BOLLINGER

"The prose is lively, replete with delightful repartee and a smattering of French phrases. (Trying to explain 'recently disgorged' to Cyril Ray feels akin to attempting to teach a cat to waltz.) Rosenberg's Lily is a vibrant, potent mix of grit and glitz, with her love of the land and her amusing fondness for all things James Bond. A secret multi-decade romance adds extra dash to her character. Fun, intriguing, and packed with historical tidbits."

— KIRKUS REVIEWS

"A gripping and immersive historical novel, *License to Thrill* brings the extraordinary life of Lily Bollinger vividly to life. With meticulous research and lush detail, Rebecca Rosenberg captures the courage, ingenuity, and resilience of a woman who defied war, Occupation, and tradition to protect her family's champagne legacy. Spanning World War II through the glamorous postwar decades, this unputdownable story blends history, intrigue, and unforgettable characters into a triumphant portrait of strength and perseverance."

— PATRICIA SANDS, AUTHOR OF *THE FRENCH EFFECT*

"*License to Thrill* sparkles with the elegant, immersive prose I've come to expect from Rebecca Rosenberg. With a clever nod to the glamorous world where champagne and fictional espionage intertwine, Rosenberg weaves two timelines into a sweeping historical novel that moves from the shadowed champagne caves of France to the streets of London and an ambitious American tour. Vital and effervescent as the champagnes she protects, Lily Bollinger emerges as a heroine defined by resilience, family, and vision. Rosenberg captures the devastation of war and the fragile promise of rebuilding with emotional depth and grace. This is a beautifully told story of legacy and perseverance, family and loyalty, and the courage to rebuild without compromise."

— RENEE RYAN, AUTHOR OF *THE LAST FASHION HOUSE IN PARIS*

"Another dazzling entry in Rebecca Rosenberg's Champagne Widows series, an intoxicating blend of glamour, grit, and historical intrigue. Moving effortlessly between Nazi-occupied France and the glamour of the 1960s, Rosenberg paints a rich portrait of Lily Bollinger, a visionary widow who defied tyranny, outmaneuvered her enemies, reinvented champagne, and built a legacy against all odds. An irresistible read, made even better with a glass of bubbly in hand."

— ELIZA KNIGHT, *USA TODAY* BESTSELLING AUTHOR OF *CONFESSIONS OF A GRAMMAR QUEEN*

"Could there be something in the bubbles that accounts for the charm, imagination, and sheer guts of the heroines in author Rebecca Rosenberg's exuberant *Champagne Widows* series? Or is it only Rosenberg's amazing talent for portraying these colorful women with all the wit and flourish that distinguished them in their respective eras? In Rosenberg's latest, *License to Thrill*, Lily Bollinger takes her well-earned place in the unforgettable gallery of pioneering women in the champagne trade who, believing in the power of innovation, fought their way through personal loss, financial crises, and war to leave a remarkable and enduring legacy. Terrific book club choice!

— ELIZABETH HUTCHISON BERNARD, AUTHOR OF THE AMAZON KINDLE #1 BESTSELLER *SISTERS OF CASTLE LEOD*

"Like the champagne she devotes her life to perfecting, Lily Bollinger is anything but simple. Beneath her elegance lies structure; beneath restraint, a quiet fire. She understands that success is built layer upon layer of patience, conviction, and resolve. Like her champagne, her effervescence bubbles and glitters with delicate yet demanding principles of knowing when to yield and when to hold fast, enticing the future sip by sip while rooted in past legacies."

— JANIS ROBINSON DALY, BESTSELLING AUTHOR OF *UNDER TWO FLAGS*

"What emerges is not merely the history of a champagne house, but the portrait of a woman whose life became inseparable from the fate of the vines she guarded. ... Celebration, we realize, rests upon vigilance. ... *License to Thrill: Lily Bollinger* thus transcends the boundaries of corporate biography."

— FIVE STARS, THIS HISTORICAL FICTION COMPANY

Sparkling with wit, drama, and crackling prose, this book reads more like a historical thriller than an account of a real person.
From the start, it's clear that Madame Bollinger—as well as Rosenberg—are experts on champagne. Readers learn why "swirling is not good for champagne" and how planting a crowd of vines, layered on top of one another, can create vintages with "soul."
Rosenberg's careful research and exacting details bring authenticity to Madame Bollinger's life and work. The sprawling vineyards and quiet landscapes are the book's heart and soul, leaving readers immersed in the "sweet scent of summer foliage and warm earth," and Madame Bollinger emerges as a formidable character whose hard work, determination, and wit draw audiences in—particularly when she urges her fellow growers to action against the Nazis. This is a striking examination of personal resilience set against the pull of family legacy.
Takeaway: Evocative, inspiring historical fiction of Lily Bollinger's life.

— BOOKLIFE REVIEWS

LICENSE TO THRILL
LILY BOLLINGER

A CHAMPAGNE WIDOWS NOVEL

REBECCA ROSENBERG

License to Thrill
Lily Bollinger

A Champagne Widows Novel

Rebecca Rosenberg
LION HEART PUBLISHING

All rights reserved. No part of this publication may be reproduced, stored in a retrieval system, or transmitted, in any form or by any means, electronic, mechanical, recorded, photocopied, graphic, or otherwise, without written permission author.

ISBN Numbers:
978-1-7329699-8-8 (print)
978-1-7329699-9-5 (ebook)

Library of Congress Control Number: Pending

Subjects:
FIC014000 FICTION / Historical /General
FIC044000 FICTION / Women
FIC014050 FICTION / Historical / 20th Century / World War II & Holocaust
FIC014090 FICTION / Historical / 20th Century / Post-World War II

Cover Design: TheBookDesigners
Author's Note: License to Thrill, Lily Bollinger, is a novel blending fiction and fact.

Printed in the United States of America
LION HEART PUBLISHING

ALSO BY REBECCA ROSENBERG

The Champagne Widows Novels
Madame Pommery
Champagne Widows

The Gold Digger Novels
Silver Echoes
Gold Digger: The Remarkable Baby Doe Tabor

The Secret Life of Mrs. London

Lavender Fields of America

THE PAST IS EVER PRESENT

1

LE TOUT POUR LE TOUT
THE ALL FOR THE ALL

1967, London. My Bulova reads 3:07. The cherished gold watch, a remembrance from my husband, offers no comfort as the snarled traffic holds my hired Bentley hostage. I'll be late for the *Observer* interview scheduled before the launch—the most important launch we've ever done at Champagne Bollinger. I urge the driver to accelerate, but the city's chaos trumps his skill. *Relax, Lily, old girl.* But I despise what this delay suggests about me. Being late is cavalier: it could imply carelessness, or, far worse, that I'm one of those grand French dames, perpetually late simply to make an entrance. They wouldn't dare start without the guest of honor. *They wouldn't dare.* My throat tightens with the cold knot.

I've spent twenty-eight years proving I am a true vintner, not just another "famous widow" on the label. My reputation rests on this moment: the launch of the Bollinger R.D., and I am all in. This gamble is the first time I've introduced a radical new champagne to our portfolio, combining tradition with inspiration. Will the critics and buyers even understand such a bold idea? Will they taste the revolution, or will they simply offer distant smiles, exchanging embarrassed looks between themselves? I pray I don't see a review tomorrow that mentions "a desperate attempt by an aging widow." My reputation is on the line. I haven't poured the marrow of my pride into this company just to watch it stall now. This isn't a gamble; it's evolution. We move forward, or we become the very thing the skeptics predicted: a dinosaur.

The Bentley's dignified crawl continues through London's undignified traffic, a stark reminder that even luxury is at the mercy of the city. The black leather seat is cool beneath my silk skirt. I close my eyes and inhale the scent of aged leather and my faint Diorissimo perfume for a fleeting moment of sanctuary.

I press my hand onto the cool velvet of the portfolio, seeking its comfort. My secret weapon is tucked safely inside. It should steady me, but I'm still haunted by that man on the airplane—the sharp English wit and the way he spoke of wine like poetry. How did I let him escape without a name, a card, or a lunch date?

I pull my skirt down over my lace slip. "Enough," I mutter, my French accent scolding. I won't let a pair of tempting eyes jeopardize two decades of work. Today is about Bollinger's destiny. I will not let a distraction impede me.

Outside, Carnaby Street erupts in a psychedelic swirl of noise, a kaleidoscope of clashing colors and discordant music, a world foreign to my peaceful vineyards in Aÿ, France. My fingers tighten around the velvet portfolio, a shield I wield going into battle.

With a soft purr, the Bentley glides to a final stop. The Savoy Hotel looms, its Edwardian façade a stoic, elegant sentinel against the street's chaos. I step out, offering a wry smile to the driver as I pay him. "You navigated that chaos like a saint driving through hell. You deserve a medal, truly."

The driver gives a curt nod as he assists me. "My pleasure, Madame Bollinger."

Chin high, I step directly into the surging throng of protesters. A suffocating fog of sweet marijuana, cloying patchouli, and the odor of unwashed bodies surrounds me. It is a churning sea of faded denim, frayed edges, and hand-painted signs. Their tangled, matted long hair is evidence of relentless protest against the war in Vietnam. Fury and hostility crackle in the air, a palpable static charge against my refined silks and jewels.

"Hey, hey, LBJ, how many kids did you kill today?" The fervent cry pierces the London clamor, sharp and guilt-inducing. A wave of sadness washes over me at the harsh reminder of that distant, yet tragic war. Haven't we learned enough after two world wars? So many precious lives lost.

Mr. Harrington, the Savoy manager—a man whose immaculate tailored suit looks utterly out of place against the mob, hurries forward to take my travel bag. His normally jovial face grimaces with concern. "Allow me, Madame Bollinger. Do try to keep your head down and keep walking."

The Savoy's heavy revolving doors, a slow, majestic wheel of polished brass and glass, seal out the street's chaos. The gentle, melancholic strains of Debussy's "Clair de Lune" from a string quartet drift through the marble lobby, a soothing balm against the street's clamor.

"Lively welcome, Madame Bollinger." Mr. Harrington's shoulders relax as we cross the lobby. The air here is a hushed blend of polished wood and exotic lilies.

"Indeed. I must admit, I admire their conviction."

"Perhaps if that conviction were applied to finding employment, the world might actually change." Harrington snorts, the sound of disdain sharp against the gentle background music. "Allow me to take this up with your bag?"

He reaches for the velvet portfolio.

"Oh, no. This stays with me." My grip tightens as I pull it away.

Leslie Seyd, my Mentzendorff agent, strides toward us with the assured grace of a jaguar on the hunt. A first-rate salesman vital to our UK expansion, he exudes the daring of the race car driver he is on weekends, his sharply-tailored suit moving with a flash of silk and power.

He dismisses the manager with a curt nod. "Thank you, Mr. Harrington. I'll escort Madame Bollinger to the River Room."

Leslie kisses my cheeks in *la bise*. The soothing scent of sandalwood and cedar is a sharp contrast to his tension—his jaw tight beneath his savoir-faire, a silent disapproval of my new vintage burning between us.

"Glad you arrived safely, Lily. I was ... concerned about you traveling alone."

"Says the man who races cars across the Sahara?" I laugh, a sharp, confident sound. My heels click rhythmically against the cool marble floor as we begin walking.

He frowns, a deep line etching between his eyes. "Lily, I must confess, I have serious reservations about the presentation today. This ... 'innovative' vintage of yours. Are you certain it conveys the Bollinger our buyers expect? They trust in our tradition, our established excellence."

I lower my voice so only he can hear. "The world is changing, Leslie. And if we don't evolve with it, Bollinger risks becoming a horse-drawn carriage on an interstate highway."

He regards me with a skeptical glint in his eye, shaking his head almost imperceptibly. "My staff has been working tirelessly to ensure everything is just as you wanted for this launch," he says. "Christian made sure of it."

I smile, hearing my nephew's name. "I want to see Christian before our customers arrive."

"He'll be down before it starts," Leslie assures me, his smile stretched thin as we stroll toward the River Room. His hand tightens on my arm, the tension between us a tightly wound spring. "Do not underestimate the risk, Lily. This launch is a gamble. Leave the gambling to the Baccarat table."

I sigh. "I can't say I don't love to gamble, but I would never gamble with Bollinger at stake. My new vintage is a sure bet. Trust me." His expression remains doubtful as we approach the heavy, ornately carved oak doors. "I intend to prove that Bollinger can give them the unparalleled quality they expect, but also the innovation and modernity that will make us relevant for a new era."

I detect his eyes glazing over.

I break his firm grip, my voice low and determined. "And you, Leslie, will ensure our buyers see it that way."

He opens the doors, and his jaw tightens. A rift I regret, but the course is set. My gauntlet cast.

"Your first press interview is with Mr. Finch, the wine critic from *The Observer*." Leslie avoids my gaze. "At three o'clock."

"Monsieur—no, Mr. Finch," I correct myself, the French slipping out unbidden. "Excellent." A surge of anticipation, sharp and exhilarating, courses through me. *The Observer* is respected, and Finch a long-time champion of Bollinger. His approval will be a victory on the battlefield of taste.

"Ready to make history, Lily?" Leslie asks, his voice tight, challenge in his eyes.

"Ready as I'll ever be." As I step into the River Room, my breath catches on the shimmering vista of the Thames, its slate-gray waters a silver ribbon winding through the city's heart—a panorama of history and modern life. Just like Bollinger. A surge of confidence bolsters my resolve. Rooted in the past, it must flow into the future. I will show Leslie, the critics, the world. Bollinger, born in 1829, will be reborn as the Bollinger of today.

Merde! I glance at my Bulova, the tiny diamonds and rubies catching the afternoon light—a subtle tick-tick against the frantic drumming of my pulse. Where is Mr. Finch? This launch, the culmination of years of meticulous planning and unwavering belief, hangs precariously on this interview, and he's late? I pace the River Room, the click of my Roger Vivier Pilgrim pumps staccato as a rifle shot. Afternoon sunlight, thin and golden, streams through the arched windows, illuminating the crystal chandeliers that dangle like frozen teardrops from the high ceiling. Everything is in perfect order—the pristine white linens, the gleaming silver coolers—a flawless façade masking the roiling unease within me. What if this defiant departure from tradition is a colossal mistake? The thought snaps down my spine, a sharp whip against my poise. My fingers instinctively seek the reassuring weight of the portfolio. The smooth nap offers a fleeting sense of calm. More than ever, the weight of Bollinger's legacy presses in on me like the incoming tide.

I check my watch again. Where's Finch? Other guests will be arriving soon.

The mahogany door bursts open with a violent rush of air, and in strides a fellow in a blazer the color of a bruised tangerine. The gaudy, synthetic fabric catches the light with a cheap sheen. He nearly trips over a small, velvet-covered reception chair. Sunglasses perch precariously on a prominent nose. A whirlwind of disarray, he fumbles with a pen and notepad, gasping for breath, and trailing a synthetic, overpowering cloud of Brut cologne.

"Madame Bollinger, I presume?" His strangely familiar British accent—a curious mix of strangled vowels and hard Rs—stops me in my tracks. He extends his hand. That same expressive hand that held my attention on the airplane. The wit, the wine knowledge... yet he never offered a card. My stomach plummets.

"Cyril Ray, from *The Observer*. Delighted to meet you ... formally." He flashes that infuriatingly charming grin—the one that had me intrigued on the plane.

"I was expecting Mr. Finch." My shock solidifies into cold, hard suspicion. "You're ... you're the gentleman from the plane?"

He raises a brow, a hint of amusement, and a knowing glint in his eyes. "The one and only, Madame Bollinger."

"But how is this possible?" My French accent thickens, my poise cracking under the pressure. "You were just on the plane. Discussing *Château Lafite* with such ... such insightful passion." He never once mentioned his profession. My hands tighten into fists.

A low chuckle—a smooth, seductive pour of aged cognac over ice. It feels manipulative. "Indeed. A most stimulating conversation, wouldn't you agree? As for my presence here, Mr. Finch suffered an unforeseen impediment. *The Observer* telegraphed me in Paris, and I wasn't about to miss this unique opportunity." He steps closer, holding my gaze with that same unnerving intensity. A sharp, assessing scrutiny.

"To do what, precisely?" I take a small, measured step back, gathering my composure.

"Why, to ensure your new Bollinger release receives the discerning attention it deserves, of course," he replies. "You see,

Madame, I recognized you the moment you boarded that flight. Your impeccable style, your *joie de vivre* ..."

A short, sharp laugh. "You recognized my *joie de vivre*?"

He has the courtesy to blush, a faint flush rising on his neck. "I may have overheard the stewardess when she seated you." His eyes gleam with mischief. "I thought a shared appreciation for fine wine might predispose you favorably to our interview."

"You deliberately withheld your identity." My voice escalates. "You ... you engaged in charming banter, knowing the stakes of this *Observer* review. And, good heavens, man." I flick his orange jacket sleeve disdainfully, the awful synthetic fabric rough under my manicure. "What happened to your handsome tweed jacket?"

He laughs a big, hardy laugh that echoes off the high ceiling. "I wore the tweed to interview the Rothschilds. I'm much more fashionable here in London." He strikes a jaunty pose, holding his jacket out with that damned twinkle in his eyes.

The flutter against my ribs is a furious heat—anger at my own naiveté and his audacious deception.

"When I realized who I was sitting with, I wanted to understand the real Bollinger, Madame. The woman behind the legend." His voice drops, matching the low, persistent hum of the river outside. "I wanted more than facts; I wanted a story, a connection."

"And you thought deception was the way to get that?" My words catch, a rare fracture in my resolve. "Am I some sort of game to you, Monsieur? Mr. Ray?"

"Not a game, Madame. A carefully orchestrated opportunity." His persuasive murmur creeps under my skin. "An opportunity for a deeper understanding ... and perhaps," his eyes warm with satisfaction, "for two intelligent people to explore a mutual curiosity."

My jaw clamps, my teeth scraping together. I should call security and expel this Cyril Ray from the River Room. But *The Observer's* review can make or break my new creation. He holds the key to the next chapter of Bollinger.

Cyril gestures toward the gleaming silver ice buckets, a challenging glint in his eyes. "So, are you going to pour me a taste of your new creation?" The tension in the room is thick, punctuated by the growing hum of the impatient crowd gathering outside the heavy oak doors.

My watch shows five minutes until the doors open. Habitually, my fingertip rubs the secret engraving under the gold casing: *To Lily, my love for all eternity.* Would Jacques have approved of this new champagne? Shoving down the doubt, I take the chilled bottle, its glass slick in my hand.

"I'd be delighted to have you be the first to taste my new champagne." I pour two generous flutes. "It is called Bollinger R.D."

He wipes his smudged glasses on his tangerine blazer. "Bloody funny name for a champagne, isn't it?"

"Enough talk, Mr. Ray." I tilt my head and smile, raising my flute to his. "Look. Smell. Taste."

Cyril Ray perches on a high-backed stool, his rumpled tangerine jacket a jarring note in the room. He attacks the Bollinger R.D. A violent swirl that beats the life out of the delicate bubbles. He watches them collapse against the crystal like surrendered soldiers.

"Good God." He stares at the lazy bubbles. "They seem to be retiring early, Madame Bollinger. Is this a sleepy champagne?" He meets my gaze, a challenge in his grin. "Or maybe fifteen years' aging has killed the vintage?"

I pluck the abused glass from his hand. "Swirling is not good for champagne, Monsieur Ray." I tip the contents into the spittoon—a hollow gurgle. I take a fresh flute and pour a generous measure. "You must let the bubbles do the work."

A faint flush creeps up his neck. "I have a confession to make." He stares at the floor, the first crack in his jaunty armor. "My experience is limited to the sharp, thin stuff they serve at weddings. Acid to prickle the stomach walls."

He lifts the fresh flute, his wrist beginning that familiar swirl. I raise a finger. He stops, a sheepish grin spreading across his face. He takes a hesitant first sip.

"Not half bad. Vibrant and fresh for an old wine." He offers a conspiratorial wink. "What's the trick, Madame Bollinger? Or are you not telling?"

I hold up the bottle. With a polished fingernail, I tap the dates on the label. "R.D. stands for *Récemment Dégorgé*." I let the French roll off my tongue. "Recently Disgorged. This 1952 vintage is fifteen years old, but was disgorged in 1967."

I pause, letting the information sink in. "It is the perfect paradox: a wine aged to magnificent maturity, yet with a dazzling, fresh vitality."

Cyril takes another, more thoughtful sip. His brow furrows. "Yes, well." A hint of defensiveness. "Sounds like hocus pocus."

A rueful smile plays on my lips. "Perhaps Bollinger R.D. does have a magic quality. Is that what you meant to say?"

He blinks, the scent of yeast swirling between us. He retreats to the window, holding the glass to the light as if the London sky might offer an explanation.

Trying to explain the brilliance of *Recently Disgorged* to Cyril Ray feels akin to teaching a cat to waltz.

A welcome distraction strides into the River Room. My nephew, Christian Bizot. My one true ally. He moves with effortless chic—a Pierre Cardin suit, iconic Yves Saint Laurent glasses. Christian consults the headwaiter, then turns. A warm smile.

"Tante Lily!" His embrace is a balm. "Everything looks good?" His glance sweeps the room. "Even Leslie seems to have calmed down."

My eyebrow arches toward our sales agent, hovering near the main doors. "Has he been filling your ear with doubt, too?"

Christian chuckles, eyes sparkling behind stylish frames. "You know Leslie. Fretting is his profession. He's convinced the quail eggs and caviar are too avant-garde for the British palate."

"Leslie needs a glass of R.D."

Leslie joins us, a blend of worry and forced politeness. "How did the interview go, Lily?"

I gesture toward Cyril, still contemplating his champagne by the window. "Gentlemen, Cyril Ray. The new critic from *The Observer*. Mr. Ray, my nephew, Christian Bizot, and our sales agent, Leslie Seyd."

Leslie offers a hesitant handshake to Cyril. "A pleasure, Mr. Ray. Though, forgive me, is Mr. Finch not joining us today?"

A sigh escapes my lips. "Unfortunately, he couldn't make it. But Mr. Ray is bringing a fresh perspective ... a palate unburdened by preconceived notions." I offer Cyril a pointedly encouraging smile.

Leslie steers me away, his face grave. "Lily, soft-pedal this. Leave yourself an exit plan in case it flops. Call it an experiment. A whim. Don't try to sell it as important."

A burst of flame hits my chest. Not just temper. It is the heat of years of experimentation—the final idea proving its worth. If I fail, the skeptics win. Bollinger stays predictable. Forever.

I hold my voice steady. "Enough, Leslie. You've tried to sandbag this from the start. I will present it exactly as it is: an extraordinary new release. It will elevate the Bollinger Maison. No more. No less."

"Lily, this is serious business!" He sputters, adjusting his cufflinks. "The reputation—the brand identity! The cost, Lily. All that extra aging. It will confuse people."

"Our reputation is enhanced by the extraordinary. R.D. isn't just champagne, Leslie. It changes the conversation."

Christian strides back, a harsh whisper. "Keep your voices down. Leslie, with all due respect, Tante Lily is right. Bollinger is about standards. R.D. is bold. Daring. It is exactly what the market needs."

Leslie starts to speak, but Christian cuts him off. "Imagine the buzz this Bollinger R.D. will create! Imagine the headlines: 'Bollinger Reinvents Champagne!' 'Lily Bollinger, the Visionary!'" Christian holds his gaze and raises an eyebrow.

Leslie straightens his tie. "I guess it's showtime," his voice tight, he strides toward the doors.

Christian cocks his head. A wink of unwavering confidence. I take his arm and step toward the opening doors.

"It is time, Christian. Let them see what fifteen years of patience tastes like."

I ascend the podium. The wood is cool under my fingertips—a grounding sensation. My chin is high, but the thrum of my heart is a frantic, hollow beat. I place the velvet portfolio down. My hands want to shake. I won't let them.

The spotlight is a harsh, relentless circle. It strips me bare. I meet the expectant gaze of the crowd, but my eyes snag on Cyril Ray. A jarring splash of orange. He is laughing, holding court with that effortless, unearned authority.

The sting of the flight returns—the way I let my guard down, leaning into his charm. I had trusted a stranger. He had worn a mask. I feel small, exposed under the heat of the lamps.

I take a breath. I am more than his opinion.

"Welcome, everyone! I am Lily Bollinger."

A ripple of applause breaks out, a polite and encouraging sound.

"Today, you are tasting not just a new vintage of Bollinger, but an entirely new concept for champagne."

I pause. The spotlight feels hotter now, beating down on my forehead.

"Since the time of Queen Victoria..." My voice gathers strength, the words resonating in the cavernous room. "Bollinger has been honored to hold the Royal Warrants of Appointment to the British Royal Family."

I open the velvet portfolio. The royal arms, resplendent in gold, dominate the certificates. A collective wave of respect washes over the audience.

"Granted by Queen Victoria and King George VI. These documents are more than history; they are a living promise of quality, renewed by every monarch—including Her Majesty Queen Elizabeth II."

Christian hands me the bottle. The label catches the spotlight, gleaming with the promise of what's inside. I hold it high, a beacon of everything I've risked. A fierce courage settles in.

"Bollinger R.D. represents a revolutionary approach. It is a fine vintage aged for fifteen years in our cellars, then disgorged just before release. The extended aging on its lees imparts a unique richness, while the recent disgorgement preserves a remarkable freshness. An unparalleled taste experience awaits."

Christian nods to the back. The staff glide through the room, serving the golden liquid. Crystal clinks. I raise my glass. "To our past, and our future."

The first sip is a triumph. Chilled to perfection.

My eyes flick toward Leslie; his crossed arms and rigid jaw are a wall of doubt. Then, a sharp, cynical voice cuts through from the Harrods' table.

"Can you explain what 'disgorged' means?"

Snickers ripple through the crowd. Is this man truly a buyer for Harrods, or did he wander in from the fish market?

"Thank you for the question." I steady my voice. "Disgorging is the process of removing the sediment to achieve clarity and sparkle."

Cyril Ray's clipped accent slices the air. "And this R.D., aged for so long... Dare I suggest it is a rather convenient way to use up your old stock?"

A flush of anger creeps up my neck, hot and immediate. He isn't attacking my wine; he is attacking my name. The spotlight feels like an interrogator's lamp.

"Ah, Mr. Ray, fear not." My voice drips with amusement. "Bollinger R.D. is not a dusty relic. Think of it as a vintage Rolls Royce—its iconic lines meticulously preserved, housing a breathtakingly powerful, modern engine. Timeless elegance with a contemporary heart." I offer a playful smirk. "A little rebellion is good for the soul."

"A bold claim," Cyril says, eyes narrowing. "One I'm sure your accountants are eager to see proven."

Christian joins me with a disarming smile. "Why don't we let your palates be the judge? Perhaps a taste will settle any lingering doubts."

A hush falls as the first sips are taken.

A woman in a stylish hat lets out a delighted gasp. "Oh my. It's absolutely divine!"

Cyril Ray's voice cuts through the praise. "Madame, has Bollinger secured any orders of significance yet? The trade needs assurance of immediate demand."

The silence stretches just long enough to sting. My heart beats hard in my throat. I reach down and close the velvet portfolio with a soft, decisive thud.

"That is an excellent, if pointed, question, Mr. Ray." I meet his gaze. "So far, only one order has been placed for the Recently Disgorged."

Cyril snickers, shaking his head. Leslie peers down at his polished shoes, and his sales team mimics him. The air in the room feels heavy with their secondhand embarrassment.

I feel a sudden, wild urge to giggle at their mortification. I lean into the microphone. "And what makes this order so special is that it was placed by the Royal Family—earmarking it for the official celebrations of the Investiture of the Prince of Wales this summer."

For a heartbeat, there is total silence. Then, a roar of applause and laughter erupts, shaking the very air of the River Room. I look at Cyril, whose smug expression has frozen into a mask of shock. He wanted to defeat me; instead, he handed me the crown.

Leslie, practically vibrating with relief and commercial zeal, steps up to the podium, projecting a cheerful tone. "Your Mentzendorff agents will be circulating to answer questions," he announces, "and to take orders, of course. Limited production, so get your orders in early."

Christian beckons me over to the table where Cyril Ray nurses a second glass of Bollinger R.D. He swirls the champagne in his glass, forgetting his lesson so soon? Then, a slow, grudging smile spreads across his face. "Well, well. This R.D. is growing on me."

"Tante Lily," Christian says, a smooth lilt to his voice. "Mr. Ray is intrigued by the process behind the R.D. Perhaps you would be so kind as to enlighten him further?"

Cyril's eyes, magnified by those tinted spectacles, gleam. "Perhaps at The Savoy Bar? Say, seven o'clock?"

It is a challenge. A blatant power play. He is relishing the chance to corner me, to find the crack in the armor.

"I'm sorry," I reply, feigning a polite regret. "I have dinner with the Mentzendorff staff this evening."

"Ah, what a shame." A sly smile creeps across his lips. "Especially considering our *Top Champagnes of the Year* list is coming out next week. And this... R.D... well, it just might make the cut."

The words hang in the air like a threat. The sheer arrogance of the man takes my breath away. Does he truly think he can buy my time with a list?

Christian steps in with his usual finesse. "Tante Lily, perhaps we can rearrange. After all, informing the media is of the utmost importance." He shoots me a look. *Play along. We need this.*

I let out a slow sigh, turning back to Cyril with a steely edge. "Seven o'clock it is, Mr. Ray. But I expect punctuality."

He leans close, his voice dropping to a seductive whisper. "Wouldn't miss it for the world, Madame Bollinger. This promises to be most enlightening."

Enlightening—or just another opportunity for him to admire his reflection in my glass? Determination hardens in my gut. This man, with his sharp tongue and questionable fashion, holds the power of the press in the palm of his hand.

2

LE MORT SAISIT LE VIF
THE DEAD SEIZE THE LIVING

1941, Paris. The absolute silence in our bedroom at 31 Avenue Hoche began with Jacques's final, ragged sigh. It was not a peace won, but a crushing stillness. I sat, suspended between feeling and thought. The incessant tick of the mantel clock was the only sound, and it told me another hour had slipped away.

I reached out, my fingers tracing the hollow of his temple. His skin was cold, the finality undeniable, a terrifying fact. I shivered, the chill seeping into my bones, a premonition of the endless, echoing future without Jacques.

The morning light was a trespasser, slicing through the tall draperies of our Parisian apartment. It illuminated the dust motes dancing over Jacques's still form, cruel in its indifference. Jacques had joined the French Air Force again, stirring the blood of the decorated fighter pilot he was in the Great War. But he was forced back to Paris, where a sudden illness claimed him instead of a German bullet.

I lay my cheek against his hand. Twenty years of shared life, a beautiful life that began when we were married in Saint Pierre de Chaillot in 1923, unraveling before my eyes. Jacques looked a mere shadow of the man he'd been. The pilot who chased clouds in a canvas cockpit. The hunter who smelled of pine needles and damp earth. He was a man of bone and sinew—not just silk and titles like the predictable gentlemen of my aristocratic youth. Jacques was dashing and brave, a man of work and passion, who built the Bollinger empire across Europe with his brother Edgar.

I remembered meeting him in Épernay after the Great War, standing by the fountain while the opulent soiree went on inside. He found me staring into the rows of pinot noir to the east.

"You don't care for the dancing, Mademoiselle?" A challenging smirk in his voice.

"The air is better out here, Monsieur Bollinger," I replied, meeting his gaze. "I was noticing the difference in the vine training. That's a high cordon, isn't it? Very different from the double guyot we use for Cabernet at home."

Jacques's smirk vanished, replaced by a sharp, focused curiosity. He leaned closer, the scent of the vineyard—damp earth and crushed leaves—clinging to his coat. "A Bordeaux aristocrat talking cordon training in Épernay?" His voice dropped, husky with a startling intensity. "Most guests see the celebration in the glass; you see the labor in the soil. You aren't looking at the label, Lily. You're looking at the struggle. You look at my vines and you see the heart of the Maison."

In that moment, we were two people who understood the same language. We were standing on the edge of the rest of our lives.

But now, that memory was impossibly distant. Jacques lay in this cold room in Paris, a shadow of the man by the fountain. My fingers brushed his cheek. "Oh, Jacques." My voice was a dry splinter. "How do I live without you?"

The longing for a son, my inability to give him one—this

was the constant, gnawing wound. The annual cycle of hope, doctors, and crushing failure had almost broken us. Yet his loyalty never fractured. He always insisted, "But I have you, Lily. That's all I need." A beautiful lie, perhaps. We both knew the cellars needed an heir, but we chose to believe the lie because the truth was too heavy.

When his brother, Edgar, died, the burden of Bollinger fell entirely to Jacques. I stepped up every way I could—in the office, the cellar, checking vineyards—until he came to trust my palate completely, and the cellars became our shared, passionate purpose.

I squeezed his *Chevalier de la Légion d'Honneur* ring, leaving it to be buried with him. No more quizzing me over the new vintage, no more corny jokes, no more off-key singing. Only silence, vast and absolute. My head rested on his motionless chest. Above the fireplace, the stern portrait of the founder loomed, the oil-painted eyes narrowing with a cold, silent judgment.

You have let the line end.

The accusation hung in the stagnant air, heavier than the drapes. The ghosts of Bollinger men stared down, their mouths set in hard, disapproving lines. To them, I was a temporary steward. A childless widow. An ending.

A cold, fiery resolve hardened in my chest. I'd failed to give Jacques the son he desperately wanted, the heir his family tradition demanded. By God, I'd let that failure fuel me. I would never let the Bollinger name slip away from us, not while I still drew breath. I would carry on this legacy, though I had no idea how. It was my debt to him, and my purpose.

I closed Jacques's eyelids. "I will not fail you again," I whispered, and leaned down for one last kiss.

The rhythmic, metallic strike of German jackboots on the

avenue sliced through the room. A cold, mechanical pulse. The world was moving on, and it was moving without Jacques.

Wiping the remnants of tears from my cheeks, I sat up, straightened my spine. I had to escape this choked city and return to Aÿ. I had to face the Boches, who were already seizing our champagne. Walking to the window, I flung open the heavy velvet drapes, letting the blinding sunlight engulf the room.

1942, Aÿ. Down in the freezing wine caves, the air was a tomb of damp earth and old oak. It was so cold our breath hitched in the shadows, a white mist between us as we debated the blend. Guy Adams, our *chef de cave*, and I blended and tasted wines from our different vineyards and vintages. Guy favored the heavy, traditional notes, while I went for the bright acidity of the northern slopes. We were two musicians playing different scores, and Jacques was no longer there to conduct us. Without Jacques's final call, I wasn't sure we had the right *cuvée*—and that worried me more than I cared to admit.

To complicate matters, we hadn't made wine last year. The German occupation had begun with chaos, and soldiers had ransacked our cellars. The Germans hadn't just stolen 180,000 bottles; they had looted our history. Empty racks stared back at us like hollow ribs. Without a 1940 vintage, the cellars felt like a house with the lights turned out. We'd go out of business, like so many smaller Maisons had already. And my promise to Jacques would be broken soon after it was made.

I needed the second opinion of our vineyard foreman on the new blend, but Pierre and his motley crew of old men and women were several kilometers away, pruning the vineyards of *Côte aux Enfants*.

I eyed the secondhand blue Peugeot bicycle with sheer trepidation. Pierre had brought it to me with a proud, expectant smile after the Germans confiscated the Bentley and Hotchkiss right out of my driveway. The indignity of it! 'Madame Jacques' reduced to wobbling about like a schoolchild.

"It's quite simple, Madame," Pierre had said when he'd tried to teach me. His weathered hands, gnarled from years of working the vines, steadied the bicycle as I tentatively mounted it. "Just push on the pedals and steer." Easy for him to say. He'd been cycling since he was a boy.

I, on the other hand, had never found the need. Jacques wouldn't dream of letting me risk life and limb on such a rickety contraption, but the war, and Jacques's death, had changed all that. The first lesson had ended in a heap on the gravel, my knees scraped and my dignity shredded. But the dust on my hands felt like the soil of the vineyards I was sworn to protect. *Get up, Lily.* Jacques's voice was a ghost in my ear. I gripped the handlebars with white-knuckled trepidation, determined to give it a second try. "It can't be that hard." With a silent prayer, I pushed off, shaking on the rutted dirt road. An afternoon drive with Jacques crossed my mind, the sheer, effortless speed of an automobile, another luxury I took for granted.

Finding a semblance of balance on the bike, for a fleeting second, exhilaration cut through my shame. "See?" I told myself, a shaky laugh escaping. "Not so bad."

But my self-congratulations were premature. The wind became a cold, vicious enemy, whipping past my ears and stinging my eyes with dust. I hadn't accounted for the steep grade ahead, and suddenly I was flying down a hill, the speed stealing my breath. The pedals spun uselessly, a blurring silver trap. 'Oh, merde!' I cried, squeezing my eyes shut. If the Boches didn't kill me, this rusted Peugeot certainly would.

A sickening lurch and the front wheel skidded on a patch of mud, tossing me aside. I landed with a thud, the air driven from my lungs. "*Mon Dieu!*" I gasped, spitting out a mouthful of grit. The taste of bitter earth coated my tongue. Mud splattered my skirt, clinging to the fine fabric like a shameful second skin. I pushed myself up, my muscles protesting. "Pull yourself together, Lily. You're the patronne of Bollinger."

Jacques would have found this hilarious. I could almost hear his booming laugh echoing across the valley. But the only sound was the wind whistling through the dormant vines. I was alone. And I had to keep going.

I remounted the bicycle, this time with more caution, and continued on my way. It was a slow, arduous journey. The rutted dirt path seemed endless beneath the leaden sky, each turn of the pedal a sharp ache in my thighs. I rounded a final, dusty bend, and the first thing I saw was the familiar, stark geometry of the pruned vines of *Côte aux Enfants*. It was late afternoon when I finally reached my destination: the vineyard where old Pierre and his meager crew were working.

"Ah, Madame Jacques," Pierre greeted me, his eyes twinkling with amusement. "I see you've had an adventure."

I couldn't help but offer a shaky, dirt-streaked smile. "A thoroughly undignified adventure, Pierre." I tried to brush off a layer of dried mud that clung to my skirt. "The kind one only has after one's Bentley has been rerouted to Berlin."

Pierre chuckled and waved me over with his weary arm, thin and trembling slightly. "Come, come. Let me work while we talk, the light is leaving us." The vineyards, their bare branches reaching like skeletal fingers, seemed to be searching for the hands of the boys who should have been here. The sons at war. The sons I never had.

"The Guyot cut?" I tried to find my footing in the rows.

Pierre didn't look up, his secateurs flashing as he clipped a cane. "Always, Madame. We need the long canes for this pinot noir. See here? The fruitful nodes are farther out. I leave the renewal spur—two buds for next year—and let the rest go."

I looked at the bare, dormant canes, thinking not just of the absent wine, but of the absent young men—the boys who should have been pruning. They were at war, and their labor was lost. I had no children to inherit this task, no sons or daughters to continue Jacques's work, and the isolation I felt was deeper than grief. Yet, I felt a fierce gratitude for these loyal, aging hands who had returned to this impossible work. The continuation of everything Jacques had built rested solely and entirely on my shoulders.

"It's not the same without Jacques, is it?" Pierre said with a raspy voice, as if his throat ached.

I shook my head, tears pricking my eyes. "No, Pierre. It's not." I swallowed the lump in my throat. "That's why I've come. Jacques always worked with you on the blend, and since he's gone, I need your input."

"You don't need my help. Jacques always relied on you to make the final call. You can do it, Madame Jacques."

Pierre's sallow complexion and rheumy eyes exposed his fatigue. Seeing the tremor in his hands, I suddenly felt the weight of my own selfishness. I was asking a man who could barely stand to help me carry the Maison.

I forced a lightness into my voice, a brittle mask over my despair. "Of course I can. Guy and I will manage the *cuvée*."

A slow, weary grin spread across his face. "Never had any doubt, Madame." He returned to cutting canes, his gnarled hands wrapped around the *secateurs*.

My mind raced, calculating the labor required for the harvest, assemblage, the bottling. A daunting task, but a necessary one. A wave of exhaustion overwhelmed me. My legs throbbed from the unaccustomed exertion, and the cold seemed to seep into my very bones. "Pierre, could I ride back in the wagon with you and the men? I'm sore from my tumble."

He chuckled, a dry, rattling sound. "Of course, Madame. Any time." He helped me load the bicycle into the back of the wagon, his movements slow and deliberate, as if each one pained him.

Later, I rode back to Aÿ with the *vignerons*, their weathered faces illuminated by the dim glow of the lantern. They shared stories of their sons and brothers lost to the war, the lack of food and fuel they faced under occupation, the constant fear and uncertainty that shadowed their lives. I listened, my heart aching for their pain, my resolve strengthening with each tale of resilience, each act of quiet defiance.

We reached the house in the deepening dark. Though the wagon was cold, their shared stories had warmed the air. But as the silhouette of the house loomed, the worry returned to their faces. It wasn't natural, this life under the scrutiny of invaders.

The oldest *vigneron* leaned toward me, his eyes red-rimmed and filled with fear. "Madame Jacques," his whisper sounded reedy and weak. "With Monsieur Jacques gone, will there be work for us after the war?" The question hit me colder than the March wind. Who could know our shared fate under the suffocating German occupation? But their faces were drawn with worry and hopelessness, a sight that broke my heart.

I reached across and gripped his calloused hand. "Bollinger has been here more than a century." My breath puffed white in the freezing air, a steady, visible proof of life. "I promise you, it will endure for another. We will survive this together. We will rebuild, and we will continue making the finest champagne we're capable of." My eyes touched each of theirs, offering a solemn promise, hope in the face of despair.

Jacques, give me strength.

The days of being Jacques's elegant wife were finished. My muddy shirt was the uniform of the *patronne*. These were my people. The heart and soul of the Maison. I would not let them down.

3

SE FAIRE ROULER DANS LA FARINE

TO BE ROLLED IN THE FLOUR

1967, London. The Savoy Bar hums with the clink of glasses and the whispered secrets of forgotten rendezvous. In a quiet corner, Cyril Ray reads a paperback that looks remarkably like the latest James Bond novel I just bought.

He rises as I approach the plush velvet booth, extending a palm to help me settle in. His impeccable manners are a far cry from the drunken, orange buffoon he played at this afternoon's R.D. launch. His sharply tailored charcoal gray suit over a black turtleneck emphasizes a lean build I hadn't fully appreciated before. Horn-rimmed glasses perch on his nose, giving him an air of worldly intelligence, once again, the intriguing gentleman I'd found myself seated next to on the plane this morning.

"This look suits you, Cyril." I dare to expose my feelings on his fashion taste. "It's a magnificent improvement over the tangerine jacket."

He tilts his head and smiles a rueful smile. "That look was intended to project a younger image among the London press."

His gaze lingers on mine. "Tonight, I am appealing to your sophistication."

My gaze falls upon the cover of his paperback, confirming my suspicion: *Octopussy*. A shared taste for Bond? His *Observer* review of Bollinger R.D. is crucial, and perhaps this surprising common ground bodes well. He's a chameleon, I thought, perhaps open-minded and teachable.

"Martini?" I nod to his paperback on the seat. "Shaken, not stirred, of course?"

A slow smile spreads across Cyril's lips, something akin to delight in his expression. "Of course, Madame Bollinger. Only the proper preparation for such an intriguing encounter." He leans closer, his gaze holding a newfound warmth in the depths. "And perhaps, something to line our stomachs? Cheeseburgers?"

I raise a questioning eyebrow, a spark of amusement dancing within me. "Cheeseburgers, Monsieur Ray? After the day's delicacies?"

He gives a conspiratorial wink, "Even 007 has been known to indulge in more, shall we say, grounded fare between missions."

With our order placed, the paperback lies between us on the plush velvet. "So," I swirl the olive in my martini. "Your thoughts on *Octopussy*?"

A broad smile spreads across Cyril's face. "Ah, Madame Bollinger, a woman of discerning taste in both champagne and espionage! I confess, I've been eagerly anticipating this release! The setting in Jamaica, the exploration of Bond's past … What is your impression of *Octopussy* herself? Her connection to Bond's father is certainly fascinating."

"A complex and alluring woman, to be sure," I reply. "A circus owner with a hidden story. Though I find her sudden shift in allegiance somewhat too convenient. And that treasure hunt in the haunted ketch?" I pick up my cocktail. "It makes one yearn for a well-made martini."

"Cheers to that." Cyril clinks my glass and laughs, a warm, inviting sound. "But you can't deny the allure of her independence, her dangerous charm. And the thrill of the chase for the treasure, the suspense. It's remarkable." He shakes his head in delighted disbelief. "I never would have guessed this shared passion between us." His face alights with fresh interest as he sips his martini.. "Best Bond girl?"

"Tatiana Romanova," A thrill running through me. "Intelligence and intrigue, a potent combination."

He nods, a thoughtful look on his face. "A solid choice! Though I've always had a soft spot for Honey Ryder." He growls playfully. "Something about her ... primal attraction."

I chuckle. "But can she hold a candle to Vesper Lynd's tragic allure?"

"Ah, Vesper," Cyril grabs his chest and sighs. "A heartbreaker, to be sure. But for sheer resilience, Tracy Bond takes the crown."

A smile tugs at my lips. "But can we both agree that Pussy Galore is a dreadful name?"

He bursts out laughing. "Absolutely dreadful! Though, I must confess, it does have a certain . . . *je ne sais quoi*."

"Perhaps that's why it's so memorable." My eyes narrow mischievously. "One certainly doesn't forget a name like Pussy Galore in a hurry."

And so it goes, our conversation flowing effortlessly, fueled by shared passion, just as our talk of wine on the airplane. More martinis arrive, sent with a thumbs up from Christian and Leslie at the bar, obviously keeping an eye on me. Thank goodness for the delicious cheeseburgers, the rich aroma adding to the atmosphere.

We've graduated to a first-name basis. Cyril is a stimulating conversationalist; I'll give him that. And undeniably attractive, with his tousled hair and roguish smile.

He leans closer, his voice dropping to a whisper. "You know, Lily," his breath warm against my ear, "you're not at all what I expected."

A quiver of desire runs down my spine, too long forgotten. "Oh?" I raise an eyebrow, intrigued. "And what did you expect?"

"A grand dame," he admits, "aloof and untouchable. Encased in an impenetrable fortress of wealth and privilege." His gaze searches mine. "But you ... you're fire and wit, intelligence and passion." His thumb brushes against the back of my hand, warm and lingering.

My breath catches in my throat, and for a moment, I entertain a fantasy of a passionate encounter. Reality crashes back in, a cold wave against my heated skin. I am sixty-seven; Cyril must be a decade younger.

"Cyril," I say gently, withdrawing my hand. "You're charming, and I've enjoyed our conversation immensely. But I'm not a woman who indulges in, hmm, complications. My focus is on Bollinger, and I prefer to keep my business ... strictly business."

He doesn't pull his hand away and amusement flickers in his eyes. "Ah, Madame Bollinger," his voice laced with intrigue, "What happen to *l'art de la séduction*? I assumed that all French women were open to a little liaison."

I'm taken aback. Was I truly complicit? If so, this ends now. "Monsieur Ray," I revert to his last name. "Perhaps we could get back to business. What did you end up thinking about Bollinger R.D.?"

"Back to business?" He raises his hands in mock surrender. "Forgive me, Madame Bollinger. I seem to have misjudged you."

I wipe my mouth with the napkin, gathering my things.

But he reaches across the table, his hand clasping mine. "I was just trying to get to know the real you, the woman behind the legend." He leans closer, his breath a warm, suggestive whisper against my cheek. "Lily, you are a complex, extraordinary blend, a depth of character far surpassing anything I could have expected." He shifts imperceptibly, his lips brushing mine with a deliberate, testing warmth.

I inhale sharply, leaning into the kiss. A forbidden warmth spreads through my chest. The moment intoxicates me; the desire is undeniable.

But my will snaps back. My hand gently presses against his chest, pushing him back a firm, steady inch. "Cyril, I appreciate the compliment, but I'm not interested." It is part lie, part professional decorum, and part coquette.

"I don't believe you." A spark of frustration crosses his face. "You must feel it too? The connection, the spark?" He runs his hand through his tousled hair. "I thought we had something special."

We sit in silence, the air simmering with unmet passion.

Finally, he clears his throat. "Well," a touch of awkwardness in his voice, "perhaps I should let you get back to your less complicated life."

"Perhaps." I felt a surprising hint of disappointment.

He leans back, another angle lighting his face. "I just finished writing a book about the Rothschilds and their wine empire. Quite the formidable family. Though, during our interviews, they did mention considering branching out. Perhaps opening a Champagne Maison of their own."

The mention of the Rothschilds encroaching on Bollinger territory hits me like a kick to the ribs. "They'd have to move to Champagne to do that, wouldn't they?" My voice laced with warning.

He chuckles, a glint of mischief in his eyes. "Ah, you of all people should know that rules are made to be broken." His voice drops to a whisper, "I recall you spearheaded that rather spirited campaign against the 'Spanish Champagne' a few years back. Perhaps you could enlighten me on that court case?"

What's he driving at? Suspicion crosses my mind, cold and sharp. "Perhaps another time, Mr. Ray. I'm afraid my schedule is rather full at the moment."

He takes my hand and kisses it, his gaze holding mine. "Another time, then."

I scoot out of the booth and stand, but he doesn't release my wrist. "You don't give up easily, do you?"

A smug smile flashes. "Perseverance is a virtue, Lily. Especially when pursuing a worthy subject."

Pointedly, I extract my hand and clasp my handbag—a decisive snap. "Your persistence is admirable, Monsieur Ray. But I'm not easily persuaded."

As I make my way through the dimly lit bar, I have to admit this encounter with Cyril Ray has tickled me. Such a complex creature, a blend of arrogance and charm, intelligence and deception. "You still got it, old girl," I mutter to myself.

Upstairs, turning the key to my room, I see my copy of *Octopussy* nestled on my bedside table. James Bond, complex, captivating, and utterly safe, is a far better choice than Monsieur Ray for tonight.

The next day, the polished brass of the Savoy's elevator doors slide open, and I practically skip across the ornate carpets of the lobby. The very air, usually a stuffy blend of old money and expensive liquor, seems to vibrate with fresh anticipation. I am eager to see how Cyril wrote about the launch of R.D. Did he capture the effervescence of the party, the very *joie de vivre* that Bollinger embodied? Did he mention our evening, the shared laughter, the surprising thrill of discovering a mutual love for James Bond? A girlish flutter, a warmth spreads through my chest. I haven't felt this lighthearted in years.

But as I purchase my copy of *The Observer* at the newsstand, the crisp, inky scent of the newsprint suddenly smells strangely sharp. The newspaper crinkles, a harsh, grating sound, between my suddenly clammy fingers. The headline screams, stark and malicious: "Champagne Elitism: A Day with the Bollinger Heiress." My stomach lurches, a wave of nausea making the elegant chandeliers above blur and tilt, their crystal prisms mocking me as they sway.

Heiress? The word slaps me in the face. The audacity of that man!

Cyril's piece isn't a balanced critique; it is a vitriolic assault, a calculated takedown of me and the event itself. He paints me as a frivolous, out-of-touch heiress, a modern-day Marie Antoinette, sipping champagne with callous disregard for the 'real world' of the working class. A wave of bitter anger, hot and sharp, courses through me. And, Cyril, the self-proclaimed socialist who requires a steady diet of martinis and cheeseburgers to sustain his outrage. He had spent the evening indulging, sharing laughter and confidences, only to turn around and condemn my lifestyle in print. Was this his plan all along? A chilling suspicion snakes through my mind. He had deliberately played the charming companion, the attentive listener, only to expose me as a symbol of bourgeois decadence. All that charm and those relentless martinis and cheeseburgers were a calculated ruse, a cold, calculated act of revenge for a perceived slight to his ego. He wanted more than conversation; I hadn't accepted his invitation to bed, and this public attack was his retaliation.

And then I see he used my famous quote, plastered across the page, my own words, twisted and weaponized against me:

> "I only drink champagne when I'm happy,
> and when I'm sad.
> Sometimes I drink it when I'm alone.
> When I have company, I consider it obligatory.
> I trifle with it if I am not hungry, and drink it when I am.
> Otherwise, I never touch it.
> Unless I'm thirsty."
>
> -Lily Bollinger

The lighthearted phrase, a piece of our family lore, stripped of its cheerful, tongue-in-cheek intention and fairly dripping with his acidic interpretation.

And to think he had the gall to suggest writing a book about Bollinger! After this hatchet job? One shudders to imagine the dedication: "To the bourgeoisie, whose outrageously expensive champagne fueled my moral outrage." Over my dead body!

The implications of his article begin to spiral out of control in my mind, each one a disastrous blow to Bollinger. Christian's inspired work to expand our markets ... Leslie's carefully cultivated relationships with distributors ... Mentzendorff's tireless salesforce ... all potentially undermined by this, this journalistic assassination.

Humiliation washes over me, hot and stinging, burning in my cheeks, but then, just as quickly, it is replaced by a cold, controlled rage. Who was he, after all? A nobody, a two-bit writer trying to make a name for himself by exploiting me and my family's legacy, no better than the paparazzi who hounded celebrities or the gossip columnists who thrived on scandal.

Utterly despicable! I fume, my blood pressure thrumming in my ears, imagining him probably gloating over his coffee, congratulating himself on his clever exposé.

I crumple the tabloid in my fists, the thin paper offering little resistance to my fury. With a disdainful flick of my wrist, I toss it into a nearby bin, the rustling sound a satisfying expulsion of my anger. I have far more important things to do than waste another thought on Cyril Ray and his treacherous pen.

But as I stride out of the hotel, my head held high, I can't help but feel a lingering sense of personal violation. The excitement and connection of last night, the laughter and shared confidences, seem like a cruel illusion, a carefully constructed trap.

A vengeful voice inside me screams for immediate retaliation, for a public evisceration of that two-faced scoundrel. But I can't indulge in this anger. I will not give him the satisfaction. I will rise above it. Bollinger has weathered far worse storms than this, and we will emerge from this one stronger than ever. Cyril Ray? He will be nothing but a fruit fly buzzing around the crushed grapes during harvest.

I throw my shoulders back, the cold certainty of my purpose snapping into place. There is no time for such cheap distractions. I look toward the future, toward the generations of family waiting to carry on this name. My duty is to the promise I made to Jacques nearly three decades ago when I took the reins: to protect this Maison. Bollinger is more than just a business; it is our legacy, the culmination of my family's passion. I will not let Cyril Ray undo what we built.

4
PÉDALER DANS LA CHOUCROUTE
TO PEDAL IN THE SAUERKRAUT

1942, Epernay. The chill of the Moët & Chandon winery cut through my coat and settled in my bones. I hugged myself. The moist air of the barrel barn carried the potent scent of fermenting grapes—a promise of decades of vintages undermined by the stark fear of the German occupation. Worried whispers filled the hall. The *vignerons* stood in tight circles, faces shadowed by the looming collapse of everything they had spent generations building. We were gathered here for a clandestine meeting of the *Comité Interprofessionnel du Vin de Champagne,* the CIVC, to discuss the latest German demands. This was my first time attending in Jacques's stead, representing Bollinger amongst this formidable assembly.

Many of these men, their faces carved with worry lines and shadowed with fatigue, had stood beside me at Jacques's graveside a year ago. Their greetings held a distinct mixture of pity and surprise; I was the only woman in a sea of dark suits. Did they assume I'd crumble under pressure, a mere widow stepping into a man's world? Defiance surged within me. I met their gazes with resolve. If they insisted on judging me by my mourning attire, they would soon see that black was merely my color of choice for battle—the color of a woman who intended to run her Maison with unflinching authority. These were Jacques's friends, his comrades in arms, who shared his love for the land that nourished our vines and the easy camaraderie that bloomed with a shared glass of champagne. Pierre Dubois nervously tapped his foot, a staccato rhythm against the damp stone floor. Old Henri Beaumont gnawed his lip, his gaze darting around the cavern like a trapped bird. My hands clenched inside my gloves, and I had to suppress a shiver that had nothing to do with the cold. Don't let them see your fear, Lily, I told myself.

Above us, the towering oak vats loomed like silent sentinels, their shadows deepening the gloom. A faint scent of pipe tobacco wafted from somewhere, and for a moment, it brought Jacques back so vividly: his booming laughter echoing through the cellars, a splash of crushed grapes staining his shirt. A wave of grief washed over me, threatening to drown me. But I pushed it back, clinging to the memory of his strength, his staunch belief in me. I will not let you down, Jacques, I vowed silently. Bollinger will survive.

I drew a steady breath, anchoring myself to the present. Among those gathered were the heads of the great Maisons: Moët & Chandon, Perrier-Jouët, Krug, Veuve Clicquot, Pommery, and others, names that echoed through history, all facing an uncertain future.

Robert Jean de Vogüé, head of Moët & Chandon, acknowledged me with a respectful nod. "Gentlemen, and Madame Bollinger." A touch of gratitude warmed me at his inclusion, yet I couldn't help but wonder if my place here was truly earned in their eyes, or if they welcomed me simply out of respect for Jacques's memory?

"We are facing a dire situation." His words hung in the air, thick with the smell of defeat emanating from my fellow winemakers. "I know many of you are still reeling from the Germans stealing two million bottles of champagne from us."

Angry exclamations rippled through the men. Two million bottles? I had no idea it was that bad. The Germans had looted our future.

"But now," De Vogüé continued, his voice grim, "the Third Reich has appointed their own Wine Führer, Otto Klaebisch, who may be a blessing in disguise. Klaebisch, as many of you know, was a German wine buyer."

They talked about Klaebisch among themselves, uncertain what to think. But I remembered that Klaebisch loved Bollinger champagne. Would that prove a good thing? Or bad?

"So, at least Herr Klaebisch is not a stranger," De Vogüé continued. "And he is knowledgeable about champagne. He has been given the orders to stop the German troops from stealing our champagne."

A cheer erupted from the men, palpable relief washing through the cavern.

De Vogüé held up his hands to quiet them. "And he will be buying half a million bottles of champagne a week."

A cold dread washed over me. Half a million? Every week? Surely that couldn't be right. The entire champagne sales figures were nowhere near that.

A hesitant cheer rippled through the group.

De Vogüé's brother, Bertrand, who ran Veuve Clicquot, scoffed. "Klaebisch is no saint, I assure you. He stole my family home in Reims as his own, forcing my family to leave. I am positive he does not plan to pay market price for our champagne. We'll be lucky if they cover the cost of the bottles themselves!" He shook his head in disgust. "Soon we'll be paying Klaebisch to take our champagne!"

I raised my hand, seeking De Vogüé's attention. "Forgive

me, Monsieur, but perhaps I am misunderstanding something? How can we possibly sustain a half a million bottles? We'll be forced to use up all our reserve champagnes from past years, and you know we can't abide that. Small Maisons will be bankrupt within a year." I tried to keep my voice steady, my mind racing with the implications. A wave of nausea gripped me. How could I protect Bollinger from the insatiable Germans?

Fear and fury boiled over into a chaotic din that shook the air. "Half a million?" Pierre Dubois shouted, his face flushed.

"Is he mad?" Old Henri Beaumont's voice a tremor of panic. "We don't even own enough bottles." Another and another echoed the sentiment until the vaulted cavern rang with their fury.

They were not wrong. Besides wiping out the champagne reserves, bottle manufacturing had slowed down with the war, without the manpower and supplies. Didn't De Vogüé realize the impossible situation we faced?

De Vogüé raised his hands, his gaze sweeping across the agitated faces, his voice a low rumble. "Shouting will resolve nothing. We must gather our wits and present a united front with demands of our own. The very purpose of our *comité* is our collective strength." He punched his fist in the air. "So, what shall be our first point of negotiation?"

"No more free samples!" someone near the front spat out, his voice thick with outrage.

A surge of agreement tightened my chest. Every bottle given freely to those brigands is a bottle stolen from our future. I nodded firmly to others who seemed equally incensed.

"And they will not lay their hands on our premier *cuvées*!" another voice declared.

Precisely. Those reserves are the foundation of our Maisons. They will not be squandered on the appetites of the occupiers.

From the back, a voice, strained with desperation, cut through the simmering anger. "Monsieur de Vogüé, we can scarce keep the lights burning! How are we to produce anything without electricity?"

"Monsieur de Vogüé," my voice clear despite the tremor of anxiety. "Many of our workers are gone, fighting. And many others have been taken to German work camps. How can we possibly meet any significant demand, let alone half a million bottles a week, when we're missing our labor in the vineyards and cellars?"

"Excellent point," De Vogüé agreed. "We must insist on the return of our workers. Furthermore, we need the return of wine bottles, and, we must have the right to sell to our loyal French clientele. This is not merely about revenue; it is about keeping the heart of Champagne beating, ensuring a future beyond this occupation," he concluded, his voice firm. "These concerns shall form the foundation of our negotiations with Herr Klaebisch."

I heaved a sigh of hope. De Vogüé was a man of action, a leader who inspired confidence. With him at the helm, perhaps we really could navigate this crisis. Still, I could not go home without voicing one crucial concern.

I waved my hand again, and De Vogüé acknowledged me. "Klaebisch was a trained buyer before the war. He will choose the very best champagnes to export, Bollinger among them." My voice faltered. "What limitations can we put in place so no Maison is irrevocably damaged?"

A tense silence fell over the room, and I feared I'd overstepped. Finally, René Lalou of Mumm spoke, his voice serious. "Madame Bollinger is right. We cannot allow the Germans to cherry-pick our best vintages. It will ruin us."

De Vogüé nodded. "We will insist on balancing the orders throughout all Maisons. And, no special reserves, no vintage champagne, no exceptions." I shot René Lalou a look of gratitude for his support. Everyone in the room knows the quality Maisons are being hit hardest, a surge of camaraderie warming me. We were all in this together.

A faint ray of sunlight, filtering through a crack in the ceiling, illuminated the cobwebs dancing in the air. Hope, fragile yet defiant, bloomed in my chest. The CIVC was not just a means of survival; it was a symbol of our resilience.

As the meeting drew to a close, I rose, my mourning dress rustling softly, a whisper of all I had lost. The men nodded at me with a newfound respect. At least I'd voiced my concerns. I'd earned my place at the table, not just as Jacques's widow, but as the unflinching owner of Bollinger.

5
TIRER À LA MÊME CORDE
TO PULL THE SAME ROPE

1969, Aÿ. I serve my nephews popcorn for the Apollo moonwalk, a silly, American treat to share for such a momentous occasion. But with the butter and salt, it pairs nicely with the Bollinger *Spécial Cuvée* I poured. The nephews settle in, and the flickering *Teleavia* casts an eerie glow upon *le salon*. This sitting room—the beating heart of Bollinger, resting directly above the tasting room and cellar—is a place I've loved for forty-five years, ever since I arrived as a bride. Oh, the secrets these walls hold! They have absorbed every major decision, every tense negotiation, and every family celebration.

But tonight, that history provides me little comfort. I feel only a sharp, cold agitation. Our business meeting just adjourned, but the residue of my nephews arguing still hangs thick and sour. The three of them sit tense on the inherited Louis XV deeply cushioned armchairs with their curved walnut legs, and their open-sided fauteuils. The worn olive-green velvet upholstery looks positively bruised. All three have their attention glued to the miracle unfolding before their very eyes, deliberately avoiding each other lest they argue again.

The small, dark-wood *Teleavia* set seems impossibly small and vulgar against the wall of fine-hewn bookshelves. The grainy images of the moon are a jarring, surreal contrast to the room's permanence. Yves and Christian are crunching popcorn, their nervous energy channeled into the snack. Claude does not partake; he detests the kernels stuck between his teeth.

I cannot help but shake my head at my three successors gathered around the screen. I refer to them as my nephews for simplicity, though our relationships are more complicated. There's Yves Moret de Rocheprise, son of Pierre, who was Jacques's cousin. He carries the soul of the vineyards. There's Christian, my sister's son, whose flair thrives in marketing and sales. And Claude, my niece Claire's husband, the operations man, only connected by marriage but indispensable, nonetheless.

"One small step for man," crackles the American announcer.

"And one small sip for us." I raise my glass with a laugh, champagne bubbles never failing to revive me. "I suspect their lunar refreshment is considerably less satisfying than ours."

I expect a laugh but get none; apparently, they're still miffed. Their eyes remain glued to the moonwalk. The analogy strikes me: my nephews are like those astronauts hurtled into the future, full of courage and dedication, to be sure, but mission control is millions of miles away. What if they were stranded with no one to help them? I've been my nephews' mission control for thirty years, always calling the shots, always with the last word to guide them.

Each of these men is tethered securely to me but entirely separate from the others. What happens when my time passes and they are on their own? That day is coming sooner than they realize. I worry they cannot be a team; they've always relied on me to be the glue. I cannot let the future of Bollinger be shredded by three conflicting trajectories.

Yves rasps, "Pah! All this fuss over a pile of moon rocks! They'll find no delicious *terroir* on that desolate dust bowl." He flicks a piece of popcorn at the screen.

Claude, with his neatly trimmed mustache, makes swift, meticulous notes on a small notepad. "Fascinating," he murmurs, without looking up. "The thermal regulation of those suits. The environment is absolute zero to two hundred degrees in a matter of hours. And the pressurization loop for the helmet—a remarkable model of operational efficiency in life support. The true success here is not the walking, but the *survival*." His focus is always the science, the techniques, the equipment.

Christian springs to his feet, mimicking the deep thwump of a cork escaping a champagne bottle. "Can't you just picture it? Bollinger, the first champagne uncorked in the cosmos! In zero gravity, the liquid would stream out in a silver torrent of stars dancing against the infinite blackness!" He tosses a handful of popcorn into the air, where it hangs briefly, creating a galaxy of white puffs.

"Let them drink Tang," Yves jokes.

Claude, without looking up from his notepad, gestures toward the floor with a cold flick of his hand. "I'm quite sure Tante Lily prefers her antique Aubusson carpet to remain unsullied by your cosmic brand vision, Christian."

Before they start bickering again, I pour more champagne all around. "Gentlemen, while the world is gazing at the moon, we have our own milestone to celebrate. Bollinger, *mes chéris*. With all your efforts, our sales have surpassed one million bottles—and this despite the challenges facing our region: the price of grapes, the tight labor market, and the constant threat of bad vintages."

"This milestone isn't just about numbers," I tell them. "It's proof of the sweat and toil you've poured into every bottle." I clink their glasses, watching their faces. Christian's triumph, Claude's calculation, and Yves's shy acknowledgment, no doubt calculating whose victory this truly is. We drink as one. I try to hold this moment of unity.

Claude cuts through the moment with sharp precision. "So, Tante Lily, does this success finally justify the capital expenditure we need? The new temperature controls? The pneumatic presses? We must replace our obsolete presses. We are sacrificing a critical margin of efficiency clinging to these antiques."

Christian scoffs. "Efficiency? That's not the language of aspiration, Claude! This is the moment to seize the market. We must launch a new luxury *tête de cuvée* and secure distribution in the Orient. Delaying volume expansion is fiscally negligent."

Yves's voice is low and firm, carrying the weight of the terroir. "Negligent? You speak of negligence while ignoring the land. Our yield standards are already at the breaking point. To chase volume is to dilute our essence! Bollinger's legacy is built on quality, not mass-market *crassier*."

The tension thickens between them, heavy as fermenting must. I feel a sharp, warning spasm in my knee as I rise. "Enough!" The familiar ache in my joints a subtle reminder of time's passage. I turn off the *Teleavia* with a decisive click, plunging the room into an intimate darkness.

A chilling premonition settles in my heart. "In two years, I retire. And I will choose one of you to succeed me." I pause. "One of you must prove to me you have the vision, the respect for our heritage, and the audacity to lead Bollinger into this new era."

Christian breaks the silence. "I can organize a full audit of the Maison's global operations to assess where the future lies."

He raises his glass. "To the next era—may the best man chart the course!"

"An audit will tell you what the market wants, Christian. It won't teach you what the vines want. That understanding can only come from personal experience, from walking in another's worn shoes." I place the bottle on the table with a decisive clack. "Do you think the astronauts walked on the moon alone? No. They were supported by thousands working in union, sharing one single objective. That is what you lack. To remedy it, each of you must spend two weeks working in each other's departments. You must become the new glue."

Claude's thin smile vanishes. "To waste two weeks of my time—and worse, two weeks of a vineyard worker's time training me—is a measurable loss to the bottom line. It's fiscally irresponsible and logistically unsound."

"Inefficient, perhaps, but essential." My voice cuts through his protest. "We have two years. We start now. You must learn to function as a team."

"You must be in the vineyards," Yves says, a hint of dark satisfaction in his voice. "Harvest is early this year, and the vines do not wait for audits. You will be ready to get your hands dirty, or you will spoil the work of a year."

Christian gleams. "A crash course in viticulture it is. And Claude, no spreadsheets on sales calls. We'll need to upgrade your wardrobe, for sure."

Claude, refusing to acknowledge the joke, turns his back and begins wiping the champagne off his polished shoe with a handkerchief.

I sense it's time for my exit; leave now or listen to another forty-five minutes of competitive sword sharpening. The heavy oak door of *le salon* closes behind me with a solid, echoing thud—a final, ceremonial punctuation mark on my announcement. I walk toward the courtyard, my fingers tracing the cold iron railing as I stare out across the fields. The mild, dry warmth of a late July night settles around me, a thick, velvet shawl carrying the sweet scent of summer foliage and warm earth.

The sour, metallic tension has escaped the house and now hangs in the courtyard air. I keep walking out through the vineyards, raising my eyes to the vast, inky blackness.

The full, bright moon hangs suspended above the vines. No longer a technical image on the screen, but a cold, indifferent orb, dazzlingly close and yet impossibly distant. I can almost trace the path of the astronauts across its desolate plains. Three astronauts, standing on the edge of a new world, completely reliant on a fragile shell of technology and thousands of unseen hands on Earth who built and manage their systems. They achieved a miracle of union, not only with each other but with an entire nation's singular will.

My own three successors are like that crew: brilliant, specialized, and encased in their own shells of ambition. Except if they were in space, they'd be fighting over who gets the window seat. They must learn a difficult truth: that a team is more valuable than any individual and can only be forged in shared struggle.

The battle for Bollinger's future begins tonight. As their distant, rising voices float on the warm summer air, I can only wait to see if they will self-destruct or blaze into glory. The entire Bollinger legacy is stacked high—dry, volatile tinder waiting for the match I've struck.

6

IL EST TOMBÉ
DANS LES POMMES
HE FELL IN THE APPLES

1942, Aÿ. Honestly, one would think the sun itself was being held captive by the Germans along with the rest of France. The weak April sunlight straining through the window could not dispel the damp chill inside. Dust settled on heavy velvet curtains—one of the few furnishings the Germans hadn't deemed worthy of requisitioning. No accounting for taste, I suppose.

A log shifted in the fireplace, sending a plume of grey ash swirling into the air like a ghostly exhale. The fire, once a roaring blaze that filled the room with warmth much like my dear Jacques, had dwindled to a timid glow. I huddled deeper into my woolen shawl, the worn fabric offering little comfort against the chill seeping through the stone blocks.

The enemy soldiers, billeted in the east wing, were a constant presence. Their guttural voices and harsh laughter rumbled through the once-tranquil corridors. Every slammed door sent a jolt through me. They seemed to kick the furniture just for the pleasure of the noise.

I forced my attention back to the ledger. The numbers

blurred, a sea of red ink and unpaid invoices. The war had crippled us, cutting off export markets and leaving loyal customers struggling to survive. Ironically, our largest client had become the Third Reich, paying a pittance for the privilege of plundering our cellars.

A sharp rap at the door jolted me. "Come in."

The door creaked open, revealing Yvonne. Behind her towered two German soldiers, their eyes hard and scrutinizing. My heart lurched. My hand instinctively covered my wrist, shielding the diamonds of the Bulova watch Jacques had given me from their predatory gaze.

The soldiers parted, and a tall figure stepped through. Herr Otto Klaebisch, der Weinführer. His arrogant authority and the reek of cigar smoke gave him away before he even spoke. He was broad, with the bravado of a man used to getting his way; his uniform strained across his chest and stomach like a fatted hog ready for market. He had a thin, cruel mouth and eyes of a pale, ice blue that bored into me, calculating my worth.

"I demand to see Herr Bollinger." The thick German vowels scraped against my eardrums.

I stiffened. "Monsieur Bollinger is not available."

Klaebisch's eyebrows shot up. "Where is he, then? Hiding like a coward?"

"My husband is dead." A shadow of something crossed Klaebisch's face—regret or satisfaction, I couldn't tell—but it vanished instantly.

He cleared his throat, his gaze sliding toward Yvonne. "Well then, perhaps I can speak to your business manager? In private."

I met his stare, refusing to look at the door. A slight nod over my shoulder dismissed Yvonne toward the back hall. "Thank you, Yvonne. That will be all. Please see to the kitchen."

She hesitated for a heartbeat, eyes flicking to the two soldiers standing like stone pillars just outside my office, before she disappeared. Klaebisch waited for the latch to click.

I gestured toward the spindly Louis XV chair. "Please, do have a seat."

He didn't sit immediately. He studied the antique with profound distrust, searching the room for a sturdier alternative. He found nothing. A month ago, his own men had hauled my guest chairs into the courtyard for the barracks. This relic was the only thing they'd deemed too worthless to take.

Realizing the absurdity of standing while I remained seated, he squeezed his wide frame into the narrow seat. The mahogany groaned. I suppressed a wince as a cabriole leg bowed outward, straining against the floorboards.

"To business." His voice dropped to a conspiratorial rasp. "The Führer has developed a great appreciation for the finest champagne. He has tasked me—and me alone—to secure ten thousand bottles of Bollinger." He pinned me with a stare. "This is a private matter. Separate from the CIVC. No paperwork. I will take custody personally."

I felt the blood drain from my face. Ten thousand bottles "under the table" was not a military requisition; it was a heist. I had heard the whispers from Épernay—stories of "lost" shipments and trucks that never reached the front. The CIVC had been formed specifically to stand between us and this kind of pillaging. By asking for a delivery outside the official allocation, Klaebisch wasn't acting for Germany. He was acting for himself.

"I'm sorry, Herr Klaebisch. Such a request is impossible." I kept my hands flat on the desk to hide their tremor. "The CIVC tracks every cork. If I provide ten thousand bottles outside our allocation, Monsieur de Vogüé will notice. I would have nothing left for the official German orders."

Klaebisch's face hardened. "You do not understand, Madame. This is the Führer's wish. Do you really want to be the woman who said 'no' to Berlin?"

"If it is his wish," I said, my eyes widening in mock awe, "then surely you have the order in writing? I should like to frame it alongside our historical documents."

The blotchy crimson climbed his collar. He had no papers. "This is a matter of international importance!" he sputtered.

"Oh, I quite agree." I leaned forward. "And surely a man with such a brilliant career wouldn't want to jeopardize his standing with a misunderstanding? If the CIVC were to notice an unrecorded gap in our cellars, they might reach the most unfortunate conclusions about where those bottles went."

He surged upward, but the chair spindles seized his hips. He remained hovering in a graceless crouch, trapped. "I assure you, Madame, my conduct is beyond reproach."

"Of course." I watched him settle back into his wooden cage. "But as a humble widow, I find I am lost without paperwork. If you could just provide a small written authorization for Monsieur de Vogüé? It would protect us both from any... administrative inquiries."

I slid a piece of stationery and a pen toward him.

He stared at the paper as if it were a death warrant. With a snort of disgust, he slammed his fist on the desk. My porcelain inkwell tipped, a bruised stain spreading across the walnut.

"Oh dear." I dabbed the ink with a linen handkerchief, my movements slow and rhythmic. "Please, do not trouble yourself further. I shall simply mention our conversation to Monsieur de Vogüé when I see him this evening. I'm sure he will be eager to help you regularize the request."

His features sharpened into something jagged. He gave a final, desperate shove. The slender legs splayed, straining until—

CRACK.

The mahogany surrendered. Klaebisch was a blur of flailing wool and polished boots as he hit the parquet. He lay there, pinned by the wreckage, the needlepoint cushion landing beside him with a soft thud.

For a fleeting second, I didn't see an officer of the Reich; I saw a clumsy, purple-faced man struggling with a cushion. A cold, sharp thrill raced through me—more intoxicating than any vintage in my cellar. Shaming him was a small, private victory in a war I was losing.

The doors burst open. His soldiers rushed in, but he swatted them away. "Don't touch me!" He scrambled to his feet, livid, trying to pull his tunic straight while shards of my mother's legacy fell from his lap. "This is outrageous! You will regret this, Madame Bollinger!"

I looked at the splintered mess. "Such a pity. That chair survived three wars, Herr Klaebisch. It seems it just could not survive a German."

"This isn't over," he spat, brushing shards from his trousers.

"I'm sure it isn't. But the champagne will move through the proper channels. I'll make certain Monsieur de Vogüé knows exactly what you... required."

He huffed and retreated, his boots echoing with a hollow rhythm down the hall. A tremor finally broke through my composure as the door clicked shut. I had him by the throat.

"Yvonne!"

The cook appeared, eyes wide at the ruin on the floor.

I leaned close, my voice barely a breath. "Go to Moët & Chandon. Find Monsieur de Vogüé. Tell him Klaebisch tried to steal ten thousand bottles under the table, and that I have sent him to the CIVC to 'verify' the order."

Yvonne simply nodded, her jaw set with a fierce understanding. She memorized the words, wiped her hands on her apron, and slipped out through the back hall.

I knelt among the splinters. The wood was beyond saving —jagged, white fractures. I retrieved the needlepoint cushion and traced a snagged silk rose, the threads frayed but the pattern still holding firm. I pressed it against my ribs like a shield. I would turn it into a pillow for my own bed.

Klaebisch had broken the wood, but in his clumsy greed, he'd handed me the only weapon I had to protect Bollinger: his own corruption.

7
SE METTRE LE DOIGT DANS L'ŒIL
TO PUT ONE'S FINGER IN ONE'S EYE

1970, Aÿ. The Europa stamp album is open, but the latest floral graphics aren't providing their usual sanctuary. I press a stamp into place, my thumb lingering too long on the paper. Cyril must be late. Again. A bad habit he seems rather fond of.

Christian left in the Peugeot after lunch to fetch Cyril from the station, and now the afternoon light is fading. The silence in the driveway is becoming deafening. It's a short drive. A simple pickup. So why am I imagining the Peugeot crumpled in a ditch?

Finally, I hear the crunch of gravel. I quickly put away my album and rise from the upholstered fauteuil near the window. I look down, past the heavy, tasseled damask curtains of *le salon*. The car's intact, at least.

The oak door bursts open. Cyril's Burberry trench billows behind him like Mick Jagger's cape in a wind fan. Underneath the dramatic coat, the eyesore reveals itself: a sport jacket in a plaid so loud it could be heard in Paris, a chaotic clash of burnt orange, deep brown, and an aggressively cheerful mustard yellow. Lapels wide enough to taxi a small plane. The Jekyll and

Hyde of his dressing habits persist: one day the tweedy English gent, the next, the rock star oenophile.

Christian trails in behind him, looking slightly wilted. "My apologies, Tante Lily. The train was behind schedule, and then our guest insisted on a detour."

Cyril ignores the fatigue in Christian's voice and bruises my cheeks with an exuberant *la bise*, exuding the same self-absorbed energy that once charmed me in London. It was a charm he readily weaponized when he twisted my words in the London Observer. I had shared my little poem with him in jest —*when I'm happy and when I'm sad*—meant as a wink between friends. Instead, he stripped away the humor and presented it as an elitist mantra, a modern "Let Them Eat Cake." He turned my joy into a caricature of corporate grandeur.

I tap the crystal on my Bulova with a manicured fingernail. "If tardiness were an Olympic sport, Cyril, you'd be draped in gold."

"Apologies. I got waylaid in a bookstore in Épernay." He flashes a mischievous glint. "I couldn't resist picking up a little something for you." He produces a first edition of *Diamonds Are Forever*, signed by Ian Fleming himself.

Playing to my weakness, sly fox. He remembers our shared appreciation for 007—the stories of espionage and intrigue that once fueled a rather memorable night ending in a stolen kiss (and an even more memorable rejection). He is offering this as a paper olive branch, a silent apology for skewering me in the press.

"A signed Fleming? Clever peace offering, Cyril. Truly. But if you think a few paper diamonds make up for the coals you dragged me over in the *Observer*, you've severely undervalued the woman you're dealing wih."

I set the book on the side table, leaving it there like an

unpaid bill. "Now, shall we see if you've come to write a book about the soul of Bollinger, or just to show off that jacket?"

He throws his head back and laughs. "Touché, Lily. Haven't lost your wit, I see."

"Nor you, your audacity," I retort, a barb hidden in my remark.

Cyril's expression softens, the bravado dropping just enough to feel real. "I haven't forgotten that night in London, Lily. Things could have been different between us."

A wave of heat rushes to my cheeks. He is disarmingly charming when he drops the critic's mask, and for a fleeting second, I remember the temptation. I also remember the cost.

Beside him, Christian shifts his weight, his eyes darting between us with profound discomfort. He clutches his keys too tightly, his face reddening at the inappropriate intimacy of Cyril's remark.

"Well then." I pull my shoulders back, the warmth receding into a cool, professional mask. "Christian, have you told Monsieur Ray about our latest innovation?"

Christian's relief is palpable as he launches into a detailed explanation. "*Vieilles Vignes Françaises.* Old French Vines. We're producing a champagne from the original, ungrafted plots that survived the phylloxera blight."

"Funny one." Cyril snickers. "Pulling my leg, are you? You almost had me, Christian."

I shake my head watching him slap his knee. What the devil?

"A champagne from ungrafted French vines?" He grins at me like I'm in on the joke. "Impossible. All vines were grafted after phylloxera."

"I assure you, I am not kidding." Christian's smile fades into a grimace. "It will be the finest wine this house has ever produced."

Cyril stops smiling and rubs his forehead. "You expect anyone to believe a few hectares in Aÿ somehow skipped the Great Wine Blight? That pesky insect systematically gnawed away the roots of the entire continent, Christian. No French vines survived—it's a biological impossibility."

My temper flares. "You're saying you need proof, Monsieur Ray?"

He leans over, tapping the polished walnut table. "I'll call your bluff and raise you."

I take a step back, girding myself against this obnoxious know-it-all. Turning toward the window, I watch inky clouds gather—a mirror to the storm brewing within me. The table, usually cool to the touch, feels charged with the electricity of his antagonism. "It is too dark for the vineyards now. You will have to see for yourself tomorrow. I don't trust myself to treat you civilly until then."

"Didn't count on me challenging the legend, did you, Lily?" A wicked grin spreads across his face.

I offer the most gracious smile I can muster, though it feels like a blade. "Christian, please see Monsieur Ray to his room. Breakfast is served at eight sharp. Do try not to be late."

That evening, my fingers test the water as it rushes into the depths of my antique porcelain tub. The rising steam is already clouding the large picture window, but I cannot tear myself away; I am fixed on the uninterrupted, glorious view of the vineyards being ravaged by the storm.

Outside, thunder rumbles—a sound like artillery fire that pulls my mind back to the years when those sounds weren't metaphors. The sky has turned a monstrous, bruised black. A sudden, violent gust slams against the house, rattling the panes and making the very stone blocks seem to shudder. Jagged lightning claws across the sky, briefly illuminating rows of skeletal vines which sway and thrash like drowning figures whipped against the trellising. It is a flash storm of pure, destructive fury, and for a helpless moment, I can only watch.

The catastrophic error of allowing Cyril, with his sharp but capricious intellect, to pen this chronicle weighs heavily upon me. My nephew Christian sees a golden opportunity for modern fame, but he fails to see that with Cyril, the ink is a gamble. He could ruin us with a single, clever stroke of his pen. The fool is unleashed, each smug assertion crackling in the charged air like a dangerous static—a chilling prelude to the words that threaten to unravel decades of dedication and tarnish our hard-won reputation. If the war taught me anything, it was that an invasion, whether by boots or by books, must be met with a superior strategy. I will not merely handle Cyril Ray; I will educate him. I will bend his wandering attention until he sees Bollinger not as a brand to be critiqued, but as the true excellence it is.

The steaming water welcomes me, offering momentary solace. I step in, the heat a delicious contrast to the icy dread in my stomach, and I sink gratefully into the burgeoning froth of lavender-scented bubbles. My gaze drifts through the steam-kissed window panes. As quickly as it came, the core of the storm passes. The sound of the wind drops from a roar to a howl. Soon, the clouds part, revealing a huge, luminous golden orb that casts its ethereal glow upon the vines, gleaming with the unexpected rain.

I realize, with a sudden, calming clarity: The storm of Cyril Ray will pass, too.

This vineyard is rooted in centuries of history, and the unyielding spirit of the land has survived blights, wars, and the arrogance of men. That is the truth he must understand. I must make him understand the profound connection we have to this heritage.

A turbulent sigh expands in my chest, creating gentle ripples in the fragrant froth that cradles me. I reach to the side table, amidst the soft glow of a single beeswax candle. A chilled coupe of Bollinger *Spécial Cuvée* beckons, its crystal catching the light. Against the glow of the mon, I watch a million tiny bubbles ascend in a tireless, delicate dance—a far more persuasive argument for perfection than any critic's pontification.

The first sip is a defiant spark, a burst of crisp green apple and bright zest. The underlying minerality whispers of the ancient earth and toasted walnut, a story Cyril's palate seems unwilling to acknowledge. The persistent, creamy mousse is a testament to the time and patience it took to make this champagne, qualities Cyril clearly lacks. With each effervescent swallow, the knot of anxiety in my chest loosens, his arrogance seeming to dissipate, as fleeting and ephemeral as the bubbles themselves.

My fingers instinctively trace the cool, smooth rubies of my Bulova watch, its steady, mechanical heartbeat against my wrist remains my most comforting anchor. I need to protect it from the water. Unclasping the delicate band, I place it near the book Cyril gave me, *Diamonds Are Forever*.

A nod to a shared appreciation for sophistication. A wry smile crosses my lips. He likely imagines himself as Bond and me as the widow he must charm. Given the climate he has brought into my home, perhaps a copy of *Thunderball* would have been more fitting.

I reach for Fleming. Let Mr. Bond keep me company until the first light of dawn, signaling the start of my new mission: to ensure that a certain opinionated wine critic finally, truly understands the heart and soul of Bollinger.

8

LE COUP DE MASSUE
THE BLOW OF THE CLUB

1943, Aÿ. The harvest had always been the predictable, reassuring culmination of a year of tending the vineyards, Mother Nature's reward for a job well done. But two weeks into this harvest felt less like a reward and more like a hopeless rescue mission. The sun radiated the heat of a furnace, threatening to cook the grand cru pinot noir grapes right on the vine unless we could get them picked and crushed before they turned to jam. The air, usually smelling of ripe promise, was thick with overripe panic. If this fruit turned to rot, it would not be the *Boches* who ruined our 1943 vintage. It would be the weather, which I found frankly insulting. One expects destruction from the enemy, not from Mother Nature's temper tantrum.

And old Pierre, our vineyard director whom I'd relied on to run the harvest, was in his sickbed with a wasting illness, his breaths growing shallower each day. Our true labor force, the strong, able-bodied, and decidedly male *vendangeurs*, knowledgeable and skilled grape pickers, were still scattered across the continent, fighting in this terrible war or rotting in prison camps. Their absence was why this job fell to my new crew: a small, unfortunate army of necessity. We had the town's adolescents, sullen and clumsy, doing the work of men; the old men whose joints snapped like brittle twigs; and the townswomen who'd previously only managed the gentle weight of a silver tea service. They were untrained, they were slow, but they were here. Every bent back, mine included, was a declaration that necessity was a harsh taskmaster, and that we must salvage this harvest, no matter what it took, right under the noses of the Occupation.

Grit ground between my teeth. The cloying scent of grapes made me feel dizzy, but the defiance in the women's voices kept me moving. They sang folk songs, fragile shields against oppression. This might not be the finest crew, but they were my crew, and we were determined not to let the vintage surrender first.

A sudden scent in the breeze, sharper than the dusty fruit, made the singing falter. It was the smell of cheap gasoline and distant coal smoke, the noxious perfume of the enemy. On the ridge of the next vineyard a German patrol vehicle, a squat, aggressive thing, drove slowly along the perimeter road surveying their assets. Every vine, every cluster, was merely a future source of requisitioned profit in their ledger. They treated the rows like a bank vault they'd stumbled into, oblivious to the fact that champagne was our heritage, our livelihood, our very souls.

The vehicle passed without slowing, the grinding sound of their engine a reminder that none of this truly belonged to us anymore. It was the cruelest business arrangement I could imagine. We provided the labor and expertise, and the Germans bought our prized champagne for the price the Führer set at his whim.

I straightened my back, forcing my spine to ignore the

knife-edge ache, and fixed my gaze on the next row. I would not give the *Boche* the satisfaction of seeing the *patronne* defeated. Jacques had been gone two years; his ghost still walked in the vineyards: a comfort and a torment of its own.

Then I saw her, a dark silhouette struggling against the shimmering heat rising from the red dirt path. My sister Thérèse hurried toward me, her usually vibrant face pale and drawn. Her eyes were red-rimmed, the swelling betraying her tears. My breath hitched, and a cold fist tightened around my heart. *No, no, no.* Not another loss.

I waved to Yvonne to keep our *vendangeurs* picking grapes and rushed to meet Thérèse. "What is it? What's wrong?" My voice caught in my constricted chest.

She clutched my arm, her knuckles white against my skin. "Lily ... it's Claire." Her voice broke, a raw sob escaping her lips.

My blood ran cold. Dizziness seized me, and I swayed, my hands shooting out to grip her arms for support. "What about Claire? Is she ill? Hurt?"

"Worse. The Gestapo ... they raided the Moët caves last night. Arrested everyone they found."

"Moët?" The name spun my mind. "Why there? What on earth was she doing in the Moët caves at night?"

"Claire was part of the Resistance, Lily. They were working in the sealed-off caves ... Surely you knew about them?"

The truth hit me in the chest, knocking the air from my lungs. The cloying scent of overripe grapes turned to ashes in my mouth, leaving a bitter, metallic taste of fear. "The Resistance? She's barely old enough to drink the wine, let alone fight a war."

"Who did you think works for the Resistance?" Defiance sparked in Thérèse's eyes. "They're your neighbors, your employees, your colleagues, your ..." She collapsed in my arms. "Your niece."

As she sobbed, I held her quaking shoulders. I had no idea our sweet Claire would put herself in such danger. To risk her life for us.

Thérèse straightened up and wiped her eyes. "Claire's been keeping track of the Nazi's champagne shipments, relaying the information to the British Military to determine where their armies are."

"So, the Third Reich issues orders for champagne shipments which signals where they are planning to attack." It made a chilling kind of sense.

Thérèse nodded. "She had just uncovered information about a massive shipment destined for North Africa. Seems that's where the next invasion is planned."

So hard to think of Claire in the clutches of the Nazis. My mind rebelled against the sheer horror. "They said—" Thérèse's voice faltered. "They're all being sent to a work camp in Germany. Dozens of them, dragged away in the night."

My breath hitched. "Who ... who else?"

"Robert-Jean de Vogüé and Paul Chandon-Moët for starters."

A cold shock gripped my chest. "How can that be? They head the CIVC. How could they be running the Resistance besides?"

"Maybe that was always part of their plan. But someone must have tipped off the Gestapo. They arrested everyone down there. Marie-Noëlle, old Antoine, even young Philippe." Her face dissolved in fear and grief, and I pulled her close. The familiar scent of lavender oil mingled with the sharp tang of her sweat and tears.

I place my forehead on hers, whispering fiercely. "Thérèse, listen to me. We can't let them break us." I smoothed her hair off her face. A quiet resolve hardened in my gut. "We will keep fighting however we can. For Claire, for the Champagne, for France." I sounded strong, at least I hoped to. But as I looked over her shoulder to the *vendangeurs* hard at work in the vineyard, the late afternoon sun cast long, mournful shadows across the rows. What would happen to Claire in the hands of the Nazis?

And what would happen to the champagne without our CIVC leaders? How many more would be taken from us before this endless nightmare was finally over?

9
CHERCHER MIDI À QUATORZE HEURES
TO LOOK FOR NOON AT TWO O'CLOCK

Aÿ, 1970. Another day with the absurdly curious Cyril Ray. His interview style is beginning to feel like water torture ... drip, drip, drip. The man never stops with the questions and suggestions. I'm starting to believe I must be making up for grave sins committed in another lifetime.

Since taking on the mantle of a bestselling author, a title never far from his lips, he's become even more flamboyant. Today, he's dressed less for a muddy vineyard and more for a colonial safari. He sports a cream-colored safari suit of lightweight gabardine, complete with patch pockets and a narrow belt that cinches his softening waist. The outfit, meant for the Serengeti or perhaps a London rooftop bar, is wholly impractical for the slippery, chalky slopes of Champagne. Adding to the absurdity, he wears a dramatic, brightly patterned scarf knotted around his neck. The jacket is already hopelessly dusty, and his expensive, smooth-soled chukka boots are failing miserably to grip the rocky earth.

But as we enter the stone walls of *Clos Chaudes Terres*, a deep, restorative peace settles over me. The air is thick, almost syrupy, with the sweet perfume of ripe pinot noir. My ears register the metallic *snip-snip-snip* of a dozen secateurs—the *vendangeurs* harvesting clusters in a rhythmic percussion that is the very heartbeat of the vintage.

Behind me, the labored huff of Cyril Ray trying to keep up breaks the quiet. The loose gravel crunches loudly under his boots, punctuated by his breathless, arrogant banter.

"As I told Christian, Bollinger needs to be thinking about volume! Forget your prestige labels for a moment; the mass market is where the cash is. That cheap German stuff, that Blue Nun—it's selling by the tanker load!" His face is already the shade of a ripe tomato beneath the sweat.

Trying to ignore the sacrilege of comparing Bollinger to Blue Nun, I focus on the vineyard. Sunlight streams through the leaves, dappling the rocky earth where I spot Christian and Claude at the far end of the row. Their presence brings a smile to my face. Seeing them working together makes my heart sing.

Yves has assigned each of them a crew. I watch as Christian directs his *vendangeurs*, their buckets filling with dark, heavy fruit, while Claude supervises the delicate transfer of full baskets onto the tractors. They move through the rows with concentration and harmony—a clear demonstration of the teamwork I forced upon them. Hopefully, making them work in each other's areas, their usual petty arguments have been replaced by a new, grudging respect for the unifying work of the vines. A quiet satisfaction runs through me. My succession plan is promising.

I march through the rows at a brisk clip, enjoying the familiar burn in my thighs. Cyril's progress is more of a desperate shuffle; he puffs audibly, his breath coming in short, strangled gasps that sound like a deflating tire. He forces a question out between gasps, pausing only because he's run out of oxygen.

"Madame, what's the rush? I want to examine the vines. Do you always maintain this... athletic pace?"

I keep walking, wanting him to give up and leave me to the blessed sounds of the vineyard. The September sun beats down on the white chalk, reflecting a blinding heat that usually sends tourists scurrying for the shade of the cellars.

"No time to dilly-dally, as you English say. We have 179 hectares to harvest." I throw a look over my shoulder at his crimson face. His breath coming in shallow, jagged bursts. It's almost funny—the great critic winded by a simple stroll. "A *patronne's* job is not sitting in my salon with my stamp collection eating macarons. It's being wherever the work is being done, rolling up my sleeves and diving in."

When we reach the old vines, the oldest in France, I finally slow. They are crowded together in a wild, riotous tangle, far removed from the neat, sterile lines of modern agriculture. Cyril pulls a linen handkerchief from his pocket, dabbing violently at his forehead.

"Madame Bollinger." His voice is thin, straining against the heat. "I must be frank. The vineyard appears... chaotic. It looks less like a Grand Cru and more like an overgrown field."

I scoff, popping a plump grape into my mouth. "Perhaps to an untrained eye, Monsieur. This is *vigne en foule*—a 'crowd of vines.' Each one is individually staked, stressing the plant to produce intense fruit." I keep moving, forcing him to follow as I weave through the dense greenery. "It allows the vines to be French and passionate, rather than English and terribly buttoned-up."

He stumbles over a clod of chalky earth, his boots coated in white dust. "Regimented rows, Madame, are efficient. And efficiency is what the modern market demands." He waves a hand toward the horizon, his movements becoming sluggish. "Your rivals have moved beyond the era of romanticism. Moët

& Chandon... stainless-steel tanks. Consistency. Veuve Clicquot... mechanical riddling. This is reality." He's struggling to keep pace now, his shadow swaying unevenly over the vines. "This ancient, labor-intensive technique... a luxury you cannot afford. I wonder: will Bollinger be the charming casualty of a new world? A quaint relic?"

The criticism hits like a gut punch. He's dead wrong, but if he writes those words, it will be devastating. I stop abruptly and pluck a cluster of grapes—small, dense, and sun-warmed. "Monsieur Ray, taste them."

His hand trembles slightly as he takes the stem. He pops a grape into his mouth, chewing with a doubtful expression, his eyes squinting against the glare.

"Bollinger does not strive for 'mass-market efficiency,' Monsieur. These vines are unique. They are propagated by the ancient method of *provinage* to amplify the flavor." I lead him deeper into the tangle. "See how the branches grow down to the ground? *Provinage* is where we bend a young shoot down, burying it, and allow the tip to resurface as a new vine. It creates a continuous root system that limits yield while focusing the energy of the earth."

I turn back to him, my voice lowering with intensity. "More importantly, Cyril, these are original, pre-phylloxera rootstock. Bollinger protected them when the bug devastated Europe. They've never been grafted with inferior modern stock. They yield a tiny amount of juice, but the concentration gives Bollinger its depth, its texture—its soul."

Monsieur Ray spits a seed into the dust. He tries to answer, his mouth opening, but only a dry wheeze emerges. "But the labor... it's... it's medieval..."

He takes one more step, his knees buckling. He reaches for a wooden stake, misses, and slides down the side of a stone terrace wall until he hits the dusty ground. His color is a frightening, pasty white. His eyes close.

Mon Dieu, I've killed the journalist right here next to my priceless vines. I kneel quickly, the dry chalk soil staining my skirt as I place a hand on his heart. Still beating. His shirt is soaked through, his safari suit clinging to him like a second, failed skin.

His eyes flutter open, unfocused. "The ... the vines ..."

"Be still, Cyril. Just breathe." I settle beside him on the warm earth, the amusement and the anger vanishing, replaced by the same protective instinct. "Let's rest here a few minutes."

His skin is gray and his chest is heaving. I take a deep, steady breath of the sweet, grape-scented air and force a smile. "No more talk about vines or competition."

"But you need to think about it, Lily."

I scoff gently. "Let's talk about James Bond. Have you read the new one, *Colonel Sun*?"

He grins sheepishly, the color seeping back into his cheeks at the mention of 007. "What do you think of this Robert Markham taking over for Fleming?"

I stand and offer him a hand, pulling him up from the dust of my heritage. "His prose is rather—turgid, don't you think?"

He grunts as he finds his feet, steadying himself on the stone wall. "Always analyzing, aren't you?"

I stand and offer him a hand, pulling him up from the dust of my heritage. "I believe we have some of Yvonne's freshly baked madeleines and a bottle of perfectly chilled Bollinger waiting for us at the house. I always drink champagne to set the world right."

He grunts, steadying himself on the wall. "You really believe that, don't you?"

Remembering his famous article about me, I tilt my head.

"You, of all people, should remember when I drink champagne."

A wry smile touches his lips. "You can thank me for making you famous for that quote."

"I forgot to add that I drink champagne in the afternoons to shut up incessant journalists." I walk him slowly down the path, my hand steadying his elbow.

"Touché, Madame Bollinger. Touché."

10

CONTRE VENTS ET MARÉES
AGAINST WINDS AND TIDES

1943, Aÿ. Pierre Moret de Rocheprise, Jacques's cousin, shuffled into my office. His back was hunched like a weary vine, his brow a landscape of deep furrows hewn by years in the sun. The earthy aroma of the vineyards clung to his worn clothes as if he were part of the soil itself. Each breath puffed out in shallow, ragged bursts as if he'd just finished a sprint.

Under normal circumstances, I would have insisted he quit without hesitation; he was far too old for this demanding labor. But with the Nazis afoot and so many of our men gone, someone had to train the crew of women and children who worked the vines. He was as unyielding as an old vine rooted deep in the terroir, refusing to abandon his post. His son Yves had confided in me about Pierre's restless nights—the frantic, skipping beat of his heart and the desperate struggle for each breath.

"Ma chérie," he rasped, his voice thin and reedy. "A young lad on a bicycle just delivered this. For you."

He handed me the note, his hand trembling. I peered out

the window to see who could've handed the note to Pierre, but the alleyway was empty.

I looked down at the message scrawled in hurried handwriting: *Urgent meeting: Eglise Notre-Dame, 7 pm. Tell no one.*

A knot of anxiety tightened in my stomach. Were the other winemakers fined by *der Weinführer* as I had been when I did not let him steal my champagne? Or was the CIVC telling us to stand down? I tried to exude a calm I didn't feel as I tucked the paper into my pocket. "Thank you, Pierre. Please, say nothing of this to anyone."

He nodded, his eyes filled with a deep, weary understanding. "Be careful, Lily. These are dangerous times." He leaned closer, his voice dropping to a conspiratorial hush. "Did you hear about what the workers are doing at Veuve Clicquot?"

I raised an eyebrow, intrigued. "What's that?"

"They mislabeled all the bottles they gave Germany." His rheumy eyes twinkled. "The Third Reich will be drinking swill, thinking it's vintage!"

"Those scoundrels!" A chuckle escaped me despite the tension. Madame Clicquot would have been proud if she were still around. "Though I doubt the Nazis have much appreciation for a good vintage anyway. They probably wouldn't know a pinot noir from a pinot gris."

"And that's not all." Pierre's voice dropped lower. "They are adding things... to make the champagne less enjoyable." He winked, a sharp glint in his eye.

"Like what, exactly?"

I knew about the acts of defiance my colleagues were employing—the delayed shipments and the faulty corks. But adding something to the champagne itself? A sacrilege. To a winemaker, the wine is sacred; even if it was destined for a Nazi's palate, the idea of corrupting the juice felt like a stain on our very souls.

"A bitter herb, perhaps." Pierre leaned heavily against a chair, his breathing becoming a little more labored. "Enough to make them wonder if their taste buds have gone awry."

I couldn't help but smile, feeling a spark of that shared rebellion. "We can't let the Germans have all the fun, can we?"

"Indeed not, ma chérie. Indeed not."

He shuffled out, leaving the weight of his warning heavy on my shoulders. My renewed sense of purpose warred with my growing unease. We were guardians of a legacy, protectors of a tradition. We'd resist in every way we could, even if it meant relying on the frail strength of men like Pierre.

Clutching the note, my mind raced. Who had sent it? Was it related to our acts of defiance, or had something else happened? Had our sabotage gone too far? Were the Germans retaliating? The hours leading up to the meeting were agonizing. I tried to focus on work, but the note burned a hole in my pocket, a harbinger of the unknown danger lurking ahead.

The office had grown cold, the shadows lengthening across my desk. Every groan of the old timber floorboards sounded like a footfall, a reminder that in Aÿ, even the walls seemed to have ears for the Reich. I reached for my coat, the heavy iron key to the main gate cold against my palm. As the clock struck seven, the chimes were swallowed by the heavy, damp silence of the evening. I slipped out into the darkness. The town felt hollowed out, a skeleton of itself under the curfew. I kept my head down, my fingers rubbing the note in my pocket, moving with the quiet gait of a woman who'd spent a lifetime navigating the dark of the cellars. Fear was a bitter taste at the back of my throat, but it was anchored by a cold, sharpening resolve.

The familiar silhouette of Église Notre-Dame loomed against the indigo sky, its ancient Gothic spires seeming to pierce the oppressive atmosphere that had settled over Épernay. I had risked the tense journey from Aÿ, moving through a landscape that felt increasingly like an armed camp. I slipped through a heavy side door, the cold iron of the latch biting into my gloved hand. Every creak of the ancient building echoed like a warning. Outside, the wind howled like a hungry predator, rattling the leaded stained-glass windows—a mocking contrast to the raw turmoil churning within me.

The biting November wind seeped through the stone, mingling with the ghostly scents of faint incense and sweet candle wax. Hushed whispers rippled through the cavernous space. The heads of the great Maisons and growers were shadowed with worry, illuminated by the unsteady dance of candlelight. We looked like a congregation of ghosts, clinging to the shadows.

Monsieur Dubois stood near the altar, his knuckles stark white as he gripped the rail. "Thank you all for coming. We have grave news." His voice was a strained whisper. "As you may have heard, Robert-Jean de Vogüé and Claude Fourmon have been arrested, as well as a dozen others."

A gasp swept through the sanctuary like the wind catching in the eaves. Robert-Jean, too? He was our beacon in this encroaching darkness, our steadfast symbol of defiance.

"Fourmon has been sent to Buchenwald." Dubois's head dropped to his chest, his voice heavy with a weight no man should carry. "And Robert-Jean was sent to a military tribunal. I am grieved to tell you, they've sentenced him to death by firing squad. In two days."

The air was suddenly too thin to breathe. The room seemed to tilt, the candles blurring into streaks of light. First our sweet Claire, now Robert-Jean and Fourmon. Despair sank its claws into my heart.

Monsieur Lefevre stepped forward, his shoulders vibrating with barely suppressed rage. "Klaebisch has seized control of Moët & Chandon. Other Maisons, too—their leaders sent to prison camps. Piper-Heidsieck is completely under German control."

The news tightened like a noose around my throat. I stepped into the light, my voice cutting through the rising panic. "Monsieur de Vogüé is the heart of the CIVC. Without him, there is no trade. There is only the systematic gutting of our cellars and the sight of our life's work being bled dry to toast a German victory. We will be left with nothing but the dust on our racks and the rot in our soil."

Lefevre shook his head, his voice a low, jagged warning. "If we push now, Lily, they'll take our land."

"They will take it anyway!" I spun toward the other *vendangeurs*, forcing them to meet my eyes. "We are the guardians of this legacy, and we are being hunted. I say we march together to the Hôtel de Ville tomorrow. Stand united before the Weinführer and give him a choice: Robert-Jean lives, or the cellars go silent."

Bernard de Nonancourt stepped forward, his face pale in the flickering light. He was young, his shoulders not yet broad enough for the weight of the Laurent-Perrier name, and his eyes were wide with a terror he couldn't mask. "No more shipments? No more cooperation? That's suicide. It's our livelihood you're gambling with."

I addressed the entire group, my voice ringing against the vaulted stone. "If they kill de Vogüé, they kill the soul of Champagne. We stand together to tell Klaebisch: No Robert-Jean, no Champagne. Let him explain that to Berlin."

The words had barely left my lips when a low, rough

murmur rose from the back pews. It started with the growers, a sea of *"Oui"* and *"C'est vrai"* that swelled until the cavernous sanctuary hummed. They didn't wait for Dubois to lead; they surged forward, their heavy work coats rustling like a tide against the masonry—a wall of gray wool and grim faces illuminated by the guttering tapers.

Dubois looked at the men who tilled the soil and the men who owned the labels, seeing a unified front he couldn't have dared hope for minutes ago. He nodded, a sharp, decisive movement. "Eight o'clock tomorrow morning, then. The Hôtel de Ville."

"Bring everyone," I told them as they began to leave in a rush of frantic whispers. "Your wives, your children, your cellarmen, and your vineyard workers. If he wants to execute the heart of Champagne, he can do it in front of all of us."

I stood by the side door, nodding and gripping calloused hands until the last of them had vanished into the night. Only when the cathedral fell silent did the mask slip.

My knees buckled. My palms were slick, and the cold air suddenly seared my lungs. I hadn't just called for a protest; I might have just invited my neighbors to a massacre.

Outside the tall iron gates of the Hôtel de Ville, I was wedged into a crush of angry vineyard and cellar workers, women clutching infants, and young boys clinging to their fathers' coats. Beside me, old Pierre leaned heavily onto his stick. Yves gripped his other arm, his eyes fixed on the second-story balcony where the Nazi flag snapped in the wind like a whip.

"Again, harder!" DuBois yelled. A dozen men, their faces purple and bulging with exertion, rammed a massive oak timber against the barrier. The iron groaned, shuddering against the rhythmic, bone-deep thuds. With a final, agonizing shriek of twisting metal, the hinges snapped—a sound like a human scream.

The gates flew wide, scraping across the stone.

The pressure of the mass behind me propelled us forward with a roar of vengeance. We weren't a crowd anymore; we were a wave of human desperation spilling into the courtyard.

Above us, the French doors of the balcony burst open. Otto Klaebisch stepped out, a rigid silhouette flanked by the dark, menacing weight of soldiers. He looked down at us with a cold, disgusted detachment. He raised a gloved hand and snapped it downward.

Crack-crack-crack.

A dozen barrels flashed, spitting lead into the winter sky. The roar of the crowd turned to a strangled gasp. We instinctively ducked, the air suddenly heavy with the stinging, metallic scent of cordite. The soldiers didn't lower their weapons; they leveled them at our chests, the polished steel glinting like ice. One more snap of Klaebisch's wrist and the stones beneath us would be stained forever.

Unbelievably, Le Fevre and DuBois stepped ahead of the mob. They stood as two gray-haired pillars of the Marne facing down the balcony. I noticed the back of Le Fevre's coat was frayed at the seam—a small, fragile detail in the face of so much steel.

"Release de Vogüé!" Le Fevre's voice was a solitary blade.

"Free him," DuBois added, his voice carrying the authority of a hundred harvests. "Or we shut down the houses. Every cellar, every press, every bottle. No more champagne for Germany until you free de Vogüé."

"Free de Vogüé!" we shouted in unison, pumping our fists.

The chant grew, a rhythmic thrumming that shook the air. "Free de Vogüé! Free de Vogüé!"

Klaebisch leaned over the rail. His face was a sickly, translucent white, his leather gloves gripping the stone railing. He could end us all with his next breath. He looked at the shattered gates, then at the two men below, his eyes narrowed as he weighed the cost of his anger. Without us, there was no more champagne. Without champagne, he was a failure to Berlin.

"Silence!"

The command boomed, distorted and cold. "I will not release a criminal. But I will stay his execution. De Vogüé will be imprisoned. He lives only as long as you Champenoise continue to comply. If a single bottle is withheld, he dies!"

Imprisoned. A stunned silence fell, broken only by the ragged, freezing breaths of hundreds of bruised souls. He lived. The air felt thinner, the immediate threat of a massacre receding only to be replaced by a different kind of terror. We were no longer a mob; we were a collective ransom.

"Did you hear him?" I whispered, my voice trembling not with fear, but with a strange, cold electricity.

"De Vogue's still a prisoner, Lily," Yves rasped, his knuckles white on Pierre's arm.

"At least he's a living one." We hadn't won his freedom, but we had bought him time.

"Disperse them! Move!" Klaebisch's order was a jagged bark.

A low, guttural murmur rippled through the courtyard—the sound of hundreds of people turning their backs on the rifles.

"Come on," I told Yves and Pierre, my voice low and urgent. "Don't give him a reason to change his mind. Move out. Now."

We turned to leave, but the Gestapo surged from the

arched shadows—a wall of black leather and silver-capped caps. They didn't speak; they simply swung. Heavy, weighted batons sliced through the air. A young woman near me crumpled, a dark stain blooming in her fair hair as a baton connected with her temple with a sickening *thwack*. Her husband scooped her up and ran blindly for the street.

I did this, the thought burned through me. *I brought them to this courtyard.*

A hulking officer shoved Pierre, sending the old man sprawling. Before I could reach him, the baton swung again, catching me squarely in the shoulder. A muffled thump preceded a white-hot explosion of pain that stole my breath. The officer didn't stop to look; he simply moved on, reaping his way through the crowd.

"Papa!" Yves's voice was a raw tear in the chaos. Together, we hauled Pierre to his feet. He was shaking, his eyes vacant with shock, but he was upright.

"Let's get you home." I wrapped my good arm around his waist, and Yves slung Pierre's arm over his own shoulders.

We limped away as the weak morning sun cast long, distorted shadows over the cobbles. The street outside was quiet, indifferent to the blood we had left behind on the courtyard stones. My shoulder throbbed with every heartbeat, and the taste in my mouth was iron and dirt. But beneath the pain, a cold, hard flame of triumph flickered. Robert-Jean lived. We had stood our ground, and we had won.

11

C'EST L'HOMME
QUI FAIT LA TERRE
IT'S THE MAN WHO MAKES THE LAND

1970, Aÿ. I glance out the tall window of the dining room—my home for nearly fifty years. Outside, the vineyard-covered slopes unfurl in a spectacular expanse of green. It is the best view on the property, and I have seated Cyril Ray specifically to appreciate it. After eleven months of his research visits, I would think his book on Bollinger would be finished, bound, and already gathering dust in a London warehouse. But he's here again at meal time, just in time for a splash of champagne.

Cyril sits opposite me in his rumpled chartreuse sport coat with wide lapels, an eyesore against the patinated dark wood paneling behind him. His face exudes that keen curiosity that I've long since ceased to find charming. I suspect the real reason for his continued visits lies an ocean away: His wife, whom I've never met, is touring America with her own book deal, and Cyril has become lonely. My dining room has apparently morphed into his personal, well-stocked bachelor pad.

The fire settles into a gentle hiss in the stone hearth behind me, casting a warm glow that does nothing to warm my patience. It is *goûter*, a simple afternoon affair, but every detail is planned, right down to the secret reinforcement I've invited, Marcel Clément. The eldest of our Bollinger vineyard staff, a man who's worked for Bollinger since he was a boy, unlike independent *vignerons* who own their land. His hands gnarled and thick, rest on the white linen cloth. I catch his eye and give him a tiny, encouraging nod. I have grown so weary of Cyril's interrogation, I've deployed the nuclear option, a direct source.

I remind myself that Cyril Ray isn't just any journalist. He's writing a book on Bollinger. His impression will be a lasting one. A terrifying thought, but then, it wouldn't be Bollinger without a touch of risk. I have to ensure he hears the right story about the Champagne Riots, from a source he can't possibly doubt.

Yvonne, her cheeks flushed from the heat of the kitchen, enters bearing a tray laden with food, the air suddenly rich with the scent of freshly baked bread and savory herbs. She's no longer the girl I hired twenty years ago, though neither am I. A wince crosses her face as she strains to set down the tray. Must be her aching back again. I must insist on getting her some help; this is too much for her.

On the tray, a small mountain of *gougères*, the golden cheese puffs, still warm from the oven. Platters of creamy *rillettes*, tiny, crisp *cornichons*, and a selection of cheeses that would make even the most discerning connoisseur swoon: a ripe Camembert, a nutty Comté, and a tangy goat cheese drizzled with honey. A shiver of success runs through me as I see Cyril Ray's eyes abandon all pretense of journalism and light up with pure delight. A well-fed journalist, I've observed, is a far more agreeable one. Operation Charm the Journalist. I smile at my 007 analogy.

"I've chosen the Spécial *Cuvée* for our *goûter* today." I twist open the wire cage, and the cork releases with a sigh. "Its fine bubbles and crisp character are the perfect foil for the richness of the rillettes and the savory *gourmandise* of the *gougères*. It is the very soul of the Maison, proof of our commitment to the timeless art of blending," I say for the twenty-eleventh time, hoping to see my words in print very soon.

I pour a pale stream of champagne into our glasses, the delicate fizzing of the bubbles adding a delicious layer of aroma to the handsome spread before us. I raise my glass. "To tradition, to resilience, and to the soul of Champagne itself," I toast with a small smile.

Cyril raises his glass to his lips. He takes a slow, deliberate sip. His keen, bird-like eyes gleam, a nod of professional recognition. He's an Englishman, after all; effusive praise never his style. But the subtle shift in his expression is all the victory I need. He wastes no time in piling his plate high with *gougères, rillettes, cornichons,* and a generous wedge of Camembert.

A gentle smile touches my lips. "Marcel, Mr. Ray is quite keen to hear about the Champagne Riots, a rather spirited period in our history."

Marcel chuckles, like dry leaves rustling, and his old gaze drifts back in time. "Ah, *les révoltes*." He fills his plate with a modest selection and a sliver of Comté. "I was but a lad then, full of youthful exuberance."

Cyril pulls out a pen like a magician with a quarter. "You were actually there?"

"It was a political betrayal!" Marcel's eyes burned with the memory. "The small independent growers were already starving from the frost and the vine-blight. They were desperate, and the big houses knew it. The big houses used that desperation like a blade, threatening to buy cheap grapes from outside the region just to force the local prices down."

Marcel took a bite of a *gougère*, deep in thought as he finished it. He pointed a finger at the table for emphasis.

"The government tried to fix it with the 1908 law, but they

only created a loophole. They drew a border that excluded the Aube district. Because the Aube was off the official map, those grapes were 'foreign' and cheap. The big houses bought them for pennies, spiked them with a bit of Marne juice, and slapped a Champagne label on the bottle. It was a legal swindle." Marcel leaned in, his voice dropping. "Those houses got rich on outside grapes while the local harvests rotted in the fields. That's what sparked the 1911 riots. It was about the families of the Marne watching the big owners steal the bread from their tables."

He points an unsteady finger toward the window. "We saw them coming down the road from Épernay—a wall of hundreds of *vignerons* with torches. Their faces were black with soot, twisted by a fury I have never seen since. I could hear the chant of *'Death to the Thieves!'* before I could even see the flames."

I listen not just to his words, but to the memory in his voice, the raw emotion.

"They didn't just smash barrels; they tore down buildings and torched the cellars of every house that had betrayed them." The air was thick with the smell of smoke and sour wine." He swallows hard, the memory still fresh. "But when they reached Bollinger, they didn't touch a single vine, a single vat. They knew we never bought cheap grapes to make a fraudulent bottle, and never laid off one of our own to hire a stranger. Their silence at our gates... that was the testament to this family's integrity."

Living proof of our family's values; my heart swells with pride. But across the table, Cyril's pen remains poised, his eyes unblinking.

"A moving story, Madame Bollinger." His voice is as dry as parchment. "But one could just as easily call it a calculated business strategy. Bollinger watching from the sidelines while competitors were burned to the ground—an elegant way to corner the market, wouldn't you say?"

My smile feels thin, stretched across bone. "Monsieur, I was a child in 1911. That is precisely why I brought Marcel here. He is the living witness to a truth you seem determined to ignore." I sip my champagne, but it's turned woefully warm.

Cyril props his elbows on the table, a cardinal sin in any French home. "Then let us speak of the present, Madame. What have you done to earn that kind of fealty? Or does the Bollinger reputation rely entirely on the ghosts of those who came before you?"

Heat rushes to my face, but my voice is ice. "Why don't you ask my hundred and twenty employees? They will tell you that while we now sell a million bottles a year, I do not cut corners to chase volume or impress investors."

He gulps his champagne, his eyes darting away.

"Our standards guide how we treat the wine, and how we treat each other. Wouldn't you agree, Marcel?"

"Absolutely, Madame Jacques." Marcel's eyes lock onto Cyril's with a look that would wither a lesser man.

"Perhaps you'd do well to write a chapter on integrity, Monsieur Ray." I place my folded napkin on the table and rise, the movement sharp and final. "It might be a refreshing change for your readers."

Cyril opens his mouth to retort, but I do not give him the floor.

"Now, if you'll excuse me. The vineyards await me." I nod to Marcel. "You'll see Monsieur Ray to the gate? I believe he's heard enough for today."

I walk out, my heels clicking a sharp, triumphant rhythm against the stone tiles—the stride of a woman who has just defended a fortress.

12

AVOIR LA PEUR AU VENTRE
TO HAVE FEAR IN THE BELLY

1944, Aÿ. Four long, gray years of occupation had leeched the color from my life. The enemy had infested the west wing of my home, a scavenging presence that made the very air feel filthy. From dawn to dusk, the house throbbed with the grinding noise of their intrusion: the clumsy thud of boots scraping my parquet floors and the guttural thunder of a language I refused to learn. Keeping Bollinger running was an exhausting battle against a lack of labor, corks, and labels—a numb survival amidst the suffocating stench of cheap tobacco, stale grease, and the chemical sting of the petroleum jelly they used on their gear. It was the smell of infestation.

But lately, the news had turned from a nuisance into a death knell.

We had saved Robert-Jean from the firing squad, but the price was a slow death elsewhere. He was deported to Ziegenhain, and the whispers filtering back were grim: critically ill, emaciated, a ghost of the man who had led us. And then there was Claire. My niece, sent to a work camp for a Resistance cause I hadn't even known she claimed. I found myself crossing my arms as if to hold my own soul together. I had been so focused on the vines that I hadn't seen the fire burning in my own family.

Now, the nightmare was shifting toward the house itself. I knew the Nazis had seized Moët & Chandon, but because of Robert-Jean's "crimes," they had declared the estate a security risk. Otto Klaebisch, the Weinführer himself, was now the head of Moët.

The man who had spent years bleeding our cellars dry now had his boots firmly planted in the halls of the greatest house in Champagne. If they could take Moët, they could take us. It was no longer about quotas; it was about erasure. I could almost feel Klaebisch's eyes turning toward Aÿ, his pen poised to scratch our name off the map and rewrite Bollinger as a Nazi asset.

A scorching August morning. The air was thick and still, the heat a brutal, suffocating blanket. I had just come up from the cellars, my notebook tucked inside my apron, having verified the cases for the latest Nazi requisition. The weight of that theft was a boulder on my chest. Outside, Marie was hanging linens, her movements quick as she raced against the high sun.

The distant drone of engines—a slippery hope for Allied planes—sharpened into a visceral whine that shook the ground. Marie dropped a sheet, her eyes wide.

Above the vineyards, the sky tore apart. The silver silhouettes of American B-17s, marked with white stars, tangled with the dark, predatory shapes of German Messerschmitts and their black crosses. Two airborne armies clashing in a whirlwind of steel. The air shredded with the metallic *tat-tat-tat* of machine-gun fire, a jagged rhythm that signaled the end. This wasn't salvation; it was a slaughter.

German soldiers swarmed out of the west wing like vermin. The cracking of Mauser rifles and the sickening rip of an MG42 tore through the pinot noir rows, a curtain of fire aimed skyward. The odor of scorched oil drifted over the wet laundry.

My breath caught. A plane was falling—a brilliant, terrible torch. The B-17 corkscrewed into the earth just past the east wing. A column of oily black smoke punched into the sky, smelling of high-octane fuel and melting rubber.

"Inside!" I hauled Marie toward the back door. We weren't just escaping the crash; we were fleeing the gray wave of soldiers surging toward the wreckage.

Inside the scullery, I threw the bolt. Marie huddled in the corner, clutching her damp linens like a rag doll. The domesticity of the white laundry felt grotesque against the violence bleeding through the window. I peered out, my heart hammering. The vineyards were crawling with Germans, their rifles raised as they hunted the rows for survivors. This was no longer my land; it was a killing field. The thought of Jacques, swallowed by the last war, and of Claire, trapped in a desolate camp, hardened into a cold knot in my stomach.

A frantic hammering jolted me. A heavy, uneven thud. The rasp of rough canvas and the scrape of buckles as bodies leaned against the wood. The latch rattled with a frantic, metallic chatter.

"Madame Jacques," Marie squeaked, then bit into her fist.

I risked a glance through the side window. Three figures huddled against the door, their khaki American uniforms blackened by soot and blood.

I flung the door open. They stumbled across the threshold, bringing the copper tang of fresh blood into the yeasty air of the kitchen. The tallest one leaned against the frame, his breath a ragged hitch. "Please, Madame! Hide us!"

"Marie, take them to the attic. Hurry!"

I shoved them toward the narrow servants' stairs in the back of the pantry. They moved with an agonizing slowness: the tall one cradled a slumped shoulder, the second pressed a bloodied rag to his face, and the third dragged a mangled ankle, leaving a dark, glistening smear across the stone floor.

I watched them start the climb just as a violent crash splintered the front door. The Germans hadn't knocked—they had kicked their way in.

Panic clawed at my throat. I hissed up the stairwell. "Not a sound."

I stood at the pantry door, my ears straining until I heard the faint, metallic scrape of the trapdoor bolt overhead. I looked down at the dark blood trailing across the floor and, with a surge of desperate resolve, kicked a heavy rug over the worst of it.

Two German soldiers stood in my hallway amidst the splintered wreckage of my door. The Feldwebel stepped forward, his tunic stained with dark salt-rings at the armpits and vineyard dust clinging to his boots. The smell of him was overwhelming: the sour tang of old sweat and the stale, acrid reek of cheap tobacco.

"Frau! We are searching for escaped flyers. You must have seen them fall."

"No one has come through here." I forced myself to meet his eyes. "Your own troops live in my west wing. The Allies would not hide here."

The younger soldier studied my face, his jaw taut. He looked hungry for a catch. "We will search anyway."

He pushed past me, his boot heels snapping on the stone like gunfire. They moved through the ground floor like a scythe, throwing open closets and overturning chairs. I pictured the Americans hidden above us, only a thin wooden board separating them from a firing squad.

When the Germans reached the cellar door, I led them down into the cool, damp darkness. They moved with a predatory, focused silence. Usually, the scent of chalk and aging yeast brought me peace; now, the tunnels felt like a trap.

The younger soldier's flashlight beam cut through the dust, darting behind the heavy oak riddling racks. He paused, his jaw tightening as he focused on a shadow in the corner. With a sudden, violent surge, he lunged forward and shoved a heavy rack aside to clear his line of sight.

The massive rack scraped harshly against the stone, the shock causing the bottles to rattle and chatter in their holes like teeth. One bottle, jarred loose, slipped and smashed against the floor. He didn't even look at the mess. He kept his rifle leveled at the shadows, his eyes searching for a target that wasn't there.

A noise cracked through the silence from upstairs. A sharp, heavy thump, followed by the rolling sound of something metallic across the stone floor. My blood turned to slush.

The soldiers lunged for the stairs. I scrambled after them, my lungs burning. I burst into the scullery to find two rifles trained on Yvonne. She stood frozen, a basket of white eggs clutched to her chest, her eyes wide with fury rather than fear. At her feet lay a heavy copper pot, still wobbling on the stone.

"What are they doing?" she demanded in French, her voice trembling with indignation. "The door is ruined! Are they animals?"

"Silence, *Mädchen*!" The Feldwebel barked, though his shoulders slumped. The excitement of the hunt had vanished.

"My cook," I spoke in German, stepping between the rifles and her. "She is clumsy when she is frightened. She is harmless."

The younger soldier didn't lower his weapon. He reached into the basket, pulled out an egg, and held it to the light as if it were a jewel. With a grin, he cracked it on his teeth and sucked the contents down in one disgusting gulp. He tossed the shell; it crunched under his boot like a bone.

"Contact us if you see the Americans," the Feldwebel ordered.

They left, their rigid strides fading down the street. Yvonne's legs gave way, and she slid down the wall, clutching the basket to her chest. I dropped to my knees and pulled her into my arms, propping us both against the heavy oak table. We sat on the cold stone, two women anchored to each other, finally releasing the breath we'd been holding since the first tank rolled across the border.

The attic had become a silent, secret hospital hovering like a ghost directly above the lions' den. It was a fever on my brain, an agonizing calculation of inches. While the German soldiers billeted in the west wing laughed over stolen Schnapps and cleaned their Mausers, three American heartbeats pulsed just above their heads, separated only by a few layers of aging lath and plaster.

I climbed the narrow, screaming stairs to find Marie already crouched among the rafters. She held a single candle with the steady hand of a statue, her gaze fixed on the men with the fierce, quiet concentration of a diamond-cutter. The airmen—Lieutenant Carter, Sergeant Davis, and Ensign Jones—had become our shared burden. This makeshift ward was a profound, terrifying secret that turned every floorboard creak into a potential death sentence.

I knelt beside the pilot, my knees cracking against the old wood. "Move the shoulder, Carter. Slowly. I didn't risk my house for you to let that joint set like mortar."

Carter's face clenched, his skin the color of wet ash as he fought to rotate the arm. He nursed a fracture that would have sidelined a man in any other world; here, it was a liability he had to breathe through. Beside him, Davis winced as I took a rag from Marie. She had already soaked it in high-proof *eau-de-vie* from the cellars. I dabbed the jagged gash on his forehead with a firm, practiced hand.

"The cellar antiseptic stings like the devil," I murmured.

Davis tried to smile through the burn. "Compared to the flak we flew through, Madame, it's a kiss."

Ten men had gone up in that B-17; only these three had come down. They had no way of knowing if their comrades were corpses in a field or prisoners in a cage. I felt a fierce, maternal protectiveness, but I hid it behind a mask of brisk efficiency. I'd learned that in a war, pity is a distraction. Competence is the only thing that keeps the gallows empty.

Jones's ankle remained the greatest threat to my little hospital. It was swollen tight as a drum, a mottled landscape of blue-black bruising. He couldn't bear weight. If we had to flee on a second's notice, Jones would be an anchor dragging us all down.

I kept the secret from Yvonne for three days, until she caught me on the back stairs with a bundle of bloodied linens.

"There are three Americans in the rafters, Yvonne. They

are wounded, they are hungry, and if they are found, we will all hang from the same beam in the barn."

From that moment, Yvonne's complicity was absolute. She began a campaign of culinary triage. The rich, savory scent of her slow-rendered chicken stock and herb-heavy stews became the airmen's salvation and our most terrifying liability. I had to walk through the house, opening windows to catch the breeze, terrified that a German sergeant with a keen nose would ask why our scanty occupation rations suddenly smelled like a Parisian bistro.

Every tray Marie carried up those stairs was a tightrope walk over an abyss. She moved like a shadow, her footsteps light enough to be mistaken for the natural settling of an old house.

The days blurred into ten. We stabilized their fevers, but the world outside was closing in. I put out feelers through my colleagues at the CIVC—whispers passed during official wine audits. Finally, on a moonless night, a shadow detached itself from the vineyard. A Resistance courier, smelling of damp earth and tobacco.

We led the men out of the attic into a starless sky as black as a funeral shroud. They moved like ghosts, leaning on us, their borrowed French coats hanging loose on their frames. At the edge of the woods, where the vines ended and the wild thicket began, we handed them over.

"Godspeed, *mes amis*." I embraced each one, the rough wool scratchy against my cheek. As they vanished into the trees, the silence of the night rushed back in, cold and absolute.

13

GAGNER LA BATAILLE, MAIS PERDRE LA GUERRE
TO WIN THE BATTLE, BUT LOSE THE WAR

1970, Aÿ. I push open the heavy oak door, stepping out of the cellar's chill into the glare of the October sun. Cyril Ray is at my shoulder, a shadow I cannot shake. The silence of the caves is instantly consumed by sounds of the harvest, screaming hydraulics, idling engines, and the raw, rhythmic shouts of the pickers.

Then, a sharper sound: my nephews. Their voices rise in a jagged argument that cuts through the machinery.

I glance at Cyril. His expression has shifted; that journalistic thirst is written across his face, a hunger no vintage could satisfy. I have to kill this spectacle now. If I don't, this family drama won't just be a memory—it will be a chapter in his next book, no doubt.

Christian, dressed inappropriately in his perfectly tailored Savile Row suit, stands dangerously close to the sorting tables, heckling Claude about the book. Cyril's book. Of course. What else has distracted us from business for a year? Christian could be strolling the Parisian markets on Sunday instead of working in the Pressior. He projects an air of confidence and infallible charm. His lips curl into a broad, engaging smile while pointing out the benefits of Cyril's book on Bollinger.

Claude waves him away like a pesky fly, simultaneously flagging a new truck into the unloading bay, shouting instructions to the sorters above the din, and relaying pressure adjustments to the pressmen. His dark scowl, deep and purple as the pinot noir juice they are crushing, is driven by the urgency to control the output of every machine and every man. Christian is a tornado, creating chaos in Claude's perfect order.

Yves, the vineyard manager, usually so steady, plants his boots right beside Claude. I'm shocked to see him so mad; his face is red and tight as he frantically jabs his thumb back at the fields, desperate to get Claude's attention. The rising volume of their voices hits my chest like a timpani drum.

"Christian, can't you see I'm busy? Enough with the book, alright? The book is a damned waste of all of our time." His tone was sheared wire, coiled tight and dangerous to touch. "Maybe you should spend less time telling my pressmen how far to lower the Pressior and more time entertaining Monsieur Ray with champagne up at the Maison. Isn't that your job? That would be infinitely more useful than getting in my way."

Christian ignores the chaos, flashing us a smile. "Lighten up Claude. You run the Pressior like a military formation. I'm trying to impress upon Cyril that making champagne is a fine art. Don't reduce the process to temperatures, brix, timing, press speed. *Yeech!*"

Yves holds his palms up as if talking to God. "Why aren't you listening to me, Claude? The crisis in the Croix Rouge vineyard is real." His voice cracks with anxiety. "The fruit needs to be harvested right now or we'll write off the entire parcel for the year."

Claude whips around, his face pure frustration. "If you're

so concerned, Yves, perhaps you should have followed my harvest schedule."

Yves jabs a finger toward his chest. "You have this all wrong, Claude. The grapes tell us when to harvest, not your schedule."

I've heard enough. I march into the middle of them. "Gentlemen, this is a Pressior pad, not a theatre. If you three wanted to audition for a French farce, you should have at least dressed the part." I raise a sculpted eyebrow, letting the humor slice through the din. "Perhaps we can reserve the passionate soliloquies until after the harvest? Monsieur Ray is here to chronicle Bollinger's secrets for success, not to referee a family drama."

Cyril steps forward, a vicious gleam in his eye. "Madame Bollinger, don't worry about me. I confess, this conflict defines the greatest Maisons. The grower against the maker against the seller. What could be more vital to my book?" He is lighting a fuse, waiting for the explosion.

My composure dissipates like bubbles left out too long. When I speak, my voice has the grit of cellar limestone, cold and heavy. "You confuse friction with vitality, Cyril. What is vital is the wine. Everything else—the shouting, the egos, your book—is merely the sediment we filter out before the cork is driven home. Now, unless you wish to help with the press, leave me to filter this out."

I turn to my nephews. "Yves, you're in charge of the vineyards. Why are you bothering Claude about your work? Order the tractors out to Croix Rouge and bring in those grapes."

Yves hesitates, glancing at Claude.

"Go. That's what you wanted. Now get to it."

Yves bolts toward the trucks. Claude stands rigid for a heartbeat, his jaw tight enough to snap. He doesn't look at me, but the fight has drained out of him, replaced by a cold, industrial focus.

"Then the *pressoir* schedule is useless. I'll have to rework them for Yves."

"Then I suggest you go and be brilliant, Claude. That's what we all count on you for."

Claude grins and disappears into his office.

Cyril Ray turns a satisfied smirk on me. "So, you still run the show, it seems."

I allow myself a frosty smile. "My dear Monsieur Ray, when my directors have a squabble, I merely offer a perspective. But I assure you, my 'running the show' is far less fascinating than watching the next generation succeed. You must try not to ruin the ending of my story before it's been written."

But Cyril's amused observation is dead right. In my rush to save the harvest and to control the spectacle, I've sabotaged the one thing I truly want. I haven't forced them to collaborate; I merely asserted my dominance, validating their reliance on me and ensuring their bickering will continue the moment I step away. My intervention was a catastrophic failure of my real mission. I should have stopped them from their work and made them figure out what was best for the company, for Bollinger. Bad habits die hard.

Christian's charm snaps back into place. "My apologies, Monsieur Ray. Harvest is a busy time, I'm sure you understand. Come," he guides Cyril away from the crush pad toward the barrel room. "How would you like to do a barrel tasting to check the progress of the fermentation?"

I bless that boy for taking Cyril off my hands. Yves will be back in a few hours with the first truckloads of grapes. Better get these grapes pressed, or Claude will have too many grapes to press at once. I join the women at the sorting table, picking through with great care. They stand straighter with my presence. After a while, feeling the grapes under my fingertips, moving in rhythm with the women, baskets of grapes going into the Pressior, my heart, which has been tight with dread, finally begins to ease.

This is the truth I must hold onto: The future of Bollinger doesn't rest on one person's shoulders, but on three—marketing, production, and vineyard. They have to realize they are stronger together than they are apart. And I must let them find their way without me.

14

UN COUP DU SORT
A BLOW OF FATE

1944, Aÿ. A monstrous crash shattered the night, flinging me into darkness. I gasped for breath, my heart a violent fist punching up my throat, my mind reeling. Disoriented, I fumbled for the bedside lamp, but the power was out. The house electricity, and perhaps the whole town, had gone dark. Dear God, what was happening? The darkness swam around me, thick and nauseating, and I gripped the edge of the nightstand for support. I scrambled out of bed, my bare feet hitting the cold floor, the chill creeping into my bones.

Another explosion sent a vicious tremor through the house. The windows rattled violently, and plaster rained down from the ceiling, dust swirling around me in a ghostly fog. A raw, animal shriek tore through the haze. Marie slammed into my side, her desperate hands clamping onto my bare arm. A blast sent a blinding white flash across the windows, revealing her face—chalky white and contorted with fear. Her fingernails dug into my skin; the pain intensified the panic that gripped us both.

"The Germans!" Marie's voice tore from her throat, raw and animal. "They're bombing us!"

Germans? Confusion warred with terror. Why would the Germans bomb their occupied territory? But through the cracked window, the bursting light of the explosions illuminated the scene outside. German soldiers tumbled out of the wings of my house that they occupied, fleeing in a chaotic scatter into the night. A distant, guttural shouting rose above the din of the explosions, the unmistakable sound of panic in German.

A chilling realization stole my breath. It wasn't the Germans bombing us. It was the Allies. Our liberators were bombing us? That knowledge, thick and nauseating, was a cruel irony, a bitter twist of fate.

Hastily, I pulled on my clothes, my fingers fumbling with the buttons. My hands shook so hard I lost all sense of the fabric. "Marie, we need to get out of here!" The words clawed from my throat.

The house groaned, the walls seemed to sway, and a jagged terror gripped me, a visceral fear that choked my breath. We tumbled down the stairs, the walls shaking violently around us. Dust choked the air, thick with the smell of burning wood and pulverized stone. Another flash, and a portrait of Jacques tore from its hook in the hallway, its glass shattering with a tragic crash. Splintered on the stone floor. A pang of sadness pierced my fear, and in a stupid, desperate reflex, I snatched the broken frame to my chest, its sharp edges biting my palm. I couldn't leave him here.

We burst into the kitchen, finding Yvonne huddled low against the stone larder. Just as a tremor forced the cupboards to fly open and spew their contents across the tiled floor, Yvonne let out a brief, muffled shriek. Plates I'd inherited from Jacques's mother, delicate porcelain edged in gold, hit the stone floor and exploded into a thousand pieces. Crystal glasses, some dating back to the Napoleonic era, smashed into shards that glittered ominously under the flashes of light. I looked at the wreckage: the proof that Jacques's sacrifice, and his faith in a lasting peace, was meaningless. Are we forever doomed to repeat this cycle of domination?

A high-pitched screech interrupted my thoughts, growing louder and closer. The unmistakable scream of a bomb hurtling toward us. I felt the blood rush from my head, a wave of nausea rising in my throat.

"Under the table!" I dragged Marie with me. We dove beneath the pastry table, our bodies trembling, our ears ringing, the whistling intensifying with every passing second. The tabletop shook, fragile as a pie crust fresh from the oven. The kitchen, our sanctuary of warmth and comfort, was delicate shelter between us and impending doom. I pulled Marie close, her shoulders trembling.

A roar swallowed the world. Dishes shattered in the kitchen; the floor bucked with the fury of an earthquake. Dust and debris rained from the ceiling, thick and gritty on my tongue. The smell of sulfur burned.

Each impact was a promise of the end. The house groaned, wood screaming as the weight shifted above us. I gripped Marie's hand, our fingers locking.

This is how we die. Buried under the rubble of my own home.

The foundation shuddered, rattling my teeth and my faith. Where was mercy? I wanted to scream into the dark. Why do men kill us with their wars?

We huddled there in our funeral cocoon, the chaos stretching into an unbearable eternity. The floor tilted violently, and Marie let out a choked sob that was instantly drowned out. Then, finally, the noise grew fainter. The violent shaking subsided, replaced by a terrible, hollow silence. Only the crackling of flames in the distance and the wailing cries of the injured broke the quiet.

Cautiously, we emerged from under the table, our bodies stiff and aching. Yvonne crawled out from behind the larder. We were alive.

The sight of the kitchen was a second blow. A disaster of crumbling plaster and debris. Pottery shards littered the floor, cupboards hung precariously from their hinges, and a thick layer of dust coated everything, turning the familiar room into a ghostly tableau. It was the sight of a stable world gone mad.

Yvonne grabbed a broom from behind the door. Mindlessly, stupidly, she and Marie tried to restore some semblance of order to the chaos, sweeping the floors, wiping the cupboards clean, gathering the rubble to throw out.

Old Pierre and Yves stumbled into the kitchen, their faces ashen. Yves was supporting his father, hobbling in pain. Pierre's trousers were torn, dark blood staining the fabric, and his leg was twisted at an unnatural angle.

"Lily, are you alright?" A wet, choking wheeze came from Pierre's chest.

I grasped my old friend's hand. "What in God's name is happening?"

"It's the Allies." Pierre's voice was a rasp of disbelief. "They bombed Aÿ. Everyone is in the streets... homes, businesses... everything." He shifted his weight, biting back a groan. "A family was trapped. I lifted some timber... it fell on my leg."

His eyes held a hollow, helpless look that sent a chill through my ribs. "The Dubois' house. It's burning." His voice trailed off, lost in the ruin of his world.

I knelt and covered his hands. They were like marble.

"Yves and I will go help the others." The words felt small against the smoke rising outside. "We'll bring them to the church, or back here. Anywhere with a roof."

I looked to Marie. She didn't flinch, her face a mask of grim resolve.

"Marie, are you okay? Can you clean Pierre's leg? Wrap it in sheets?"

"Yes, Madame," she turned to find supplies.

Yvonne stepped forward, her voice steady. "Bring the injured here. We will be ready."

Yves bent to his father. "You'll be safe here, Papa." He grimaced as he said it, knowing the lie. None of us were safe. Not even from our allies.

My pulse throbbed against my throat. We had to move before the grief paralyzed us. "We'll be back soon." I gripped Yves's hand and headed out the kitchen door.

The town we knew was gone, replaced by a jagged landscape of ash and irony. If the world was ending, we would spend the final hours pulling others from the dark.

I was thankful for Yves's company. Thirty-six, tall and strong from working the vineyards, he moved with a quiet, steady determination that was a stark contrast to my reeling emotions. Together, we stepped out into the chaos. The night air was thick with the smell of smoke and the cries of the injured.

The familiar streets of Aÿ were unrecognizable, transformed into a nightmarish landscape of devastation. The bakery, where I bought my morning croissants, was now just a pile of charred bricks, the sweet scent of baking bread replaced by the stench of ashes. Madame Perrin's flower shop, always bursting with colorful blooms, was a blackened husk. Fires raged where homes once stood, casting shadows that danced a macabre rhythm on the crumbling walls. The air, thick with smoke and the cloying sweetness of burnt grapevines, filled my lungs with each choked breath. A low, mournful wailing seemed to emanate from the very earth itself, despair echoing through the shattered remnants of our town.

We had survived the Germans, only to be butchered by our own liberators. Was this the price of freedom? To be crushed between two warring forces, pawns in a game we never asked to play? Anger warred with grief, a bitter brew of emotions churning within me.

As we made our way through the debris, Yves moved with a purpose, instinctively taking the lead, his broad back a shield against the worst of the chaos. He shifted a fallen beam off the path, his muscles straining, and then turned back, his hand on my arm, guiding me away from a crumbling wall.

The true cost of this 'liberation' became horrifyingly clear. The building at *7 rue de l'Huilerie*, another of my properties that the German soldiers had occupied, was a smoldering ruin. I noted that they escaped before the bombs hit, but a wave of dread washed over me. Who else had been caught in the blast? Each shattered window, each crumbling wall, was a reminder of the indiscriminate nature of war.

We passed two young men, really just boys in ill-fitting uniforms, lying partially beneath a fallen piece of roof timber. They wore the gray of the Wehrmacht, the hated enemy who had been our unwanted guests for years, but their faces were clean of stubble, frozen in the same bewildered shock as the others. One boy's hand was still curled around a tattered leather-bound notebook, his thumb resting on the ribbon bookmark. The other lay with his steel helmet beside him. His fingers, stiffened in death, clutched a small, crude wooden bird, its wing slightly splintered. Seeing the dead Germans who were someone's sons, pulled a fresh, agonizing layer of grief over my anger.

We found more bodies, half-buried in the debris, each one horrific evidence of the nightmare. My hand felt for a pulse on a wrist under a pile of bricks, a young woman whose face was contorted in a silent scream. No hint of life under her skin. A sob tore through my chest. Yves knelt beside me, helping me up gently, and moved on. He didn't say a word, but his presence was a quiet comfort, a shared burden.

Nearby, a child lay sprawled on the pavement, a doll clutched in her lifeless hand. I turned away, the guilt for leaving the dead behind settling deep in my gut. My stomach churned with nausea at the thought of how many lives, how many dreams, had been extinguished today.

The sight of our supply barn burning sent a jolt through me that overrode the terror. "Yves, the barn!"

We ran. My boots skidded on the grit, my lungs burning as we raced toward the structure. It was the lifeline of the estate—housing the tools, the crates, and the entrance to the hidden vault. If we could just reach the water barrels, if we could stave off the edges of the heat...

But as we drew closer, the heat hit us like a physical wall, forcing us to shield our faces with our arms. The heavy timber skeleton had bucked and splintered, snapped like dry kindling.

It was already over.

Flames licked at the gaping maw where the roof had caved in. The air roared—a wall of scorched oxygen that tasted of burning oak and a sickening, boiled sweetness. Below the barn was my secret, the vault carved deep into the chalk, hidden beneath these very floorboards to keep our finest vintages safe from German pillage. I had outsmarted the Occupation for years, only for this.

I jolted forward. "Maybe the champagne is not be ruined?"

Yeves held me back from the flames. "Listen, Tante Lily."

Pop. Crack. Shatter.

The fire turned the bottles into grenades, shards whistling through the smoke. Each explosion was a legacy dying. Years of painstaking work, hidden from the enemy in the dark, now bled into the ash.

My stomach lurched. "No!" The word consumed by the fire's roar. Yves held my quaking shoulders and watched the flames with me. The heart of Bollinger, the lifeblood of Aÿ ... This was where Jacques and I had shared our dreams. Even after his death, I'd gathered a family here, a team bound by blood or soul. Now, it was being consumed, the precious wine boiling into nothingness. I could only hope the other cellars were intact. I watched the flames, helplessly. watching the fire devour the one thing I thought I had saved.

Guilt hit me—a cold, sharp rebuke. How could I grieve for bottles when the world was bleeding?

I pulled Yves away from the heat. "There's nothing we can do here. Let's go help the survivors."

The roar of the burning barn warmed our backs as we reached a woman on the street. Her eyes were wide, filled with a hollow panic as she clutched a crying baby to her breast.

"Come with us." My voice was hoarse, tasting of sulfur and smoke. "We'll find you shelter."

I didn't wait for her to agree. I hauled her up while Yves knelt to an elderly woman, lifting her as if she were a bale of vineyard clippings. His face softened as he cradled his precious cargo.

"The church," I gestured toward the spire. "We'll take them there."

We moved through the wreckage of Aÿ, our boots crunching on broken glass and pulverized brick. We passed men carrying a sheet-covered body toward the graveyard, their heads bowed.

But as we rounded the corner, my hope died. The church

doors were flung wide, but the vestibule was a crush of people. Wails echoed off the stone. The injured were lying on the cold floor between pews stretching all the way to the altar. The priest stood in the center, his vestments torn, shaking his head at a line of people still trying to push inside.

"There's no room, Tante." Yves looked at me, the weight of the woman in his arms making his breath hitch.

"To the house, then." I gestured for our procession to follow. "We're taking you home."

We trudged down the cobblestone streets to the courtyard, dreading the climb up the long, sweeping staircase. Marie stood at the top, waving us away. Her voice was listless, exhausted. "Madame. Others have come to us. The house is full now."

"Then we'll make room, Marie." My voice cracked. "We must make room for all of them."

I looked back at the faces following me up the stairs—eyes dull with smoke and shock, bodies slumped with exhaustion in the shimmering glow. Tomorrow, we'd figure out how to feed them.

A small boy, no older than five, was clutching my skirt, his eyes wide with terror, his small body trembling. Where was his mother who was with him? But asking him would only cause him further distress.

"Come, child." I scooped him up, his small body light in my arms. Sobs wracked his tiny frame, and I held him close, whispering soothing words in his ear. "Everything will be alright."

I prayed it was not a lie.

15
L'HEURE DE VÉRITÉ
THE HOUR OF TRUTH

1971, Aÿ. The cellar air is a constant 12°C, yet my ears burn with the slow-building heat of a woman kept waiting. Today is the day I allow Cyril Ray to taste the *Vieilles Vignes Françaises* —the creation I guarded like a lioness from the very man who called these ancient, ungrafted vines "relics of a delusional past."

He thinks he is here for a drink; I am here for a reckoning.

He has pestered me for a taste on every visit for a year. Christian suggested that having Guy Adam, our *chef de cave*, present would "manage" the Englishman, but I loathe submitting Guy to the torture of a critic dissecting our treasure like a specimen in a biology class.

These grapes were picked on my seventieth birthday: October 2, 1969. I had planned to keep the bottles sleeping until my seventy-fifth, God willing, but Cyril's book is already at the publisher. The danger of his mockery has passed; the ink is dry. The wine requires three more years to reach its zenith, but even a critic as cynical as Ray should be able to glimpse the glory it will become.

The vaulted tunnels usually soothe me with their tapestry of damp stone and yeasty fermentation, but today they feel less like a sanctuary and more like a stage. Dozens of candles cast dancing shadows across the bottles—slumbering sentinels of history.

In a small alcove, the table is a study in white linen and polished glass. Christian, Yves, and Claude wait in the soft light, their faces taut. But the chair for Cyril remains empty.

A figure emerges from the gloom, carrying a small lamp: Guy Adam. He bears the magnum of *Vieilles Vignes Françaises* with the reverence of a high priest. As he sets the bottle down, I glance at my Bulova.

"Where is Monsieur Ray, Christian?" My voice is dry as the chalk walls.

Christian begins a polite excuse, but I cut him off with a look. "He has waited two years for this. Can he not manage to be—"

A sudden, impossible gust of wind tears through the alcove. The candle flames whip wildly and die. Absolute darkness falls—thick, heavy, and smelling of old earth.

"My apologies, Madame Bollinger!" Cyril Ray's voice tears through the stillness like lightning. "I fear my lateness has been so offensive it extinguished all the light in the world!"

I calmly produce a small, silver lighter. With a flick of my thumb, a single flame springs to life. I relight the candles one by one, their golden glow banishing the shadows from his grinning face.

"Monsieur Ray, I see you have once again arrived just in time to be late. I was about to toast your absence." I nod to Guy. "Do not let our guest's dramatic entrance delay the wine any longer."

Guy removes the muselet with a practiced motion. He eases the cork out with a soft *pfft*—the sound of a sacred act.

He pours a delicate measure into each glass, the wine catching the light as a pale, fleeting gold.

Cyril holds the glass to the candlelight, his frown deepening. He inhales with a sharp, professional sniff and takes a sip. He grimaces. "I taste the earth, certainly. Chalk and minerals... but it is a skeleton, Madame. Lean, acidic, and frankly, a bit thin. I am afraid I see a significant risk here. It is quite... unformed."

A tense quiet falls. Christian shifts, and Claude's lips curl into a surly smile.

I let out a soft, elegant laugh. "My dear Monsieur Ray, you are judging the impact of *Live and Let Die* by its opening page." I hold his gaze, unblinking. "What you taste is the subtle intrigue—the beginning of a grand design. The artistry is in the promise. The challenge is not to write about a perfect wine that has already arrived; the challenge is to recognize a masterpiece while it is still a work of fiction. Take another sip, Monsieur. Stop looking for the period at the end of the sentence and taste the verbs."

He hesitates. A long silence stretches between us, the only sound the faint drip of water from a distant wall. He takes another, longer sip, pondering my words.

I turn from the table, a calm smile on my face. "Remember walking these vineyards, Cyril? You called the layout a shambles. But there is a reason we plant *en foule*—in a crowd. These vines are not polite, modern rows. They are a dense, fighting chaos. They must struggle against one another to reach the chalk, and that struggle is exactly what you are tasting. It is the grit required to survive."

I gesture toward the darkness beyond our circle of light. "The second tradition is *provignage*. We do not use grafts. We bury a cane while it is still attached to the mother. It takes root while still drawing breath from the parent. It is an umbilical cord of wood and sap."

I turn to my nephews. "You are those canes. You draw your strength from the same heart that beat a century ago. You aren't just heirs; you are the original stock renewed. Whether by blood or by soul, you are cultivated in Bollinger's values. That is what it means to be a Bollinger."

Christian nods, his gaze fixed on his glass. "It is the essence of the original stock," he whispers. "Renewed."

Yves says nothing, but his eyes shine in the candlelight as he looks at the labels on the racks. He doesn't need to say he tastes the roots; he *is* the roots.

Then Claude leans forward, his hand trembling slightly. "When I came to you after the war, I was broken. I thought this champagne was a folly of a bygone era. I was wrong." He lifts his glass to the light. "I don't just taste the wine, Tante Lily. I taste the woman who taught me how to live again."

Cyril is silent for a long moment, watching the bubbles rise like tiny pearls. The crusty skepticism finally cracks. "Madame Bollinger, I must admit... I was looking for a wine, but I found a biography. I taste the future, and it is far more stubborn than I gave it credit for."

I lift my glass, meeting their eyes one by one. This is the moment a soul is laid bare and acknowledged. We drink. We inhale the cold chalk, the old yeast, and the fierce, unyielding promise of centuries.

16

PETIT À PETIT, L'OISEAU FAIT SON NID
LITTLE BY LITTLE, THE BIRD MAKES ITS NEST

January, 1945, Aÿ. The final truck rumbled past the gates, an olive-drab ghost vanishing into the biting white fog that had swallowed the road to Belgium. I watched them go—my Americans—and felt a fierce, maternal ache twist in my chest. The faces I had come to know over shared rations were now masks of grim determination, disappearing one by one into the mist.

The winter wind bit at my face, driving flurries of ice against the stone, but a deeper cold settled in my stomach. They were heading for the Ardennes, thrown into a hole in the line where a surprise German counteroffensive had turned the forest into a slaughterhouse. How many of these boys, barely men, would be lost to the deep snow? How many mothers would weep over letters I had watched them write? The thought chilled me more than the frost.

I stepped back inside, where the silence was so heavy it felt like a physical weight. Just days ago, these halls had echoed with boisterous laughter and the warm, comforting scent of damp wool and endless coffee. Now, the rooms harbored only the thin, dusty ghost of their absence. A tremor hit me, and I pulled my worn shawl tighter against the sudden draft.

On the stone porch, a beat-up harmonica lay forgotten, its chrome glinting faintly in the weak winter sun. I picked it up; the metal was biting, cold as a coin, but I tucked it into my pocket. It was a small, silver memento of a life that might never return.

Standing in the center of the dining room, the memories flooded back—the low, frantic murmurs of officers huddled over maps on my mahogany table. "Ardennes... cut off... Bastogne is critical." I hadn't understood their strategy, but the cold terror in those hushed voices was a language I knew intimately. It was the final, ferocious gasp of an enemy we thought was beaten, and their fear mirrored my own.

I looked at the ballroom, once a place of celebration, now still smelling faintly of the antiseptic I'd used in the makeshift infirmary. I could still see the young British lad who had shown me a picture of his sweetheart, his shy smile full of a hope I wasn't sure he could afford. We had cleaned their wounds and mended their clothes, offering words of comfort to hold back the dark. Now, the only sound was the fading groan of the trucks, leaving us alone with the ghosts of what we had tried to save.

My sisters, Guillemette and Thérèse, joined me at the window, their breath fogging the cold glass.

"Do you think they'll be all right?" Guillemette whispered.

I watched the last truck vanish, my heart a heavy stone. "They are young and they are angry. That is a formidable combination." The words felt like a shield I was holding up for them, and for myself. How much more blood must the Ardennes drink before this madness ended?

I stayed there until the last vibration of the engines bled out of the air. The silence that followed was a physical weight—the sound of a house holding its breath. I turned from the window and took my sisters' hands, our fingers interlacing. We were a circle of three in a cold, quiet Maison, but we were the roots that would not move.

March, 1945. Aÿ. The stationery was a taunt—a vast, snowy expanse that mirrored my own barren desk. I stared at the white page, my pen hovering like pruning shears over a dormant vine, deciding where to cut and what was worth saving.

My American agent, Richard Blum's request for champagne had arrived with the post, written with the breezy optimism of a man who watched the war through newsreels. To Richard, the Allied crossing of the Rhine at Remagen earlier this month meant the gates of Europe were flung open for business. He lived in a world of effortless abundance; to me, the world was still this strange, hollow netherworld. The American soldiers who had filled my halls with the scent of Lucky Strikes and dirty socks were long gone. They had survived the bloodbath of the Ardennes in January only to be funneled east, their blood soaking into German soil to finish a war that refused to die.

They had left us in a sudden, jarring silence, leaving behind only scarred floorboards and a house that felt hollow. We were caught in the breath between a nightmare and a morning that refused to arrive.

LICENSE TO THRILL: LILY BOLLINGER

Dear Richard,

I began. My knuckles were a map of red, angry cracks.

I must first express the gratitude of France for your country's part in our liberation. It is a joy beyond words, though a joy currently tempered by a great deal of masonry.

I paused, the nib of my pen trembling. My gaze drifted to the window. Across the courtyard, our storage buildings stood like hollowed skulls, their roofs punched in by aerial thermite. Beyond them, the vineyards were a graveyard of gnarled wood. My *vendangeurs*—the men who knew every curve of these hills—were gone. Some were behind barbed wire; others were simply... gone. I had no idea how to replace a century of intuition with the few weary hands left in Aÿ.

The truth is, Richard, the infrastructure of Champagne is a shattered glass.

I wrote, the scratch of the pen loud in my bare office.

We are not just rebuilding walls; we are waiting for a generation to return. It appears even our corks have decided to go on holiday. The Wehrmacht managed to liberate 70,000 of our bottles before the Allies could liberate us. You ask for a shipment, but I am currently an architect of ruins. However, do not mistake our scars for defeat. Bollinger will be ready. The wine, like the woman, is recovering. We are battered, but the roots are deep. With any luck, after the next harvest, we should be able to rebound with some beautiful Bollinger champagnes for your clients. That is our joyous promise to you. 1945 should be a much better year for all of us, God willing.

I pressed the Bollinger wax into the seal, the smoky scent briefly masking the hospital smells from the ballroom below. I stayed there for a moment, my hand resting on the cooling wax, caught in the tension of a war that had moved on but hadn't yet ended.

A soft rap at the door announced Thérèse. She didn't wait for an invitation, pushing the door open just enough to let a sliver of warm light from the hallway cut across my barren desk.

"You've been at this since dinner, Lily. The ink is probably frozen in the well, and you aren't far behind it."

I looked up, rubbing my eyes. "The Americans are restless for their wine. Richard Blum thinks the crossing of the Rhine means we're ready to celebrate."

"Richard Blum isn't the one shivering in a drafty office." She crossed the room to rest a hand on my shoulder. Her touch was the first bit of warmth I'd felt in hours. "Leave the ruins and the bureaucrats for tonight. Guillemette has managed to coax a real flame out of the hearth, and the children are asking for their Tante Lily. Come. Put the pen down."

I looked at the sealed letter, my "joyous promise" to the

world, and felt the weight of the day finally settle in my bones. "You're right. I'm starting to see ghosts in the margins."

I followed her down the hall, past the scarred wainscoting where soldiers' heavy kits had scraped the wood raw. We entered the salon, a sanctuary that smelled of beeswax and a well-tended hearth. The shift in atmosphere was a welcome relief; the heavy velvet curtains were drawn tight, a final barricade against the biting fog and the sight of the ruins outside.

My sister Guillemette sat by the fire, her needle moving with hypnotic grace. At her feet, her grandchildren—the new shoots of our family tree—built imaginary chateaus out of smooth river stones on the rug. I sat between my sisters, the warmth of the fire finally reaching my marrow.

"You finished the letter?" Guillemette asked, not looking up from her work.

"I did. I told him the truth—that the sap is rising, but the vine is still scarred." I picked up my needlework tray, the familiar shape a comfort. "Thérèse, have you had any word from the Red Cross? Any news of Claire?"

Thérèse's hands stilled over her linen. Claire, her youngest, was somewhere in the frozen nightmare of the concentration camps. "Nothing," she whispered. "The radio says the camps are being liberated as the armies move east, but the lists are so slow. I wake up in the middle of the night and I can't breathe because I imagine her in the cold."

I reached over and took her hand. "She has your heart, Thérèse. She is a Lauriche. We have always been a family that knows how to survive a hard winter."

"But this isn't a winter." A tear dragged through the fine lines of her cheek. "It's an apocalypse."

Guillemette leaned over, squeezing her arm.

"We have to have faith." I steadied my voice. "Faith is not pretending the danger isn't there. It is refusing to let the darkness have the final word. We kept this house standing while the boots of the enemy rang on our floors. We will keep the lamps lit until Claire walks through that gate."

The *prick-prick-prick* of our needles became a rhythmic, domestic defiance. Outside, the world was still a landscape of mud and uncertainty, and our boys were crossing the Rhine into the unknown, but in this room, we were building something the war couldn't touch.

17

C'EST EN FORGEANT QU'ON DEVIENT FORGERON

IT IS BY FORGING THAT ONE BECOMES A BLACKSMITH

1971, Aÿ. Claude stops at the oak doors of the cooperage, his hand hovering over the iron latch. He throws a narrow, impatient gaze toward Cyril, who's dabbing at his forehead with a monogrammed handkerchief.

"Is this truly necessary, Madame?" Claude's voice is a low rumble of discontent. "We have three casks to finish before the fête tomorrow. We don't have time for a tour."

"Monsieur Ray is here to understand the importance of the oak barrels to Bollinger champagne, Claude."

He huffs and heaves the door open.

"Egads," Cyril gasps, stepping into the threshold. "Like walking into a sauna. Hotter in here than outside."

"Embrace the heat. Think of it as a small penance for the divine complexity the barrels add to the champagne." The dry, intense heat of the high-ceilinged cooperage is so thick it presses against the very drums of my ears. Yet I adore it. It is a necessary, deliberate heat, a testament to tradition. The air is a swirling, complex vapor: the coarse scent of raw sawdust, the sweet heart of fire-laced French oak, and the sharp tang of iron. How can anyone not be amazed?

The rhythmic, metallic *ping* of a cooper's hammer, tapping a hoop into place, echoes off the walls ... the very pulse of Bollinger, primitive and ceaseless. A few high windows shoot shafts of golden light through the haze, illuminating dancing dust motes above the massive stacks of heavy staves.

But Cyril is beginning to liquefy. Why on earth had he chosen a three-piece Savile Row wool for a midsummer trek through a furnace? A masterpiece of tailoring, no doubt, but utterly suicidal in a room where the air is more steam than oxygen.

He fusses with his bowtie—a silk foulard that has gone limp as a dead fish. His fingers fumbling against the starch of a high-collared cotton shirt. A jagged map of the British Empire is blooming across his chest, the fine blue fabric clinging to his ribs. He grips his Smythson leather notebook as if it's a life raft, though even the gold-edged pages look ready to curl and surrender.

"Impressive, isn't it?" I gesture to a mountain of raw barrel staves. "We've been making our own barrels right here since 1829. We're nearly the only ones who still do this, Cyril."

He tugs his collar open, exposing a throat flushed a violent shade of pink. "Can't imagine why. It's positively medieval, Lily. The rest of the world has moved to stainless steel tanks. It's cleaner, easier to control, and doesn't require a bonfire in July. This is old-fashioned to the point of masochism."

Claude doesn't slow his pace, his boots crunching decisively through the wood shavings. He's endured Cyril's company enough times to know that the man is all garnish and no steak, and today "Steel tanks are sterile tombs, Monsieur." Claude keeps his arms locked across his chest, his gaze fixed forward. "Oak allows the wine to breathe, to oxygenate, to find its structure."

"Structure?" Cyril snorts, flicking a stray splinter off his damp sleeve. "Why trust a vintage to a porous piece of timber and hope for the best when you could have the precision of a laboratory?"

Claude stops dead beside a stack of timber. I see his lips moving slightly, counting to ten to control his temper. When he speaks again, his voice is low and controlled, ignoring Cyril's comment entirely.

"Every stave you see is aged for three years in the open air, surrendered to the rain and the sun to leach out the bitter tannins." Claude runs a calloused thumb over the rough wood. "The oak takes the harshness out of the wine, and in return, it gives it a soul."

"A soul," Cyril daubs his neck with his sodden handkerchief. "I believe the technical term is 'phenolic extraction,' but do let him continue his poetry."

"It's about keeping the micro-flora." I step over a pile of shavings. "We even repair our own casks, some nearly a century old, to preserve the ecosystem of yeasts that exist nowhere else. You can't buy that in a catalog. You have to earn it through time."

Claude leads us into the toasting area, where his coopers heat the curved staves over an open fire. He stands near the flames, seemingly immune to the temperature, while Cyril keeps his distance.

"Oh... I get your game, now, Lily. Clever." Cyril traces the scorched rim of a barrel, his mouth curling. "It's not a cellar you're running, it's a secret munitions factory disguised as a Champagne House. If one of these babies were to go up in flames, what would 007 call the vintage? *Goldsinge*? Or perhaps... *The Man with the Golden Burn*?"

Despite his absurdity, a smile tugs at my lips. "Are you suggesting we aim for a vintage that tastes like an explosion? This is champagne, Cyril—not clandestine arson. I won't name our bottles after Bond escapades. No 'Toastapussy' in my cellar."

Cyril doesn't flinch. "You must admit that a very heavy over-toast could be a unique marketing scheme. You could call it 'Live and Let Fry.'"

"Or we leave the roasting to British spies and stick to our traditional techniques." I tap the charred wood, ash staining my fingertip.

"Ah, but the best wines are always stressed to the max, are they not? Greatness requires a spark of danger." The brazier's orange light catches the twist in Cyril's smile. "Give me a barrel that flirts with the flashpoint. After all, 'You Only Toast Twice'—once for the grape, and once for the oak."

"And risk the whole vintage?" The heat flares in my cheeks, a jolt of adrenaline at the challenge. "That's not winemaking, Cyril; that's betting the house at *Casino Royale*. One wrong spark and this cooperage ends in a very expensive ball of fire."

Claude's gaze bounces between us. Beside him, the young cooper has stopped his rhythmic rotation of the staves, mesmerized by Cyril's performance.

"Risk is the primary ingredient, Lily." Cyril gestures grandly toward the brazier. "A little controlled danger to create something truly explosive. 'Dr. No-Toast?', 'The Spy Who Loved My—"

A violent crackle cuts him off as the oak flashes into open flame. A pillar of fire roars toward the rafters. The cooper yelps, stumbling back as the heat hits us like a physical blow.

Claude is a blur of motion. He yanks a red canister from the wall. The sharp, mechanical hiss of the extinguisher drowns out the fire, coating the charred barrel in a thick cloud of white chemical snow.

The young cooper looks up, face pale. "I am so sorry, Monsieur Claude, I—I got distracted."

Claude lowers the nozzle, the hiss of the extinguisher dying into a heavy, chemical silence. White powder clings to his soot-stained shirt like unseasonable snow. He doesn't look at the trembling apprentice; his eyes are fixed on Cyril as he gestures to the chemical-covered mess that used to be a thousand-franc barrel.

"Is this the 'profound reaction' you were looking for, Monsieur?" Claude's voice is a low, dangerous vibration. "Or can we go back to talking about wine?"

Cyril's pristine Savile Row wool is caked in chalky grit, his hair a wild nest of grey dust. A smarter man would be apologetic. A quieter man would be mortified. But Cyril doesn't even flinch. He simply raises a finger, eyes twinkling through the grime.

"'License to Ignite?'"

A laugh bubbles up before I can choke it back with my sense of propriety. It's an atrocious joke, delivered at the exact moment I should be calculating the replacement cost of a hand-hewn barrel, yet the timing is impeccable.

I match his grin, feeling the residual heat still glowing on my cheeks. Despite the acrid sting of smoke in my lungs and the ruined barrel at my feet, the man is brilliant. Irritating, brash, and a total liability to my insurance—but certainly, brilliant.

Christian rushes through the cooperage entrance, then stops short, his nose wrinkling at the acrid sting of the air. He looks from the scorched barrel to Cyril, who stands frozen like a marble statue—if the statue were dressed in a ruined Savile Row suit and dusted head-to-toe in white fire-retardant powder.

"What in the name of God happened in here?" Christian demands.

"A brief flirtation with the flashpoint." I find a wicked satisfaction in seeing Cyril's flamboyant dignity smothered in chemical snow. "The result of too much Bond and not enough focus."

Christian shakes his head, waving away a lingering cloud of dust. "More bad news, I'm afraid. The *Fête de la Saint-Jean* cask race is tomorrow, and we're down a man. It's Yves's last race, so we cannot forfeit, but we have no one left to pull from the floor."

Cyril blinks, a puff of white powder falling from his eyelashes like fresh snowflakes. "A cask race? Some sort of... competitive drinking? Count me in!"

"It is a relay, Monsieur," Christian snaps, his patience clearly evaporated. "We roll two-hundred-kilogram oak barrels through the streets of Aÿ, uphill over the cobblestones, as fast as humanly possible. Then we pass the barrel to the next man."

Cyril's enthusiasm vanishes instantly. A calculation clicks into place in my mind. It's a gamble, certainly ... Cyril has the muscle tone of a poached pear ... but it's exactly the penance he deserves.

"This is your chance, Cyril." I plant my hands on his shoulders, feeling the chalky grit against damp wool. I can feel him trembling, or perhaps it's just the heat finally getting to him. "You nearly burned down the heart of this house with your distractions. You owe us, Cyril. You owe Claude, and you owe the boys."

"Me?" he squeaks. He tries to peel his sodden, powdered linen shirt from his chest with two fingers. "Lily, I'm a creature of the men's club. I haven't exercised since primary school athletics. My heart is strictly for metropolitan use."

"The Cask Race is an opportunity to feel the process like you never imagined." I lean in, letting the dry steel of my resolve meet his frantic gaze. "Time to experience the people of Champagne, their traditions, their celebrations."

Claude looms over him, his eyes narrowed in predatory glee. "You judge the work of the coopers from the safety of your notebook, Monsieur." His voice is a low rumble. "Join us. Get your hands dirty for once instead of just passing judgment."

Christian doesn't wait for an answer. He seizes Cyril's hands, shaking them so fiercely a cloud of white powder puffs off the Englishman's sleeves like a Victorian wig. "I'm telling Yves we've got a new teammate!" He spins on his heel and rushes back toward the vineyard.

I catch the faint trace of a smile on Claude's face as he turns back to the ruined barrel.

Cyril stares after Christian, looking like a ghost that's seen a ghost. "Lily, I've never rolled anything but a coin!"

I smile and pat his powdered, sweating cheek, leaving clean smudges on his face. My heart is still racing from the fire, but the thrill of the trap is better than any brandy. "Tomorrow, Cyril, you will finally understand the true, glorious inefficiency of oak. I suggest you roll it straight. Bollinger only races for gold."

LICENSE TO THRILL: LILY BOLLINGER

June 24th, the *Fête de la Saint-Jean*. The morning sun is a relentless, blinding orb in the azure sky, searing the meticulously tended vines of Aÿ until the air itself seems to shimmer. From my vantage point on the rooftop terrace—a limestone sanctuary I reclaimed from the rubble of the war—the world below is a vibrating tapestry of noise and heat. The stones beneath my shoes are pleasantly cool, but the air carries the heavy, mineral scent of the chalky soil and the faint, tart promise of pinot noir grapes ripening in the July heat.

I snap open a silk-edged hand fan, the rhythmic *thwack* a sharp punctuation against the rising roar of the village. Beside me, my sisters, Guillemette and Thérèse, are already fluttering theirs with a frantic, ladylike desperation. My niece, Claire, leans precariously over the stone parapet, her eyes shaded by a gloved hand.

"Isn't it thrilling?" I gesture toward the streets of Aÿ, where a river of white shirts and colorful skirts has begun to surge against the chalk lines of the course. "This race is a cherished tradition, older than those church bells."

"The English press calls it a Midsummer's celebration," Thérèse murmurs, her voice thin through the humidity.

"It is more than a celebration," I correct her, my eyes scanning the relay points marked by festive banners. "It is an audit of mastery. The coopers roll the new barrels through the town to bless them, but for the houses, it's about the wood. The winning team gets the first selection of the reserve *pièce*—the finest cut of oak set aside for the next year's vintage. It is the only time a cellar master is allowed to be greedy."

Claire's knuckles are white as she grips the railing. "I hope Claude won't get hurt. He hasn't run like this in years, Lily. That man will do anything for a trophy."

"It isn't the trophy he wants, Claire. It's the oak."

I raise my binoculars, the lenses catching the glare. The teams are taking their marks, a vibrant spectrum of winery colors: Ayala, Deutz, Gosset, and our own men in the deep purple of the pinot. Claude d'Hauteville stands at the second relay point, his knees working like pistons even as he waits. Christian is at the start, radiating a competitive zeal that makes him look like a greyhound in the slips.

Then, there is the albatross.

Cyril Ray stands at the final leg, looking like a man awaiting a firing squad. He is stuffed into a borrowed Bollinger shirt that strains so violently across his midsection I fear the buttons might become projectiles. His dark trousers are rolled messily at the ankle, and—most tragically—he is wearing his thin, ridiculous London city shoes.

A sharp pang of regret stings me. If he breaks a hip on my cobblestones, I'll have the British embassy at my door by nightfall.

"Monsieur Ray looks as though he's about to faint," Guillemette observes, her fan slowing as she takes him in.

"He is about to learn the difference between criticizing a barrel and mastering one," I say, though my laugh feels a bit hollow. The sight of those polished leather soles against the dusty track is a recipe for disaster.

The church bells suddenly cease. The silence that follows is sharp, heavy with the smell of sawdust and sweat.

"Oooo, they're starting," Claire whispers, crossing herself as she leans over the parapet. "On your marks... get set..."

A single, shrill whistle blasts.

"GO!"

The roar from the streets surges up the limestone walls, a physical force. A cloud of fine, white chalk dust erupts at the start, momentarily obscuring the runners. I hand the binoculars to Guillemette. "Look at your boy go."

We watch Christian take the first leg down the *Rue du Cadran*. He is a purple blur, his barrel thundering over the cobblestones with a dull, rhythmic boom. He is untouchable, setting a blistering pace that leaves the Gosset runner in the dust.

He makes the hand-off to Claude. Claire snatches the glasses from her mother, her breath hitching. "My turn."

Claude maintains the lead with a precision that is almost mechanical. He runs the dirt track through the young vines as if the barrel were an extension of his own skeleton, his gaze fixed on the loop back toward town. He is pulling further ahead, a gap of ten, fifteen meters opening between Bollinger and Ayala.

"Go, Claude, go!" Claire screams, her voice cracking over the parapet.

The hand-off to Yves is clean. Yves, despite looking pale earlier, manages the steep rise of the hill with a practiced, long-striding grace. We are ahead by a comfortable margin. It is a locked victory.

And then, there is Cyril.

I take the binoculars back. He is hunched over, his face already the color of an over-oaked Claret. He takes the hand-off from Yves with a panicked jerk. He starts to run, his city shoes sliding on the loose gravel, his too-small shirt hiked up to his ribs. He looks up, sees the town square thick with cheering villagers, and for a moment, I see the light of vanity in his eyes. He realizes he is winning.

In his excitement, he gives the barrel a straight, forceful shove—a rookie's mistake.

The two-hundred-kilogram *pièce* veers violently to the left. It slams into the vineyard trellis with a sickening metallic *crack*. A hoop springs loose, rolling away into the barbed wire. Cyril stops. He actually stops to look for the hoop as the Ayala runner, a burly, seasoned cooper, surges past him in a blur of motion.

"No! Cyril! Keep going!" I am on my feet now, leaning so far over the railing that Thérèse has to grab my waist. "Abandon the hoop! Move!"

The win, the oak, the honor—it all begins to vanish in that agonizing hesitation. Cyril drops his head, abandons the iron ring, and begins to chase his barrel. He takes a bold, desperate risk, cutting a corner of the path to regain ground.

It is a disaster. The barrel ends up behind him on the slope, a rogue cylinder of oak chasing him down the hill. His legs flail, uncoordinated. He gives a high-pitched cry, simply running to keep from being crushed by his own charge. Dust billows around him in a suffocating shroud.

Just as the Ayala man begins his final, straight sprint toward the finish line, Cyril stumbles. He doesn't fall. Instead, his right hand catches the upper edge of the careening barrel. He instinctively throws his full body weight against the top arc. It isn't a push; it's a desperate, perfect brake.

In that split second, his brain seems to bypass exhaustion. He isn't fighting the barrel's speed; he is exerting an opposing force on the higher radius to stabilize the roll. He is steering the momentum. The cask straightens, its velocity surging under this accidental, brilliant control. He rockets past Gosset. Ayala is feet away.

Cyril lets out a guttural, primal sound and slams the barrel forward, beating the Ayala man by a hair's breadth.

The crowd explodes.

Cyril keeps moving for three more paces and utterly collapses, rolling onto his back with his arms splayed like a fallen soldier. His barrel rolls harmlessly into the throng as the roar of victory turns into a collective shout of concern.

"My God!" I push away from the railing, my heart hammering against my ribs. "Is he alright?"

I shove past my sisters, rushing for the narrow staircase. My breath catches in my throat as I fight through the press of bodies in the square—the scent of sweat and sun-warmed wool is suffocating. I push past a woman clutching a baby, a knot of genuine fear tightening in my chest. He has pushed himself too far. If I've killed him for the sake of a race, I will never forgive myself.

Straining to see over the shoulders of the crowd, I find them. Christian and Claude are grinning, lifting Cyril from the dirt. He hangs between them, limp as a wet dishcloth, his face ghostly pale but wearing a triumphant, dazed smile.

They hoist him onto their shoulders, carrying him high above the jubilant crowd—a dust-covered, disheveled hero. The cheers erupt anew, "Bollinger! Bollinger!" Yves, looking drained and grey, gives Claude a quick nod and slips away into the shadows of the cellar entrance, his part in the victory finished.

I stand at the edge of the circle, unable to decide whether to laugh or cry. I watch Cyril's exhausted, soot-streaked face bouncing on my nephew's shoulders, his dignity discarded somewhere back on the Rue du Cadran. A sudden, cold prick of shame stings my conscience. I have been too rough on him. I've treated him like a nuisance to be managed rather than a guest to be hosted, casting him as the villain in my own story simply because he was inconvenient. Yet, he has just nearly martyred himself for a tradition he doesn't even understand.

Cyril has earned his place at my table, not through charm, but through grit. He paid his debt to the house in sweat and bruised pride, and in doing so, he proved he's more than a collection of quips and mind-boggling critiques. Perhaps he is worth the effort after all.

18

APRÈS LA PLUIE, LE BEAU TEMPS
AFTER THE RAIN, THE GOOD WEATHER

May 8, 1945. V-E Day. The meager fire in the salon cast dull shadows on the walls, illuminating the quiet industry of the women gathered there. My grand room, once a stage for elegant gatherings and the bright chime of crystal, now echoed only with the soft, repetitive click of crochet hooks. My neighbors and friends sat hunched over our work, our spines curved like the winter vines we'd spent all day tending. Our hands, roughened by years of vineyard and cellar work, moved with a mechanical, desperate grace.

We were unraveling old wool sweaters, the fibers worn thin at the elbows and grayed by years of use. As I pulled the thread, the yarn kinked and spiraled, holding the shape of the man who'd once worn it. We were transforming these ghosts into tiny garments for the newborns arriving this season—babies conceived in the brief, frantic leaves of soldiers who would never know them. It was a strange rebirth, this knitting of new life out of death. Each stitch was a silent prayer, a small act of creation meant to defy the overwhelming destruction that had become our horizon.

Since the troops had left for the Ardennes, a heaviness had settled over the town, thick with the smell of woodsmoke and foreboding. We gathered every evening like this, huddling for warmth as the fuel stocks dwindled to dust. The chill permeated the limestone walls until it seeped into our very bones, a constant reminder of the young men facing unimaginable hardships in the frozen north. Outside, the wind rattled the windows, carrying the imagined cries of the wounded across the dark hectares of vines. The air itself tasted of ash and the stale, metallic tang of fear.

I looked at the women—the hollows under their cheekbones and the dirt etched into the cracks of their knuckles. A fierce, maternal surge of determination rose in me. I was the steward of the only thing they had left. I would keep these vines alive until their husbands and sons crawled back to us from the camps or the trenches.

Our ears were tuned to the static of the radio, a boxy relic from better times that sat like a shrine on the sideboard. We listened with a hunger that food could no longer satisfy, desperate for any sign that our boys were still fighting, still breathing. One certainly had to be patient with the French infrastructure; even a world war couldn't improve the broadcasting.

"Any word from Claire?" Guillemette's voice was a thin thread of sound in the gloom.

Thérèse's hands stilled; the unraveled yarn dangling from her fingers like a broken vein. She bit her lip, her eyes flashing with a sharp, defensive bitterness. "Do you think I wouldn't have told you?"

Suddenly, the music cut off. A voice, crisp and clear, sounded like a forgotten dream. It was General de Gaulle. Even through the crackle of the airwaves, his tone carried a weight that silenced the chatter.

"Mes amis, la guerre est finie."
I felt my heart hitch, then hammer against my ribs. The war was over. We froze, a gallery of statues, every muscle locked tight by years of bracing for bad news. We stared at the radio, afraid to breathe lest we shatter the moment. It seemed highly improbable that the heavy, suffocating blanket of the last six years could be lifted so cleanly with a single sentence. The "Wine-Führers" had long since retreated, but we had remained in a state of suspended animation—waiting for the other shoe to drop. Now, the bureaucrats had finally surrendered their hold.

A small, sharp sound broke the spell—the clatter of a crochet hook hitting the stone floor as Thérèse's hands went slack. A collective, ragged gasp tore through the room. Slowly, a smile spread across Guillemette's face, her eyes welling with tears of pure, agonizing relief.

"Claire can come home." She reached for Thérèse, her voice thick and choked.

The relief was a violent, shocking thing. It erupted from within, a frantic, ecstatic heat that made my blood sing. I stood up, my legs trembling, and hugged my sisters to my chest. Then, the radio erupted. Not the garbled static of the last six years, but the soaring, defiant opening of *La Marseillaise.* The anthem—forbidden for so long—surged through the room with a triumphant, brassy roar.

The feeling was too overwhelming to hold. I grabbed Thérèse's hand, pulling her up with a strength I didn't know I still possessed. I snatched Guillemette's arm. The ecstatic surge of it demanded movement—a total rejection of the stillness we had lived in for so long.

We began to dance. Not a waltz, nor a proper jig, but a furious, stumbling, giddy shuffle. The three of us were a blur of worn wool and flying tears, a mad, ungraceful whirl around the meager fire. Madame Vautrin and Madame Petit, the baker's wife, dropped their knitting with a clatter and stumbled to their feet, their faces split by radiant, unbelievable smiles.

The silence of the last six years shattered. Sobbing laughter and the rhythmic, clumsy slap of shoes on cold stone replaced the clicking needles. We were dancing to the urgent, vital dream of a future where we didn't have to hide our wine or our words. My legs, which had been weak and tired moments before, felt invincible. My throat, scorched by years of unshed grief, sang out in an intoxicating, crazy relief.

This was an utterly ridiculous spectacle. A Bollinger hostess losing herself in a desperate, frantic jig around a smoky salon. Wildly improper. Wildly undignified. I didn't care. I wanted to howl with it.

Every twirl was a thumb pressed to the eye of the Reich, a rejection of the Germans who had occupied our homes, and a defiance of the Vichy government who had tried to domesticate our spirits. We danced until our cheeks were flushed, our shawls were askew, and our breath came in ragged, triumphant gasps.

Our dance was our true humanity coming out to play after years of hiding in the dark. It was our instinctive way to celebrate the return of our people and the final vanquishing of a seeping evil. The war was truly, gloriously over.

News of returning soldiers and prisoners trickled in like fire and rain—the burning heat of joy for some, the cold, drenching downpour of grief for others. It was a gut-wrenching, disorienting thing to carry. So many were not coming home. Every morning, I watched the faces of my workers as they arrived at the vines, looking for a light that had been extinguished. Their families were bereft, and I, as their employer and their neighbor, felt the weight of every empty chair in Aÿ.

The war had stripped Bollinger to its bones. Our cellars were depleted, our equipment was rusted or stolen, and the global market for luxury was a memory. I looked at the sprawling hectares of vines and knew that the real battle was only beginning. We didn't just need to make wine; we had to restore a legacy. I needed to find glass for bottles, corks for sealing, and, most importantly, I had to find the will to convince a broken world that there was still something worth celebrating.

Robert-Jean de Vogüé was liberated by Allied forces in May 1945. He was, as we feared, a shadow of the man who had led the Resistance in the cellars. He had barely survived the camps, his body brittle and his eyes haunted by things no man should see. But he was home. Despite his broken state, he was a beacon for all of us. Hopefully, he would resume his leadership of Moët & Chandon, but his return was a somber reminder of the price of our defiance.

And then there was our own miracle. Claire, our beautiful Claire, finally came home.

The girl who walked through the doors was a phantom. She weighed little more than an empty harvest basket, her frame so slight I feared the spring wind might shatter her. Her skin was the color of old chalk, drained of the vitality that had once defined her. The vibrant red hair she had inherited from her father, the hair that used to catch the sun in the vineyards, had been sheared off. She wore a shapeless cap to hide the jagged edges of her spirit. Her hands, once so deft and lyrical at the piano, were raw and perpetually shaking, as if they were still trying to ward off the cold of the work camp.

She did not speak much at first. Only a word or two. The

silence in the house was no longer the silence of waiting; it was the silence of a wound trying to close.

My sister, Thérèse, simply held her and fed her broth, spoonful by agonizing spoonful. It would take many, many months for Claire to resurface, and the camp had left its permanent, unseen scars on her heart. But she was here, within my walls, under my protection. And that was enough to stoke the fire in me.

I looked at my niece and then out at the vines. I was no longer just protecting a name; I was rebuilding a world for her to live in. I wanted Bollinger to be more than a business; I wanted it to be a fortress of stability. I would work until my hands were as raw as Claire's to ensure that this House flourished again. We would plant, we would harvest, and we would wait for the bubbles to return to the wine.

19
LA FORTUNE SOURIT AUX AUDACIEUX
FORTUNE SMILES UPON THE AUDACIOUS

1971, Monte Carlo. The door of the black Citroën DS—the hotel's private car—is held open by a driver in pristine white gloves. I step out into a world that has quite clearly gone mad. Behind me, the car pulls away to return to the Hermitage, the Belle Époque jewel where Christian had booked me a suite overlooking the sea.

Everything has been arranged to the letter. Christian is nothing if not a master of the grand gesture: the flight, the silk-lined rooms, the private transport—all designed to whisk me into the heart of the action without a single ruffled feather. But as the Citroën disappears into the swirl of traffic, I realize the Grand Prix has outgrown my memories. It is no longer a mere race; it is a sprawling, chrome-plated beast.

I stand for a moment on the edge of the Place du Casino, feeling the sheer scale of it. The moment my heels click against the sun-baked asphalt, the event doesn't just assault my senses; it invades them with a terrifying, ecstatic feast of noise. It is a mechanical scream that tears through the salt air, vibrating in my very marrow. The engines are a continuous, tearing shriek

—each piston fire an intense promise of speed that travels straight down the spine. This sound is intoxicating. It wraps around my bones, shuddering in my belly, pulling me along with its sheer, frantic energy.

I take a deep breath, and the air is a complex, almost overwhelming perfume. The lilting scent of expensive French florals from the passing crowds mingles with the raw, masculine bite of burning rubber and high-octane racing fuel. It is the only place in the world where that mixture feels like freedom. I giggle to myself, the sound instantly swallowed by a downshift of gears on the track nearby. If I have to choose a way to lose my head at seventy, it might as well be through an overdose of glamour and gasoline.

I have to navigate the human current—linen suits, silk scarves, and the glint of expensive watches—to find our place in this madness. Christian had sent a map, but in this fray, maps are useless. I follow the sound of the water and the unmistakable, high-pitched chatter of the elite carrying me deeper into the harbor. I scan the line of luxury tents and corporate boxes, my heart doing a little nervous dance. I am bracing for what Christian considers "modern." I half-expect a neon sign or something equally garish.

Then, my eyes snag on it, positioned right at the water's edge.

Not our usual discreet Bollinger box, a quiet, tasteful corner where one can sip in peace. No, this is a sprawling terrace draped in shimmering white organza that billows like the sails of a racing yacht. Emblazoned across the top, in letters so bold they demand a salute from every billionaire in the harbor, are the words: "The Bollinger Experience."

Christian, you rascal.

I move toward it, my trepidation turning into a sharp, electric curiosity. As I step onto the terrace, the pavilion reveals itself as a masterpiece of modern theater. It is a total rejection of the dusty, oak-paneled dignity of Aÿ. Avant-garde ice sculptures drip in the sunlight, carved into jagged, frozen waves that overflow with Bollinger bottles like futuristic fountains.

Then I see the furniture. Olivier Mourgue's Djinn chairs —in shades of tangerine, lime, and sky blue—look like they've been plucked from the set of a space station and dropped onto the French Riviera. Their playful, skeletal elegance is a delightful, neon slap in the face to the traditional grandstands. The engines of the cars scream past just yards away, a continuous, tearing shriek that makes the crystal flutes on the tables ring.

It is a spectacle. Utterly magnificent. A very Christian spectacle. And as I stand there, taking in the chrome, the glass, and the sheer audacity of it all, I realize I'm not just smiling—I'm beaming. I am no longer the *Grande Dame* of the cellars, minding the dust; I am the guest of honor at the center of the world.

Christian, the ringmaster of this glamorous circus, weaves through the crowd to envelop me in a hug, planting kisses on both cheeks. His cologne hits me—something avant-garde and daring, a racy, elegant scent that belongs precisely here.

"Tante Lily, darling! Welcome to the Bollinger Experience!" His voice booms with an infectious enthusiasm. He gestures toward the terrace with a flourish, nearly knocking over a champagne flute held by a passing countess. "A surprise, just for you!"

"I don't like surprises." The skepticism in my voice is betrayed by the twinkle in my eye.

He chuckles, unfazed, the picture of carefree nonchalance in his cream linen suit. "Ah, Tante Lily, wait until you see who is here! I think you'll approve." He lowers his voice, his eyes sparking with mischief. "Bollinger has to project the right image to this crowd, and it's working. Prince Rainier himself has requested a case brought to the Royal Box."

That boy... he knows exactly how to play me. Mention royalty and the future of the House, and my reservations melt like the ice sculptures in the Monaco sun.

Christian leads me through billowing white curtains, and I gasp. It a space-age oasis amidst the Grand Prix frenzy. The shimmering ice sculptures and low tables with smoked glass tops and chrome legs—it is all so modern, so unlike the heavy oak and dust of Aÿ. A wave of dizziness washes over me, and for a moment, the vibrant colors blur. The undulating red Djinn series, the cocoon-like Bouloum chaises, and the reflective aluminum petals of his famous flower lamps fuse into a single swash of motion. It is a triumph of Pop Art shapes in scarlet, orange, and electric blue, and the effect is nothing less than astounding. I grip the arm of a chair to steady myself. Am I already an artifact of a bygone era, while the world speeds past me in a blur of chrome and neon?

Christian sweeps his hand forward to introduce the man standing in the center of the vibrance: Olivier Mourgue himself.

The sight of him is as striking as his furniture. The legendary designer, known for pioneering the sleek, futuristic world of *2001: A Space Odyssey*, is instantly recognizable. He wears a jaunty, dark green tam o' shanter perched above a perfectly tailored, plum-colored velvet blazer. The look—a bold blend of traditional whimsy and Parisian swagger only adds to the modern shock value. Mourgue, carrying himself with an utterly confident air and a boyish enthusiasm, takes my hand and kisses it with a theatrical flourish.

"Enchanté, Madame Bollinger."

"I'm afraid I've never seen our champagne displayed quite like this before," I reply, taking in the playful elegance of his creations. "You are, quite simply, a revolutionary, Monsieur. But how on earth does Christian convince you to lend your genius to our pavilion?"

A rogue's grin crosses his face. "We met on the James Bond film set, you see. After all, a certain secret agent requires a certain *je ne sais quoi*, no?"

"Of course." My eyebrow arches, a spark of amusement in my chest. "I should have known any partnership involving a certain secret agent would be well-chaired."

A waiter materializes with chilled flutes of Bollinger R.D. for the three of us, a delicious, frigid shock compared to the white heat of the track. I need a toast, *tout de suite*. But what do the silent caves of Aÿ have to do with this glass-and-chrome oasis? How are they tethered by this single, golden liquid?

A revelation bubbles up, sharp and persistent as the wine itself. I clink their glasses with verve.

"To the awakening!" My voice rings over the mechanical howl of the engines. "This R.D. is a rare vintage, fifteen years in the dark of the chalk, recently disgorged to find fresh life."

We drink the cold, complex fire of the champagne. Mourgue's face alights. "Magnifique! The old is always the seed for the new. Style born from tradition; substance reinvented."

Christian's face lights with the glee of a master provocateur. "You heard her, Maurice. This wine is a time capsule with a fuse. We've spent fifteen years prepping the launch, and today we finally sparked the ignition." He grins, the sunlight catching the blur of passing chrome in his flute as he raises it to the track. "To the legend—out of the caves and into the stratosphere!"

I laugh, a genuine, startled sound that surprises even me. I feel a sudden, sharp urge to floor it, to let the noise and the glamour carry me into this new world.

Christian excuses us and steers me toward a group

lounging in the Djinn chairs. "Tante Lily, look who's here... Brigitte!"

Brigitte Bardot, all feline grace and effortless glamour, is draped in a tangerine Djinn chair like a sleek, golden lioness. Her bare feet are propped on a low chrome table, and a flute is held loosely in her hand. Christian bends and kisses her cheeks, the scent of her perfume—something musky, sun-warmed, and provocative—drifting toward me like a cloud.

"May I present my Tante, Madame Lily Bollinger."

She looks up at me with a playful smile, her eyes sparkling with that famous, heavy-lidded electricity. "Madame Bollinger," she purrs, her voice a low, melodic growl. "This champagne is absolutely divine, darling. So much *soul*, and yet so fresh." She takes a sip, her gaze lingering on the steady bead of bubbles. "It's the only way to celebrate when your driver, Leslie Seyd, makes you a winner, *n'est-ce pas?*" She arches a perfectly sculpted eyebrow, the question hanging like a challenge.

"Indeed," I reply, my smile polite but sharpened by a lifetime of leading a House. "Though I suspect with you in the pits, Monsieur Seyd has all the incentive he needs to reach the finish line first."

She laughs, a throaty, genuine sound. Then her gaze turns serious. "I simply must have this for my home champagne. This is it. This is the one."

Christian, overhearing, smiles with practiced apology. "I'm so sorry, Brigitte, but we are completely sold out. Our R.D. is in very high demand."

Bardot fixes me with a theatrical pout that has surely brought empires to their knees. "So, you mean to tell me I simply can't have this exquisite champagne? Not even a drop?"

I feel a strange swell of affection for her—this beautiful, brazen woman who is so wonderfully direct. She is

Champagne disgorgement personified: explosive and crystal clear.

"Perhaps," I say, a small smile playing on my lips. "A small case could be found. I'm certain my private cellar could be persuaded to part with a few bottles for you."

Her pout melts into a blinding, triumphant smile. "Oh, Madame Bollinger!" She leans forward, her eyes dancing. "Do you mind if I call you Tante Lily, too?"

Can life get any more surreal? A strange exhilaration tingles through me. I'm here, trading wit and favors with a cinematic icon while the engines roar just yards away. I am no longer just watching the future; I am part of the engine.

Christian introduces me next to Roger Moore, turning to another guest before I can protest. I feel a subtle flutter in my chest—he really is a remarkably handsome man.

Roger's voice is smooth as the champagne he's swirling in his glass. "This R.D. is quite exceptional," he purrs, his eyes twinkling over the rim. "The finest things in life should never be left to chance, should they?" He takes a sip, nodding with appreciation. "A perfect accompaniment to a man of discerning taste."

He acts like the world is a stage set just for him. His beautiful, manicured hand continues to swirl the glass like a brandy snifter, a habit as graceful as a well-rehearsed line. He's practicing, I realize with a jolt. Every smooth, deliberate rotation of the wrist is a performance, calibrated for the cameras and the crowd.

I watch the glass circle one, two, three times. It is more than I can bear; I simply cannot let him continue swirling the bubbles out of my R.D.

"Ah, Mr. Moore." I reach out and grip the stem of his glass. The movement is quick and decisive, halting the motion instantly. "Champagne is not brandy; one does not swirl." My voice drops to a whisper. "The bubbles need to be seduced. They are delicate and fragile, meant to keep coming to delight the tastebuds to the very last sip. You are making them dizzy."

A slow, knowing smile spreads across his face. "Madame," his voice is a low chuckle. "I'm delighted to receive such a private lesson." His gaze holds a deep twinkle of self-awareness. He knows he's being watched, and he enjoys the new script I've given him.

I meet his gaze, my hand a little less steady than it should be. Christian returns and whisks me away. "What did you say to make Roger Moore blush?"

I pat his arm, looking back over my shoulder at the actor. "That is between me and Roger."

The afternoon unfolds in a whirlwind of introductions and effusive praise. I meet film stars, royalty, and captains of industry, all of them captivated by the Bollinger Experience. It is exhilarating ... and utterly exhausting.

I take a moment to lean back against a lime-green Djinn chair, watching Christian as he moves through the crowd. He is a marvel. He doesn't just walk; he glides, his cream linen suit a bright beacon against the neon-and-chrome backdrop. He leans in to whisper a joke to a princess, throws a head-back laugh at a financier's story, and expertly refills Brigitte's glass without ever breaking eye contact. He has that rare, dangerous magnetism that makes everyone in his orbit feel like the only person in Monte Carlo.

He is the ringmaster of this high-octane circus, and for the first time, I see the absolute necessity of his theatre.

Beneath the glamour, a nagging realization persists. Christian's methods are bold, untraditional, and terrifyingly expensive. But as I watch him command the room with that effortless starpower, I see that he has the drive and the charisma to make Bollinger the champagne of the new world. I am the roots, gnarled and deep in the chalky soil of Aÿ, the quiet strength that has endured the frost and the fire.

But Christian? He is the vigorous new vine, reaching toward the sun with a wild, hungry energy. He is the fruit that will burst with the sharp, electric flavor of this jet-set age.

Mon Dieu, I think, watching him raise a glass to the crowd as the engines scream past on the track. This will be a vintage for the history books.

The qualifying heats are over; the posturing is done. Below the Bollinger terrace, twenty machines idle on the starting grid, a vibrating phalanx of fiberglass, magnesium, and heat. The air is a heavy soup of unburnt fuel and scorched rubber that rises like incense. I can feel the vibration in the soles of my shoes, a low-frequency tremor that makes the iron railing beneath my hands shiver.

The French Tricolour snaps downward.

Twenty engines scream in unison—a wall of sound that hits the chest like a physical blow. The thunder swallows the terrace, obliterating the clink of champagne flutes and the gay, silvered laughter of the elite.

Leslie Seyd's ruby-red March 711 lunges from fifth position, its bizarre, elevated front wing cutting through the haze like a blade. As it streaks past the terrace, a blur of ruby and gold, my heart stops. Painted across the sleek machine in flowing golden script is one word: *Lily*.

I turn to Christian, my voice nearly lost in the thunder. "Did you have anything to do with this?"

Christian doesn't flinch. He leans into the spray of grit, his gaze locked on the track. "Why do you think I filled this terrace with the most influential voices in France? To witness a moment they'll recount at every party for a decade. The day Bollinger won the Grand Prix with a car named *Lily*."

I grip the iron railing until the metal bites into my palms. "And if we lose? My name—will be a laughingstock by sunset."

A cocky spark leaps to his eyes, but the clench of his plastered smile and the way his breath hitches give him away. His nerves are fraying right before my eyes—a man watching his own life hang by a thread.

"I know how you love a good bet, Tante. The higher the stakes, the better."

He's as terrified as I am.

The race dissolves into a mechanical dogfight. Lap after lap, the heat radiates off the track in shimmering waves, distorted by the oily haze of twenty exhausts. On the third lap, the high-speed rhythm of the back straight is ripped apart. A silver McLaren clips a Ferrari at the hairpin. Fiberglass shards explode like shrapnel with a bone-shaking screech. The McLaren spins—a jagged, smoking wreck that vomits oil and hot coolant across the line, forcing the field to scatter in a desperate hunt for a line.

Leslie is forced onto the soft verge. The ruby car fishtails wildly, the wide rear slicks searching for grip in the dirt and clods of earth that mask the car entirely. On the slick turf, the March 711 bucks, nearly spinning into the catch-fencing. When he finally emerges, clawing back onto the asphalt, he's lost three positions.

"He's falling back!" My fingernails pierce my palm, leaving white moons.

Christian's leaning so far over the railing I'm afraid he'll tumble onto the track. His jaw is set so tight the tendons in his neck stand out like cords. He's muttering, a frantic, rhythmic prayer under his breath that the V8s nearly drown out. "Move," he hisses, his body jerking. "Inside, Leslie. Take the gap. Take it."

The mid-point of the race becomes a slow-motion nightmare. Leslie is boxed in, a prisoner of his own momentum. Two massive blue Tyrrells from the Elf team weave across the straightaway, a wall of metal blocking his every move. A tactical execution. Every time Leslie tries to peak inside, they shut the door, forcing him to stand on his brakes. The screech of his tires echoes up to the terrace, a desperate plea for space that never comes.

The laps are bleeding away. Six left... Four... Two.

The finish line looms, and the leader is a distant, blue speck, pulling further ahead with every second. On the terrace, our guests have gone silent. The branding on the car—my name—now feels like a neon sign pointing at our impending failure. A cold, leaden weight settles behind my ribs. It isn't just the money or the brand; it is the intimacy of seeing my own identity dragged through the grit, failing in front of this crowd.

Christian has gone white as linen beside me, bouncing up and down on his toes as he did as a boy. How will he survive this loss? And Leslie. I look down at the ruby blur of the March 711 and wonder what drives a man to hunt a gap that doesn't exist. Is it for the glory, or is Leslie just as desperate as we are, possessed by the same terror of being ordinary?

Coming into the final, lethal curve, the two blue Tyrrells begin their wide arc to sweep the bend. They move as a pair, certain they have marginalized the ruby car and blocked any path to the finish. Most drivers would concede. But Leslie goes mad.

He downshifts with a violent, mechanical shriek and dives for the narrow, debris-strewn shoulder—a strip of gravel no wider than his tires. The move is so sudden that the trailing Tyrrell has to jerk his wheel to avoid clipping him. The 'blue wall' shatters as the trailing car swerves, and in that heartbeat of chaos, Leslie finds his opening.

Leslie's March 711 bucks and skips, its suspension groaning against the uneven stones. For a split second, the outside wheels hit a jagged piece of wreckage and vault into the air. The car nearly flips inward, balanced on a knife-edge of physics and prayer. My throat constricts, a sharp ache as my breath locks tight. I am no longer watching a machine; I am watching a man gamble his life to save my reputation.

Leslie screams past the first blue car, then draws level with the leader. He is sandwiched between the lead blue Tyrrell and the metal guardrail, his chassis inches from the steel. A spray of sparks ignites as his magnesium rim scrapes the barrier, a trail of white-hot fire in his wake. My skin pricks with a sudden, electric heat—the visceral shock of watching a man cheat death by a fraction of an inch.

He finds the grip. The car slingshots out of the bend, catching the leader's draft. The engine whine hits a pitch I didn't know was possible—a high, thin vibration that rattles my teeth and makes the very marrow of my bones shiver. He pulls out to the left for one final, desperate surge of speed.

The two cars—the ruby and the blue—cross the line as one, a blur so fused by speed that the eye cannot separate them.

A collective gasp ripples through the crowd, followed by a heartbeat of breathless silence so absolute I can hear the snap of the wind in the flags. No one moves. No one cheers. The entire terrace is suspended in a terrible, agonizing vacuum, eyes locked on the empty stretch of track where the cars have already vanished into the distance.

Beside me, Christian is a statue. His hand finds mine, his grip so fierce it feels like he might crush my bones, but his skin is clammy and cold. He doesn't breathe. He doesn't blink. Waiting for a verdict that will either crown us or bury us.

My pulse thrums in my throat, a frantic, jagged rhythm that refuses to settle. I feel hollowed out, as if my own blood has been replaced by the same volatile fuel burning in that engine. My lungs burn from the fumes, yet I cannot bring myself to draw air.

The silence is so heavy it feels like it might crack the marble of the terrace. Then, the speakers crackle with a sharp, electric hiss. A voice, distorted by static and raw emotion, screams the result over the PA system.

"*C'est Seyd! Victoire pour Bollinger!*"

The sound of my own name—no longer a target, but a triumph—is instantly swallowed by a sudden, violent surge of noise from the crowd below. It is a physical wave of sound, a roar of disbelief that the underdog has actually snatched the win.

Christian's face shatters. A ragged, raw sound rips from his throat—half-sob, half-roar. He lets go of my hand and spins, his eyes wild and shimmering with a terrifying, manic relief. He grabs my shoulders, his grip bruising, and shakes me.

"Did you see it?" he bellows, his voice cracking. "Tante, did you see what he did?"

He throws his head back and crows with laughter. The terrace erupts. The same people who'd looked away in embarrassment moments ago now surge forward, a tidal wave of expensive silk and the sharp, yeasty scent of freshly uncorked champagne.

"Lily, darling! Masterful!"

"A stroke of genius, Christian! Truly!"

Faces press in, hands reaching to touch my arm, my shoulder, as if success is a contagious fever. Christian is swallowed by them, lost in a sea of back-slapping and raised flutes. He's radiant, basking in the noise.

A lump forms in my throat, thick and unexpected. We

survived the gamble, but more than that, he has proven himself. For the first time, I don't see a protégé or a nephew.

I reach out and catch his hand, squeezing it with a fierce, silent pride. He looks at me for a split second—a flash of the boy behind the man he's become—and he knows. He's done it. At long last, the boy who was terrified of being ordinary has conquered the world.

Christian whispers in my ear. "See that man in the tan suit? That's Cubby Broccoli. We're going to say hello."

The name clicks instantly. I've read every Fleming novel, seen every movie. A producer of his caliber is true royalty. Christian maneuvers us through the press of silk and linen with the grace of a predator.

"Christian, you lucky dog!" Broccoli's voice booms over the music. He's a man of immense, solid presence, looking like he was carved out of granite and poured into a tan suit. He claps Christian on the back with a heavy, rhythmic thud. "I saw that ruby car of yours. You nearly gave my heart a permanent rest. A hell of a race, boy. A hell of a race."

Christian laughs with effortless warmth. "A finish like that ... it's the kind of drama not even you can script. And congratulations on *Diamonds Are Forever*. It's a spectacular film."

"It's doing well, it's doing well." Broccoli winks, then turns to me.

Christian ushers me forward. "Meet the famous Lily, my tante, Madame Bollinger."

Broccoli raises his glass in a silent toast. "Congratulations on the race. And the champagne." A sharp look of appreciation crosses his face. "Killer, Madame. That R.D. is stunning. Risky. Brilliantly played."

"Thank you, Mr. Broccoli. I'm a forever fan of James Bond; I simply can't get enough."

"Speaking of 007..." Christian's voice drops to a whisper. "Have you ever considered that he should drink a signature champagne? One that truly defines his style?"

The sheer audacity of the pitch makes my skin prickle. Broccoli chucks his thumb at Christian but keeps his eyes on me. "Did you put him up to this, Madame Bollinger?"

"Certainly not. His cockamamie ideas are all on his own, I'm afraid." I squeeze Christian's arm, a silent command to retreat.

He ignores my signal. "Seriously, Cubby. A man of mystery deserves a special vintage. It's the perfect backstory. Bond only drinks Bollinger."

"Let Monsieur Broccoli enjoy the party, Christian."

Christian snatches a bottle of R.D. from a passing waiter and hands it to Broccoli. "Think of the image, Cubby. Look at the bottle, then look at that car. Sophisticated, fast, dangerous. That is Bond."

Broccoli holds up a palm, a twinkle of amusement in his eyes. "Alright, alright, Christian. Enough. I appreciate the fire. I'll give it some thought." He winks at me. "No promises, mind you."

As we step away, the heat rises up my neck. "Christian Bizot, you're incorrigible! I ought to—"

He flashes a disarming grin. "I planted the seed. Now, we just let it germinate."

"Germinate? You practically bombarded the man."

"A touch of passion never hurts. Besides, you have to admit, he seemed intrigued. Bond ... Bollinger. Could be legendary."

My exasperation gives way to a new respect. I smooth the lapel of his cream linen suit. "No more impromptu pitches. Bollinger has a reputation to uphold."

"Of course, Tante. Whatever you say."

I excuse myself to sit in my favorite lime green Djin chair. I watch him move through this sun-drenched world, seducing the glittering crowd with a mix of wit and raw intelligence. Christian, with his fearless schemes, may be exactly what Bollinger needs to navigate these modern times.

Or he'll fling us into oblivion.

20

LA LUNE AVEC LES DENTS
CATCH THE MOON WITH YOUR TEETH

1946, Paris. The war was over, but the battle for Bollinger's future was just beginning. The city was a ghost of its former self, shivering in the wake of the Occupation, yet the world was reawakening. People were thirsty for joy, for celebration, and for the taste of something that hadn't been tainted by the struggle. I knew I had to move. I had to launch a daring offensive of my own, or Bollinger would be relegated to a memory, a relic of the "before" times.

America was the key. They had embraced us before the shadows fell, and I needed to reignite that passion. I had to remind them that Bollinger wasn't just a drink; it was the very epitome of French elegance and a symbol of survival.

Richard Blum, my American agent, had been relentless. His latest letter practically threw down the gauntlet across the Atlantic.

"Come to America, Lily," he'd written. "The market is wide open, and the curiosity is peaked. We'll arrange interviews, meetings, high-society parties—a full-scale offensive to reclaim your crown!"

The words felt monumental. I stared at the letter until the ink blurred. Could I really sail across an ocean by myself? English wasn't the barrier—my nannies had drilled the language into me until it was second nature—but traversing a continent as vast and loud as America was something else entirely. It was a gamble. A massive, perilous leap of faith for a woman who had spent the last five years dodging requisitions and hiding bottles from the Wehrmacht.

And what about the winery? The thought of leaving it for months on end filled me with a gnawing anxiety. I'd just managed to get Yves and Claude working in a fragile harmony. If I left, would the discipline hold? Would the cellars remain as I left them?

But the harvest would be over in October. The vines would sleep, and so must my fears. That was the time, while the world was still rebuilding its soul and looking for a reason to toast the future.

I walked to the village post, the gravel of Aÿ's streets crunching under my boots—a sound of permanence in an uncertain world. The post office was small, smelling of stale tobacco and damp paper, but it was my link to the world beyond the vineyards. My hands trembled as I wrote out the message, not with fear, but with a fierce, almost terrifying resolve. I handed the paper to the clerk. He didn't look up, his fingers simply tapping out a series of sharp, mechanical clicks that seemed to echo in the small room:

PREPARE AN ITINERARY FOR NOVEMBER. THE QUEEN ELIZABETH AWAITS.

As I stepped back out into the cool air, the weight of the decision settled into my marrow. God help me. What was I doing? A woman couldn't single-handedly charm a continent, could she? If I was to lead a successful campaign in the States, I couldn't arrive looking like a widow of the Occupation; I had to arrive as the Queen of Champagne.

The polished brass doorknob of Jacques Heim's designer salon felt cool and smooth beneath my gloved fingers. A familiar flutter, not quite nausea but akin to it, rose in my throat. It wasn't the fear of war this time, but the daunting prospect of America. Vast, influential, and absolutely crucial to Bollinger's future. It was a bit like stepping onto a stage for a performance I hadn't yet rehearsed, where the only critics were the millions of Americans whose tastes were notoriously fickle.

Richard Blum, bless his tireless efforts, had secured those all-important interviews: *The New York Times*, *The Wall Street Journal*, and even that newfangled television program, *Toast of the Town*. The thought of facing those sharp-eyed American journalists, those titans of industry, in my patched-up, wartime wardrobe was enough to make me reach for a calming glass of our finest. Preferably a magnum.

Dignity above all. Maman's voice echoed in my memory, a reminder that true lineage was marked by restraint, not display. Extravagance had never been the Bollinger way; we left ostentation to those who had something to prove. Now, with France shivering through recovery, every franc spent on a whim felt like a betrayal of the land that fed our vines.

Yet, I was the guardian of a legacy. To conquer America, to convince those thirsty Yanks that our bottles held the very soul of France, I couldn't arrive as a war-weary widow. I needed to project an image of effortless command and timeless grace. I needed to step off that ship not as a supplicant, but as the sovereign of the great Champagne Bollinger.

With a resolute sniff, I pushed open the heavy oak doors. The familiar, comforting scents of Guerlain perfume and freshly brewed coffee mingled with the subtle, almost masculine aroma of Jacques' cologne—something spicy with a hint of leather. The salon, though bearing the subtle scars of war, a slightly faded tapestry here, a repaired chair there, still radiated an air of understated elegance. Sunlight streamed through the tall windows, illuminating the pale cream walls and plush beige carpet. Several mannequins, draped in Jacques' latest creations, stood like silent sentinels. Their clean, architectural lines hinted at the glamorous lives they represented, proving style could thrive even with an economy of fabric. At a small work table tucked in a corner, a young woman with dark hair pulled back in a neat bun diligently worked a sewing machine, the rhythmic whirring a calming counterpoint to the frantic beating of my heart.

"Lily! What a delightful surprise!" Jacques himself, the epitome of Parisian chic, emerged from behind a screen, his tall, slender frame in an impeccably tailored charcoal suit. His neatly trimmed mustache and piercing blue eyes gave him an air of authority, while his warm smile softened the sharp angles of his face. He greeted me with a kiss on each cheek, his hand, cool and dry, clasping mine for a moment longer than usual. "To what do I owe the pleasure?"

"Jacques, darling, I'm in a bit of a predicament." I sank into a worn velvet armchair, its familiar softness a welcome relief. "I need to look presentable for my American trip, press interviews, business lunches, and gala dinners. But these post-war prices! One practically needs a bank loan for a simple frock."

Jacques chuckled, a low, resonant sound. "Ah, Lily, I understand completely." He took my hand, gentle but reassuring, and led me to a secluded corner of the salon I hadn't noticed before. "But fret not, my dear, I have just the solution." He spread his arms as if unveiling a masterpiece. "My new collection has the same impeccable craftsmanship, the same luxurious fabrics, but... shall we say, a touch more sensible."

"Sensible? Jacques Heim and sensible in the same sentence? Is this some kind of clever conspiracy?"

He explained that post-war elegance lay in being smart and thrifty, not ostentatious. His designs looked custom-made yet were practical enough for his burgeoning ready-to-wear lines. He began presenting a series of outfits, each beautifully tailored and elegant, yet without unnecessary embellishment. He held each garment up against me, stepping back to assess the effect with a critical eye.

"For your luncheon with those newspapermen at the Waldorf." He held up a crisp linen suit in a subtle shade of dove grey, "this, with a silk scarf, perhaps a simple, classic print. Understated elegance. Perfect."

"And for an evening cocktail party..." He unveiled a flowing gown of midnight blue silk jersey that shimmered under the salon lights. "This elegant design will flatter your figure without being ostentatious. Sophisticated, yet comfortable. Ideal for an American soiree."

"For travel, this smart wool coat with a velvet collar. Practical, yet undeniably chic." He pointed out the discreetly placed pockets and the elegant line of the coat. "Warm, stylish, and ready for anything."

"Including international intrigue, one assumes," I replied, a smirk playing on my lips.

Finally, with a wicked grin, he presented a classic one-piece swimsuit in navy blue. "And for those leisurely afternoons by the pool in California..."

"Jacques, darling, you know I prefer a brisk walk in the vineyards to baking by the pool."

He tilted his head, observing me with his piercing blue eyes. "Wait, *ma chérie*." He gently turned me toward the large, gilt-edged mirror. "Just one more thing to make Lily the height of glamour."

He reached for a brush and deftly began to gather my hair, twisting it up from my neck and arranging it in a smooth, faultless French chignon. He opened a small, leather-bound box and removed a breathtaking piece: a delicate, antique hair ornament carved from translucent, amber-toned horn, its head inlaid with a huge black pearl and a wing of shimmering, sculpted glass.

"A special gift, *chérie*," he murmured, securing the pin in the shining knot of hair. "This little Parisian ornament was designed by René Lalique. When you wear it, you carry the beauty, resilience, and courage of Paris itself. The Americans, my dear, will be drinking champagne out of your hand."

"A glass will do just fine." I laughed and squeezed his hand in gratitude. Turning my head to the side, the gleam of carved horn and sculpted glass seemed like a magic talisman to my soul, softening the loss and hardship of the war, and giving me courage. *Watch out, America*, I thought. *Lily Bollinger is coming, and I'm dressed for my close-up.*

The last of the harvest was in. A cool air, smelling of fallen leaves and damp earth, slipped through the dining room window. It was October, and for the first time in years, the weight of the war seemed to lift.

But for me, the peace felt false. My sisters, Guillemette and Thérèse, sat across from me, deserving a truth I had yet to give them. I hadn't mentioned America; I knew the chorus of voices that would tell me I couldn't go. But the ship was booked and the parties were scheduled.

Claire sat by her mother's side, a quiet flame in her eyes. I'd watched that fire ignite years ago when she began running messages for the Resistance. Now, Thérèse watched her daughter with an unending relief that the girl had returned from the German labor camps at all. Opposite Claire sat Claude, our cellar master. From the quick, nervous way their glances met, I knew the rumors of their romance were true.

Yves sat next to Guillemette, with her son, Christian, opposite them. Christian had recently abandoned a safe bank position to intern at Veuve Clicquot. I saw his risk as a perfect education; secretly, I hoped to bring him home to Bollinger.

Our dinner was modest—simple chicken and roasted root vegetables—but any meal on the table was a blessing.

"So," Guillemette said, breaking the comfortable silence. "Was it a good yield?"

"The Veuve Clicquot harvest was better than expected," Christian was quick to answer.

My gaze went to Yves, who had managed our estate seamlessly since his father passed in the spring. "The Bollinger harvest looks very good," Yves added with quiet pride. "Both in quantity and in quality."

"A hard-won victory," I said, letting a smile reach my eyes. "After so much looting and bombing."

Christian held up his glass. "To victory, Tante Lily!"

We clinked our glasses. I set mine down, a small gesture to command the room. A panic, sharp as the Occupation, fluttered in my stomach. The love for my family felt like a weight anchoring me to the chair. The thought of sailing alone terrified me, but the thought of Bollinger's decline was worse.

"I am going to America."

Christian's fork scraped loudly against his plate, the sound echoing in the sudden vacuum of the room. Thérèse didn't breathe; she simply stared at the steam rising from the chicken as if the world had frozen over. The stillness was sudden and deafening.

"America? Now?" Thérèse finally found her voice, her hand flying to her throat. "Lily, why?"

"The market is recovering," I said, forcing a bright tone as my heart pounded. "The Americans have a new thirst for French wine. It's a chance to meet our clients face-to-face."

"But... November?" Guillemette's voice was tight. "Wait until spring."

"Begging your pardon, madame, but you're leaving in November?" Claude's gaze flickered to Claire. "That's when fermentation begins. We must get it right this year."

"Ah, Claude. Fermentation is mostly up to the grapes themselves. A little trust is what a vintage needs."

The truth was that fear was the war's lingering ghost—the same panic I'd seen when the Germans first rolled up the drive. I had to push past it. I had to force my family to find their own courage.

"I'm putting you in charge of operations, Claude, with Claire assisting you. You understand the cellars better than anyone."

Claire's head snapped up. "No. That's too much, Tante Lily. To risk a mistake now—"

"She's right," Yves added, his voice trembling. "We need you here."

I held their gazes, a wrenching desire to stay fighting my resolve. I saw Claude's hand shift under the table, likely searching for Claire's. He wasn't just afraid for the wine; he was afraid of failing in front of her. I was giving them the keys to the kingdom, but I was also giving them the weight of it.

"Listen to me. You will not make a mistake. Yves, you know

the land. Claire, your mind is sharp and your courage is beyond question. Claude, I trust you completely. You have each other."

"I can come help on the weekends," Christian piped in.

I smiled at him. "I'm sure Claude would appreciate that."

They exchanged wary glances, debating whether that was true. Forcing down the knot in my throat, I smoothed the tablecloth.

"I'll be home after Christmas. We will celebrate the New Year together, ready to face the next year, stronger than ever."

I squeezed my sisters' hands. They would have each other. Who would I have?

21

RIEN NE SERT DE COURIR; IL FAUT PARTIR À POINT
NO USE RUSHING; ONE MUST SIMPLY START AT THE PERFECT MOMENT

1971, Aÿ, France. The pink dawn paints the sky as a gaggle of geese fly in formation overhead. A gentle wind brushes my arm, raising goosebumps. Jacques's presence washes through me, an old, familiar comfort that has walked beside me for decades, right here on *La Côte aux Enfants*. This vineyard, the cornerstone of our family legacy, begins the harvest.

The air, crisp and clean, carries the scent of damp earth mingled with the luscious aroma of ripe pinot noir grapes. Dewdrops, like tiny diamonds, cling to the crimson-tinged leaves, shimmering in the pale morning light. My gaze sweeps over the vineyard: above us, the distinctive white chalk cliff, Jacques's favorite hunting ground, catches the sun. Below, where the steep slope meets the flat ground, the *vendangeurs* are starting their rhythmic work, their voices rising in a traditional song.

I walk the rows with Yves and pluck a cluster; the berries cool against my palm. I taste it. "This block is ready." I plant a flag in the ground, marking a specific section.

Yves tastes a berry from across the tractor path where the

wagon is parked. He spits it onto the chalky soil. "Sour. Too much acid. Wait three days." He sighs, rubbing his temple. His weathered overalls are dusted with the same chalk that forms our unique *terroir*. "We need four crews here, but I only have two. My best hands are over at those new vineyards Claude bought. They should be here." He leans on the handle of his wagon, a double-barreled hunting shotgun on the door inherited from his father, Pierre. How I miss that man.

"Harvest is always stressful, *mon cher*. We will be fine. Focus on quality, not quantity, always." From his wheezing breath and sallow skin, I sense the deeper toll our vineyard expansion is taking on his health.

Just then, a vicious roar tears through the morning quiet. A utility tractor rockets up the steep slope far too fast. It kicks up a dense cloud of white chalk dust that instantly coats the precious fruit we just inspected. The dust cloud rolls over the *vendangeurs* below, who cough and shield their faces.

Yves explodes. "That thoughtless *connard*!" He shakes his fist. "Kicking up chalk dust to coat the fruit right as we begin? He's ruining the flavor before it even touches the press."

The vehicle skids to a stop. Christian jumps off, the engine still roaring. He marches toward us.

"Tante Lily, you must talk to Claude. He refuses to run the press crew in three shifts, twenty-four hours a day. He's letting the equipment sit idle for eight hours while the competition is crushing. I've already sold more futures of this year's production than the cellar can handle."

A wave of bone-deep weariness hits me. "Christian, we only have enough experienced staff for two shifts. Everyone's already pushed to the maximum. We need to stay calm and work together."

"Doesn't anyone appreciate the growth I've brought this

company?" he fumes. "You all work like it's still 1829. Same methods and small expectations. Bollinger doesn't stand a chance against Moët or Clicquot if we continue to limit our vision to what we've always done." He throws his arms out to the sides in a wide, desperate gesture. "Please, Tante Lily. Just consider it."

I meet his outburst with all the patience I can muster. "We can consider everything after the grapes are safely crushed, Christian."

He spins on his shiny boots, stomping back toward the roaring utility tractor.

Yves cups his hand to his mouth. "We could use your help up here, Christian."

Christian waves him away, but stops short of the tractor. A sounder of wild boars, dark, shaggy shapes, surrounds him from both sides. They are rooting around the tires, grunting softly, their snouts fixed on the scent of ripe fruit. He tries to shoo them with a quick, dismissive kick. "Out! Get lost, you brutal thieves!"

The massive lead boar, a *sanglier*, fixes its small, malevolent eyes on Christian, lowering its head. Christian's trapped between the machine and a wall of bristling, territorial hogs. His face goes white beneath his tan.

"The shotgun, Yves!" I order, my voice low and strained.

Yves snatches Pierre's double-barreled shotgun with the speed of a man who knows what he's doing. He sprints toward Christian and the boars.

I'm surprised when he does not aim for the animal, but fires both barrels into the ground just inches in front of its massive head.

The sound is a physical blow to my chest. The dense, compressed chalk dust explodes upward like a white geyser, blinding the *sanglier*. The boar tumbles and squeals in sudden shock and confusion, its charge derailed. The rest of the sounder scatters wildly back toward the white chalk cliff.

My ears ache from the blast. The still-running engine of the tractor is the only sound, a mechanical drone in the sudden quiet.

Yves drops the shotgun, clutching his chest, his face turning a sickly grey green. He collapses against a low stone wall.

My breath escapes in a sharp, ragged gasp. I run to him, Christian right beside me. My hand flies to his cold, clammy forehead, his eyes fluttering back.

"Yves," Christian's voice thick with alarm. "I'm taking you down to the house. We're calling a doctor."

Yves struggles for breath, his eyes fixed on the vineyard workers. "The harvest ... they need ..."

I smile and rub his cheek. "Don't worry about the fruit I'll stay with them. They'll have their hands full with this vineyard today. I've done it one or two times before."

Christian slips an arm beneath Yves's shoulders and lifts his weight, slinging Yves's arm over his shoulders.

"Papa's gun ..." Yves mumbles, pointing weakly toward the ground.

I pick up the shotgun and sling it over my shoulder. "I'll keep it handy in case the boar comes back."

Christian hauls Yves against his side, their shoulders locked as they lurch toward the utility vehicle. The rage from moments ago has vanished, replaced by a desperate, clumsy rhythm.

Yves trembling hand finds Christian's forearm, gives a quick, hard squeeze, and then falls away. Christian doesn't let go; he only tightens his grip, anchoring him. The tractor begins its slow descent down the path.

I turn to the *vendangeurs* in the vineyard. They've stopped picking and are peering down, worried. I wave them back toward the vines, yelling up the slope that Yves is fine, but we're taking him to the house. They hesitate for a moment, then, understanding the priority of the harvest, they return to their work. No songs, just the snip, snip of their *secateurs*.

The bright pink of the horizon has vanished. The light across the vineyard has turned a bruised grey. On the far horizon, dark clouds are swiftly pulling the sky shut. The stillness is profound, broken only by the tractor's lonely drone.

I look to the sheer, indifferent white of the chalk cliff above. I close my eyes, feeling the cold chalk dust on my face—the grit of this morning's chaos.

Oh Jacques. My whisper is swallowed by the wind biting at my cheeks. This is not working out as I hoped. I thought I knew the leader this house needed. I was so sure. But these boys, their constant wars and brittle truces ... it's too much. Now the storm is breaking, the grapes are still on the vine, and for the first time in thirty years, I can't find my way back. I am lost, Jacques. Utterly, completely lost.

22

LA MER REND CE QU'ELLE PREND

THE SEA GIVES BACK WHAT IT TAKES

1947, The Atlantic Ocean. The RMS Queen Elizabeth churned through the gray expanse, a titan of steel and steam fighting a heavy swell. They say the sea gives back what it takes. I watched the heave of the wake and prayed it was true; after six years without Jacques, it seemed as though the world had done nothing but take. My stomach mimicked the heave of the hull, a cold weight rising and falling with every swell. The rhythm of the engines was a constant pulse, throbbing through my body. What made me think I could do this trip on my own?

I looked out the porthole, but the tumultuous waves, whitecaps cresting and vanishing, only amplified the churning in my gut. The thick fog outside seemed to creep through the glass, a persistent cold that bit through my wool sweater and served as a dismal reminder of the distance I was putting between myself and my home. I missed the vineyards, so rooted in the earth, green and gentle, instead of this chaotic, roiling ocean.

For years, keeping Bollinger afloat had meant battling the Nazis, rebuilding from the damages of war, and making do with the chronic shortage of supplies and men. I was so used to this fight that I hadn't realized how utterly alone I felt until now ... in the middle of the gray, swirling ocean. The heavy, clenched fist in my chest was a raw wound that hadn't had time to heal. Women still couldn't legally own businesses by themselves in France unless they were widows, so keeping my business must take precedence. Still, a profound and hollow loneliness began to dominate my thoughts.

"Damn this infernal motion." I squeezed my emerald-green silk turban on my pounding head. "Enough of this pity party." I was on an Atlantic cruise to America, not a funeral barge. This was my first solo trip, the fulfillment of a solemn promise to Jacques: not just to save Bollinger, but to make it thrive. But this voyage meant more than securing Bollinger's future; it was a personal pilgrimage. I was traveling to tour America, to meet the right people, and to win them over with the elegance and quality of our champagne. It was a chance to outrun the ghosts of war, and, I hoped, the ghost of my own solitude. Jacques wouldn't have wanted me to be sad and lonely.

A colossal wave shuddered through the ship, and I stumbled, bracing myself against the wall. A hot, bilious flood rose in my throat. A knock sounded, and I pulled the door open, grateful for the distraction. It was a ship steward, holding a silver tray with a fragrant cup of tea, a couple of pills, and a single rose in a small vase.

The steward smiled. "Madame Bollinger, Commodore McCullough noticed you weren't feeling quite yourself. He sent his favorite ginger tea."

"Please thank him for me." My voice trembled.

The bone china rattled against the silver as he set the tray down. "The commodore requests the pleasure of your company this evening for the captain's dinner."

My heart leaped. For once, the flutter in my stomach wasn't pain, but a thrill.

I'd met him only briefly at the welcome tea—handsome, distinguished, a man of quiet strength. I had been so vexed when my health forced an abrupt exit; he was the only person I'd actually wanted to know.

"That would be lovely." My eyes drifted to the card on the tray. Commodore James McCullough, KBE. A Knight Commander of the British Empire. A knight in a naval uniform—there was a story there, one I was eager to hear.

The steward gave me the details. I closed the door and leaned against it, my mood shifting in the blink of an eye. I poured the tea and dunked the cookie, savoring the ginger spice and willing it to work. I took the medication, too. I wasn't going to miss this for anything.

The invitation was like a lifeline. Jacques ... *mon amour* ... A pang of guilt shot through me. What would he think?

He would have laughed, of course. *Take care of yourself, my Lily.* I could almost see the glint in his eye. *Bollinger cannot thrive if its soul is ill.* He'd always admired my fierce self-reliance, but I'd worn this veil of grief for so long it had become part of my skin. This gesture—a cup of tea and a rose—was the first crack in the armor. It was an acknowledgment of me, not just Madame Bollinger, the widow and guardian.

I reached out, my thumb tracing the velvet edge of a petal. It was a vibrant, blood-red splash against the cold silver of the tray. For six years, my life had been about the survival of the House—nothing more. But Jacques would have wanted me to live. Our champagne was a celebration of life, and yet here I was, drowning in it.

A new resolve settled over me. Tonight, I would not be the grieving widow. I was a woman on her own voyage, ready to find her way back to the land of the living. And about damn time, too.

Anticipation bubbled within me as I followed the steward down the narrow corridor, the ship's rhythm steady beneath my feet. He stopped, knocked softly, and ushered me inside.

My heart jolted. This wasn't a private dining hall. These were the commodore's quarters.

The room was spacious, paneled in dark wood, with a large porthole overlooking the roiling November sea. A fire breathed in a small fireplace, casting a honeyed amber glow over everything. The air was thick and warm, scented with pipe tobacco and expensive leather. Near the hearth, an exquisitely set table gleamed; the silverware looked like slivers of moonlight against the starched linen. A bottle of champagne sat chilling in a silver bucket.

There was no one else there. Just the commodore, standing by the porthole.

He had traded his uniform for an elegant navy jacket and a burgundy tie. He looked less like an officer and more like a gentleman at home. A warm smile touched his lips as he stepped forward, extending a hand. "I hope you don't mind, but I prefer to dispense with formalities. Please call me James."

A nervous thrill raced through me at the intimacy of the offer. "Then you must call me Lily."

The name tasted light on my tongue, almost new.

"Lily. It is an honor to have you here."

"I thought this was the captain's dinner."

A disarming smile played on his lips. "It was, until I decided to stage a small, necessary act of piracy." He winked. "I couldn't bear to share my most interesting guest with a whole table of admirers."

A blush crept up my neck. An intimate dinner with the dashing commodore, in his private quarters? Watch out what you wish for. I grinned slyly. "A dangerous game, James. I've been known to commandeer a ship myself if the company is good enough." I stood closer to the fire, the warmth chasing away the last of the sea's chill.

He pulled out my chair. As we settled in, he turned to the silver bucket. "I believe this special occasion calls for a special dispensation."

He lifted the bottle, wiping the glass with a practiced sweep of a towel. My eyes widened. The Bollinger La Grande Année 1943. I'd overseen that shipment to the Cunard line myself—a risky, post-war gamble to keep the House solvent. He wasn't just bringing me champagne; he was bringing me my own history.

"I'm impressed, James. That vintage is a rare find, even on solid ground." I traced the condensation on my glass. "I signed the manifest for this lot myself."

He returned my smile, his eyes sparking in the firelight. "My duty is to ensure my guests have only the best, Lily. I selected the finest bottle on the ship and found it was yours. After my little act of piracy, I believe we are both in need of an armistice."

He filled my glass, the bubbles rising in a whispered, shimmering column. Then he raised his own. "To the company of kindred spirits."

Our glasses met with a soft, crystal chime. "*Santé.*"

I took the first sip. The La Grande Année 1943 exploded on my tongue, a spectacular vintage indeed. Luscious and ripe, the rich fruit perfectly balanced with a sharp, cool minerality. I closed my eyes briefly, remembering. That year had produced some of the best quality grapes of the entire Occupation, a small, defiant gift from the earth that we'd guarded with our lives. How utterly different to share it at an elegant dinner with a man of honor, rather than tasting it alone in the cold, damp caves of Bollinger.

The waiter appeared as if by magic, serving small bowls of steaming cream of mushroom soup, and the quiet ritual broke the initial tension.

As we enjoyed a delicious meal of poached turbot, our conversation flowed from pleasantries to the more personal. We spoke of our lives at sea and on land, our long-held duties, our losses.

"I am widowed as well." He glanced out at the sea, a liquid blackness that stretched to the horizon. "Losing my wife was difficult enough but now the company is forcing me into mandatory retirement. I've been fine as long as I'm commanding the ship, but now when I go home, no one is there."

I squeezed his hand, a shared acknowledgment of what we had both lost. "The silence is a terrible thing. You shouldn't have to face it." I tightened my grip on my glass, shaking off the shared gloom. "After I buried my husband, I returned to a house full of Nazis. I had to fight them for the roof over my head and the vines in the soil. I wouldn't let them take the business, too."

"I can't imagine what it was like to face that alone." His eyes searched mine.

I leaned toward the hearth, the heat prickling my skin. "I kept thinking of Joan of Arc. The stoic leader who couldn't be broken." I gave a short, dry laugh. "The war is over, yet I can't seem to unbuckle the armor. Now I'm taking on a ten-city tour, launch parties, buyers, sommeliers ... what was I thinking?"

"I see what you mean." James laughed, the sound warm against the crackle of the hearth. "Joan of Arc in a fearless campaign to defend her world."

The pressure behind my ribs eased as I shared my fears with a man who seemed to understand. "You carry the weight of more than a few battles yourself, Commodore. How did you earn your knighthood?"

He sat back, his expression turning distant. "King George VI was generous. The official citation was for Dunkirk."

He shrugged, as if dismissive of the fire and the screaming. "We ferried thousands of soldiers. We traveled without escort, our only protection our speed. We were targets every minute we were at sea. But the Admiralty was kind in their write-up. They called me a good shepherd, seeing my flock home."

I was captivated by the quiet strength of the man telling the story. "You were a savior to so many."

He shrugged. "We all did what was necessary."

We finished the last course, the candlelight low and the silver gleaming in the dimming room. He poured the final glasses of champagne and stood, offering me his arm.

"The sky is clear tonight. It would be a shame not to see it from the deck. If you'll indulge me one last time?"

I nodded, feeling a lightness of spirit. He helped me into his coat, the soft wool smelling faintly of sandalwood and sea air. When we stepped outside, the biting cold gave way to an exhilarating crispness.

The vast, cold arch of the galaxy ran overhead, an endless stream of starlight against the deep well of the night sky. I'm overcome with an overwhelming sense of awe.

"Do you ever get tired of this view?" I leaned against the rail, the cold salt air stinging my cheeks.

His eyes stayed fixed on me, steady and warm. "Rather

forward of you, isn't it, Lily? Our first date and you're already asking if I'll ever get tired of you?"

The word 'date' sent a jolt through me. A laugh bubbled up, light and unburdened. The simple warmth of his hand over mine was more dazzling than the cold stars overhead.

A few days later, I decided to take a turn on the promenade deck, bundling up in a heavy wool coat over my suit. A gorgeous, rare day on the Atlantic Ocean. The sea was calm, and the fog had lifted, revealing a sun hanging like a cold coin in a brilliant sky. Its light was sharp but lacked heat, prickling against the salt-stung skin of my cheeks. As I walked, I saw the commodore standing at the rail, his dark blue uniform a sharp silhouette against the endless gray blue of the sea.

He turned with a slight salute and a smile. "Lily. A perfect day for a walk. Mind if I join you?"

"Please do." I moved closer to the rail to make room. "Otherwise, I'll be forced to look at the horizon alone, and frankly, I'm too restless for that kind of solitude."

He laughed, the sound warm as we fell into an unhurried pace. The rhythmic slap of the waves against the hull was the only sound before I spoke: "Tell me, Commodore, will you miss halcyon days like this when you retire?"

He flinched, his gaze drifting to the horizon. "When I leave this ship, I'll miss every last thing about it: the unpredictability of the wind, the salt on my lips, the way the light catches the water ... the rolling rhythm of the waves." He sighed heavily. "I've spent so much of my life on the ocean, in command, a man of quick decisions and strict routine. Now, the thought of quiet days on land seems ... overwhelming. I don't know who I am when I'm not a commodore."

His vulnerability caught me off guard. This man, who commanded a floating city, looked as lost as I felt. He wasn't just the handsome captain of the fleet; he was a man facing the end of his career without the one person he wanted to share it with. I stopped at the railing, my gaze fixed on the white foam seething against the hull. "Perhaps the journey isn't about knowing what you lost, but about discovering who you might become." He shifted his hand, and the warmth of his fingers settled over mine. We stared down at the dark water rushing below, like standing on a ledge together, two people who didn't know what lay ahead, only that they no longer faced it alone.

He let out a soft laugh that carried on the wind. "I've learned to expect the unexpected. But this ... you are a welcome surprise." His thumb stroked the back of my hand. "Tell me, Lily. You talked about fighting for your business during the war. But what's left to fight for when the enemy is gone and the only battle left is the ledger?"

He sounded strangely lost. I focused on the ceaseless motion of the waves, a small smile playing on my lips. "When the battle is won, perhaps then the real work begins. The cultivating. The aging. The waiting. The uncorking." I turned my attention back to him. "One doesn't simply rest on their laurels. One must find the next vintage. The next great challenge."

"To simply be?" He leaned heavily on the rail. "To have the very thing that defined you simply ... stop. Terrifying prospect, Lily." He gave my hand a squeeze, his skin a stark contrast to the cold metal of the rail. "Maybe that's the real journey, then? Learning who we can be when we're nothing at all."

"Nothing at all? Surely you jest." I studied the man before me—the quick wit, the take-charge attitude. "Being a commodore was just one expression of who you are, James. I suspect whatever you navigate next will be the most exciting voyage of all."

He smiled, then lifted my hand and brought it to his lips. It was a slow, soft kiss, far more commanding than any speech. The salty air and brilliant sun seemed to hold their breath; there was nothing but the rhythmic slap of the waves.

My heart hammered against my ribs. My mind was already racing, cataloging all the reasons this was a mistake—an English captain, a French matriarch—but the panicky thoughts soon quieted. Romance didn't have to mean marriage. This feeling wasn't just about him; it was about me.

The kiss was a single sip of a life that existed only here on the Atlantic, a taste of a joy I hadn't realized I was thirsting for. Now that I'd recognized the flavor, I wouldn't turn it down. It was the kind of gamble I favored. A sure bet.

23

ON N'EST JAMAIS TROP VIEUX POUR APPRENDRE
ONE IS NEVER TOO OLD TO LEARN

1971, Aÿ. The fragrant air is the first thing I notice as I open the door, carrying the complex, sweet scents of the season: lavender and wild roses blooming near the stone walls, mingled with the bright, sharp-sweet scent of grapes. It's a beautiful day for my usual vineyard meeting with Yves. My bicycle is right where I left it, propped against the courtyard's stone wall.

But my anticipation vanishes when I see Cyril Ray right beside it. His small, sheepish smile is enough to make me groan.

"Oh, Cyril. What in the world are you doing here? Did we have an appointment I've forgotten?"

He adjusts his Nehru jacket with fussy precision. "I confess I'm here under duress. Yvonne, bless her soul, mentioned she was baking croissants this morning. One simply cannot resist an ambush of flakey pastry." He lifts his nose as if to scent the air.

"I'm afraid Yvonne has defected." A satisfied smile plays on my lips. "She's delivering croissants to the *vignerons* this morning. You just missed her."

His shoulders slump, making his jacket seem several sizes too large. His gaze drops to the ground as a slow, painful flush creeps up from his neck. The man has mistaken a year of professional toleration for friendship, and my mid-season vineyard work cannot be delayed.

"Can you ride a bike?" I throw my leg over mine and gesture to the other bike perched against the wall. "If we hurry, we can catch Yvonne."

I take off down the lane. I don't need to look back to know that an Englishman who missed his breakfast will follow the croissants. When I cut into the vineyards, his determined puffing quickly degrades into a high-pitched, surprised wheeze as his tires hit the gravel. What is Cyril doing here? He's been a barnacle on my hull all year, a self-proclaimed expert pontificating about *sur lie* aging and *méthode champenoise* as if my years of experience are a mere tasting note. My patience has officially curdled.

My legs pump hard, scaling the hill. Cyril is the kind of man who enjoys critiquing someone else's work more than performing actual labor himself. He relishes the dusty romance of a wine cellar and the theatrical flourish of uncorking a bottle. But the true essence of Bollinger is here, in the dirt, the wind, the morning sun. And my aching back.

I hear a loud, startled squawk and glance back. Cyril's flabby frame is better suited to navigating the dusty racks of a wine library than the rolling hills of Champagne. His Nehru jacket is now unbuttoned and flapping like a panicked crow. He's leaning badly to the left, trying to pedal up a slight incline while simultaneously using one hand to desperately keep his fedora from blowing off his head. His face is an alarming shade of puce.

"Egads!" He gasps a strangled croak that could spoil milk.

His small, leather-bound notebook, the one he uses for

every fussy observation, slides from his pocket and tumbles into the chardonnay vines. He swerves wildly, nearly pitching himself into the opposite row.

"How much farther?" He recovers the dusty notebook.

"Not too far," I call over my shoulder, increasing my speed and leaving him to toil in my wake.

He groans, but gamely pedals on, his puffing and wheezing providing a rather amusing percussion to the birdsong. I push harder up the final stretch, frustration now a sharp knot in my chest. If I miss my meeting with Yves, it's because of this author I dragged along.

When we reach the crest of the hill where Yvonne was meeting Yves and the crew, the supply truck is gone. No one is there.

"We missed them," I snap, my voice tight. "We missed them because of your theatrical pursuit of a pastry."

I swing my leg off my bike and march right into the nearest row of vines. The leaves have been precisely trimmed back around the grape clusters—just enough to allow for optimal sun exposure and air circulation, but not so much as to risk sunburn on the fruit. It is exactly the balance I would have asked for, the very thing I was desperate to tell Yves not to overdo. He didn't need the instruction. Didn't need me.

Cyril finally reaches the top, walking his bike, his wheeze a pained, dry rasp that worries me. His red face looks like a pimento bursting out of his Nehru jacket.

"How do you know they were here already?" he puffs.

"See how the leaves are all trimmed back around the clusters?" I point out evidence of the recent defoliation. "The crew finished their work here, preparing the vines for the final push."

I expect his questions about the pruning, but he doesn't even look at the vines. Cyril collapses under a tree, his chest heaving, his shoulders slumped. His face is slick with a cold sheen of sweat.

I sit beside him on the ground. The panoramic view of the vineyards stretches out before us like a rumpled green quilt.

"Why are you still here, Cyril? The book is with your editor, is it not?"

His gaze drops to his fingers, calloused from a lifetime of holding a pen. "Yes, it is." He lets out a brittle, humorless laugh. "I'm afraid *The Observer* has deemed me a bit too old for active duty. My license to critique has been revoked."

"Is that code for me to decipher?" I offer a faint smile.

His face reddens. "It seems they've retired their James Bond. Only, I was never quite as dashing. The oldest Sunday newspaper in Britain has had quite enough of its oldest wine critic."

He was trying to put a funny face on his heartache, but the wit was too thin. I saw the same fear I find in the mirror: the clock devouring my relevance.

"I'm sure your wife is happy you're retiring." I hope the reminder of home would send him packing to London.

Cyril huffs. "My wife is on a two-month book tour in America." His voice falls to a whisper. "What am I supposed to do now? Pack up my pens and go home?"

The proud, pontificating man I spent a year tolerating is gone, replaced by someone utterly vulnerable. I see the man behind the bluster, and he's terrified.

I can't let him wallow. "Are you saying the world has heard enough from Cyril Ray?" I gesture to the gnarled, ancient vines around us. "You have decades of knowledge. You used it to critique wine. Now, use it to share what you know." I meet his gaze. "Write a new story. Start a new legacy."

He looks at me, a flicker of curiosity in his eyes. "A new vintage, then?"

"Absolutely. Every year we get the chance to make a masterpiece. How do you want your story to end? With a company watch and a pat on the back, and slinking off to lick your wounds?"

Though his wheezing chest still heaves, his eyes widen.

I stand and lend him a hand. "The crew will break for lunch at the house. Yvonne made *vichyssoise*, *salade Niçoise*, and cherry *clafoutis*. Let's go."

Cyril's grip is firm as I pull him to his feet. There isn't much in this world that can't be improved by Yvonne's cooking; that woman could spark a revolution with a single Niçoise.

24

QUI NE RISQUE RIEN N'A RIEN

WHO RISKS NOTHING HAS NOTHING

1947, New York City. I kept watch out of the massive, arched windows of the Ritz-Carlton where the lilting snowflakes had turned into a wretched blizzard. Streetlamps, their light nearly obliterated by the swirling snow, hovered like blurry halos. What had happened to Richard Blum? My American agent was supposed to be here an hour ago. Was he caught somewhere in this mess?

The party couldn't start without him.

Below, yellow taxi cabs and bus headlights cut faint swaths through the gloom, the traffic a stagnant, horn-blaring crush of steel and ice. Even the blizzard couldn't silence the city; it only huddled the masses closer under the leaking awnings. For a moment, the white expanse of the storm pulled my thoughts back to the *Queen Elizabeth* and the commodore. That romantic, empty horizon, another world entirely from the frenetic, bone-deep surge of Manhattan.

The grand ballroom shimmered, a vibration of crystal chandeliers and hand-painted cherubs. A quartet played a frenzied Gypsy Jazz tune—a frantic counterpoint to the panic buzzing beneath my skin.

I anchored myself near the entrance in emerald Jacques Heim velvet. My hair, swept into a chignon, was pinned by a Lalique wing of translucent glass and a single black pearl. The long spike had begun to scratch my neck, a prickle of annoyance in the growing tide of the evening.

Richard Blum was nowhere to be found. A ballroom of Americans loomed, waiting to be charmed—a task as punishing as the chignon pulling at my scalp.

I made small talk, a charming remark here, a witty observation there, all the while my eyes darted over the shoulder of each guest, searching for Richard. Richard had briefed me on the guest list, a who's who of New York society—the kind of people who could ruin a brand with a single raised eyebrow. Mr. Bellows, the head waiter, moved through the crowd in a handsome gold brocade vest. A tilt of his head or a subtle gesture of a silver tray aligned the names with the intimidating faces of the city's power brokers.

Babe Paley radiated a cool elegance; her head bent toward C.Z. Guest in a conspiracy of gossip. Nearby, Mrs. Astor sat regal and remote, her diamonds flashing like constellations. Then there was Peggy Guggenheim, the wild-child heiress, trailing an avant-garde entourage like a wake. A camera bulb flashed, illuminating Truman Capote's wicked smirk as he cornered William S. Paley.

They were all here. An impressive, intimidating cage of lions. And their eyes were already beginning to dart my way.

Richard's absence was a spark near a powder keg. If the rumor mill started, it would incinerate the evening before the first cork even popped. A failure in New York would poison the American tour; this party had to be more than a success—it had to be a conquest. The press must crown this launch a masterpiece and every whisper be an endorsement, or my Atlantic crossing was merely a fool's errand. I will not have Bollinger drowned out by the gossip of inferior houses. After all, as America goes, so goes the world.

Behind Mr. Bellows, the waiters stood poised, searching for a signal from Richard that was never coming. The hair ornament gave one final, sharp poke—a reminder of what Jacques Heims said when he gave it to me. "You carry the beauty, resilience, and courage of Paris itself."

I gave Mr. Bellows a definitive nod. Snatching a bottle of Bollinger from a passing tray, I strode toward the bandstand, relishing the sudden dip in conversation. I claimed the microphone from the startled leader.

"Ladies and gentlemen." My voice carried to the back of the hall. "I am Lily Bollinger. I am told Americans find the French stuffy. I am here to prove that in Aÿ, we simply know how to start a party."

I swept the Lalique ornament from my hair. The chignon collapsed in a loose wave, but my focus remained on the glass spike in my hand. A dagger of French resilience.

I aligned the edge with the seam of the bottle neck. My heart hammered a rhythm of pure, cold focus. *Now.*

A sharp, clean stroke. A flick of the wrist. The glass surrendered with a resounding *crack*.

The cork soared into the draperies, followed by a golden plume of effervescence—a fountain of joy for a thirsty room. "Voilà! That is how one opens a Bollinger."

The ballroom ignited. Laughter and applause rattled the chandeliers.

Richard appeared as the first rounds were served, soaked and flustered, snow melting in grey patches on his wool coat.

He froze at the edge of the room, taking in the scene: the cheering crowd, the frantic waiters, and the sabered bottle still fizzing in my hand. A slow smile spread across his face. He didn't try to reclaim the floor; he simply stood there, shaking his head in a mixture of relief and awe.

Bollinger hadn't just arrived in New York. It had exploded. I looked at the reporters scribbling in their notebooks and knew that by breakfast, the headlines would be as effervescent as the wine. We hadn't just made a splash; we'd started a tidal wave.

Later that night, back in my suite, I pulled out the Ritz stationery. The city glittered below, its lights blurred by the relentless snow. I uncapped my fountain pen, the nib poised above the creamy paper.

James McCullough. A steady presence of quiet competence on the *Queen Elizabeth*, a man who looked past the labels of legacy and brand to find simply ... Lily.

I smoothed my hand along my forearm, where the phantom of his touch remained—confident, commanding, and entirely unimpressed by my status. A faint laugh escaped me, echoing against the quiet walls as I recalled those final nights at sea.

I stared out the window, searching for the rhythm of waves but finding only the bleak, white churn of a Manhattan blizzard. James belonged to the salt and the spray; I was bound to the chalky soil of Aÿ. That voyage had been our only common ground, a fleeting intersection of two different worlds.

The ache was there, wistful and sharp, but it was tempered

by a new resolve. I leaned over the desk. The pen met the paper with a scratch of private victory. I began to write to the one man who understood the weight I carried, even if the letter wouldn't reach his hand for weeks.

25

L'UNION FAIT LA FORCE
THE UNION MAKES THE STRENGTH

1971, Aÿ. I look past the chilling Bollinger on my mahogany desk. I don't see three executives, I see my life's work.

My gaze lingers on Christian. Even sitting still, he vibrates. His chin tilts with that restless curiosity I've known since the day he was born—my sister's son, my own blood. I've watched him grow, knowing he expected the throne by birthright.

The keys in my pocket are an anchor I took up when Jacques died. For decades, I searched for the children I never had, until I gathered these three. My "nephews."

"When I took this seat, I promised Jacques the vines would never go dark—and they haven't. But now I must ensure that Bollinger will thrive long after I am gone. Give it a heartbeat of its own."

Christian reaches across the desk, his hand covering mine. The steadying weight of a man who thinks the kingdom is finally within reach.

For a heartbeat, my resolve wavers. My joints ache, and a part of me screams that it's too soon—that I am not ready to let go of the only thing that's kept me standing. But winter is in my bones. I leave my hand under Christian's, but I turn my face to Claude.

"I am stepping down as président."

Christian's fingers tighten on mine, a triumphant squeeze. I do not look back at him.

"Claude." The name tastes bitter. "You will become our president-directeur général."

Christian's fingers recoil as if my skin turned to ice.

Claude remains still. No flash of victory lights his eyes. He slowly closes his ledger with a soft, final thud. "I understand."

"Christian, you will be our directeur of marketing." My pulse stutters at the sight of his face. His tan has turned to ash. "You will be the voice of Bollinger." As if that is a consolation prize. "But there is a condition: you will spend one week a month here at the winery with Claude. And get your hands stained by the grapes with Yves. You'll learn the heart and soul of the wine so that your stories remain rooted in truth."

Christian looks at me as if I were a stranger.

I turn to Yves. "And you, Yves, will remain the master of our soil. You are the guardian of the vineyards, the one person who ensures the grapes are worthy of the name."

Yves nods once, a sharp, jerky movement.

I lean back, the chair suddenly feeling too large. "I will remain as chairperson of the board. I'm not leaving you to the storm; I am letting you learn to sail it while I can still reach the wheel."

The moment stretches. Christian swallows hard. Finally, the grit takes over. He rises, a man who's taken a punch but found his footing.

"Tante Lily. It is ... unexpected. But Bollinger comes first." He forces a wide grin. "Is anyone else as parched as I am?"

I retrieve the ceremonial saber from the sideboard. The blade sings as it leaves its sheath. "Who wants the honors?"

Christian snatches it, gripping the hilt loosely. "It should be mine."

I point to the seam of the bottle. "Absolute conviction, Christian. Strike the weakest point of the neck."

He swings. The blade skids across the glass with a screech and clatters onto the desk.

"I had the conviction, Tante Lily! I swear it."

Claude returns the sword to him, adjusting the younger man's wrist with firm pressure. "The angle must be true to catch the lip. Hold it steady."

Christian sights down the bottle. With a precise, clean stroke, the glass surrenders. A fountain of gold sprays high, christening us all.

We drink in a thick silence. The ingredients are all in the glass now—the ego, the ambition, the blood. Whether they meld into a fine *cuvée* or turn to vinegar remains to be seen.

26

VOULOIR, C'EST POUVOIR
TO WILL IS TO CAN

1947, San Francisco. The Fairmont gleamed atop Nob Hill, a festive palace of ivory stone standing watch over a city that refused to sleep. I stepped onto the terrace for a quick breath of air, dewy and bitingly cold. Below, the city glittered through the fog, a landscape built on the ashes of 1906. It was a place defined by its cycle of ruin and stubborn rebirth. To the west, the rust-red silhouette of the Golden Gate Bridge pierced the mist, spanning the channel between the Pacific and the bay.

Footsteps crunched on the stone behind me. Richard. "San Francisco is a city of renegades and dreamers. Hiding their gold in the fog and riding clanging iron chariots through the clouds."

He barked a laugh as he pulled his coat tighter. "Renegades in tuxedos, Lily? I thought we were here to conquer high society."

"High society dances to a different tune here." I looked out at the white, fluted column of Coit Tower. "Women don't just have tea; they build towers for firemen. A man in a bespoke suit haggles over a crate of crab, the air thick with brine and eucalyptus. And the Blue Fox? Hidden in an alleyway across from a morgue. San Francisco is a conundrum. They don't have 'history'—they have sagas."

I turned to Richard, the realization tightening my chest. "In Paris, the wine buyers haggle with a bored sense of entitlement. But here at the St. Francis and the Palace, they don't ask whether it's *premier* or *grand cru*. They ask if the champagne is as gutsy as the people."

A slow grin spread across his face. "And did Bollinger meet their expectations?"

A short, sharp laugh escaped me. "Even better. Bold. Grounded. A revolution in a bottle. These people want a champagne that can survive a Gold Rush and a world war."

Richard gestured toward the glass doors. "Shall we go inside? I suspect they're thirsty for a story."

The chill of the terrace vanished, replaced by a festive rush of Monterey pine, woodsmoke, and the vibrant hum of three hundred voices. The grand staircase was draped in boughs shimmering with mother-of-pearl, and a life-size gingerbread house dominated the lobby, its scent of sharp cinnamon and ginger sweetening the air.

I scanned the room, finding the kaleidoscope of characters: financial titans with the eyes of prospectors and North Beach artists in frayed velvet.

"The turnout is spectacular." Richard caught my elbow as we reached the staircase. "They're all here, Lily."

As I ascended the first few steps of the staircase, I was glad I'd chosen the crimson gown. It shone like a beacon of good tidings against the pale marble, a splash of fire in a room of black and white. The hum of the crowd didn't just fade—it snapped into an expectant silence as every eye turned toward the stairs.

Richard signaled to the waiters. As the first trays of crystal began to circulate, I raised my voice to address the room.

"Tonight, I do not bring you a drink for the timid." My voice carried easily to the furthest gilded chandelier. "I bring you a vintage of defiance. During the war, when the shadows of the Occupation fell over my vineyards, I hid these bottles behind false walls. I waited for a spirit that matched the wine."

I looked toward the officers in their dress uniforms—the men who had likely trained at the Presidio before shipping out to France.

"It was the American soldiers, many of whom started their journey right here in San Francisco, who roared into Aÿ on their olive-drab trucks. They chased away the darkness. I housed them in my home; I opened my cellars for them. I didn't pour for the elite; I poured for the fearless. And tonight, I look at the people of San Francisco and realize where those soldiers got their courage and spirit from."

I lifted my glass high, the bubbles catching the light like tiny sparks. "To San Francisco—the most courageous people I have ever met. May your spirit always be as bold as your city!"

The room erupted. Richard was laughing and clapping as he reached for my hand. "Lily! Where on earth did that come from?"

"It came from the heart." The ballroom hummed with the electric energy of a party in full stride, a heat generated by more than just the crowd.

I moved through the room as a hostess reviewing her ranks, lingering where the laughter was loudest and the ideas most daring. For an hour, I navigated the currents of the party, finding my guests to be exactly what I'd hoped: industrious, ingenious, and delightfully rebellious. They carried their Bollinger like banners of courage, and their energy was its own

LICENSE TO THRILL: LILY BOLLINGER

vintage, sparking a familiar fire in my chest. It seemed the heart was exactly what San Francisco was thirsty for.

The evening was peaking when Richard nudged me, steering us through a new swell of tuxedos. "Look, there's the 'Cable Car Lady,' Friedel Klussmann. The papers call her a sentimental nuisance."

Standing out among the ballgowns was a woman in a suit of charcoal wool, as stiff and functional as a soldier's uniform. She stood anchored against the tide of silk, watching the room with a flinty, surgical gaze. Richard marched us over. When I reached out, her handshake was a jolt of energy.

"Mrs. Klussmann, I've read so much about you." I did not drop her hand. "You're a woman who doesn't shy away from a fight. Admirable."

"The mayor calls the cable cars obsolete." Her voice took on a staccato rhythm, cutting through the party's hum. "He wants to rip out the tracks and choke these streets with buses."

She looked out at the room, her gaze unimpressed by the luxury. "He thinks twenty-seven women's groups are a frivolous distraction—a gaggle of housewives with a hobby. But I have forty thousand signatures in my pocket that say otherwise. We are the heartbeat of these hills, Madame. You do not stop a heart simply because you prefer the sound of an engine."

The tilt of her chin held the same steel as mine when I walked my own vineyards, protecting vines others thought too old to bear fruit. An electric prickle of an idea took hold.

"Mrs. Klussmann, if the mayor refuses to listen, stop speaking his language. A battle is not won with logic; it is won with a spectacle. One needs a stage, a touch of theater, and a public thirsty for a hero. *Non?*"

Richard's face paled as he caught the predatory curve of my smile.

"Richard, didn't we hear the mayor was throwing a holiday

party at Tadich Grill this evening? Perhaps we should bring them some Bollinger to support these frivolous women."

Mrs. Klussmann's eyes flashed with a sudden, dangerous light. "I'll go gather my committee." She marched away with new purpose.

"Lily, no." Richard leaned in close. "You're courting a disaster. The mayor is influential. You'll undo all the relationships we've built here for Bollinger."

"What mayor in his right mind would turn down French champagne for his holiday party?" I patted his arm. "If the mayor cannot value the roots of this city, I will make him taste them. One does not uproot a legacy simply because the modern world is in a hurry."

We burst from the Fairmont into the crisp Nob Hill night, a phalanx of silk, fur, and determination. The brass bell of the cable car clanged a sharp invitation. Richard hoisted a heavy wooden crate of Bollinger onto the running board with a grunt of effort as the invigorating air hit us like a shock. We scrambled aboard, the women filling the wooden benches with a flutter of excitement and expensive evening wraps. Friedel Klussmann stood among them like an anchor, her charcoal wool suit stiff and functional against our tide of shimmering gowns.

The conductor, a man with a crusher cap tilted low against the streetlights, swung along the running board. The rhythmic *click-clack* of his silver coin changer a metallic drumroll to our journey. He took our dimes with a wink, his hand already back on the heavy rear brake.

Richard leaned toward me, his knuckles white as he gripped the crate. "I hope you know what you're doing, Lily."

I tightened my hold on the brass stanchion. "What's the fun of always knowing what you are doing?"

Then came the ledge. The street ahead simply vanished into the dark, and my stomach did a slow roll as the car pitched forward. We went over the crest in a sudden, frightening plunge, the heavy wooden frame groaning as gravity claimed us, no longer passengers, but a projectile.

The elegant Victorians of Nob Hill gave way to the glowing red lanterns and ornate balconies of Grant Avenue. We plummeted toward Chinatown, the air thickening with the smells of ginger, star anise, and the salty tang of dried fish from the open markets. I gripped the stanchion as we rattled past laundry lines and the sharp hiss of a street vendor's steam. The city was screaming past us in a blur of neon and shadow, the tracks beneath us humming with a frantic energy.

"Look, Madame Bollinger." Mrs. Klussmann pointed ahead, her arm cutting through the wind. "Old St. Mary's. My grandfather said its bells were the city's heartbeat. She survived the fire and the earthquake—she isn't going anywhere."

I looked at the stone spire and then at the woman beside me. Her resilience was as unyielding as the cathedral.

The tracks finally leveled out, and the conductor threw his weight into the brake, and the car screeched to a halt at Battery Street. We disembarked in a blur of motion, stepping onto the very pavement the mayor had claimed for his own. Richard snatched the champagne crate from the floorboards, carrying it like a treasure chest.

A line of sleek black limousines choked the curb outside Tadich Grill, disgorging a stream of dark overcoats and tailored tuxedos. The mayor stood at the center of this monochrome world, playing the perfect host to an exclusively male assembly. He caught each guest with a practiced handshake while a solid wall of trench-coated reporters captured the staged greeting for the morning news.

As we approached, the flashbulbs became a constant, blinding stutter, turning the sidewalk into a strobe-lit stage. The mayor's gaze shifted, his smile faltering as he caught the silk army led by the formidable Mrs. Klussmann. His eyes narrowed, flickering with recognition; these weren't just activists—many were the wives of the very men standing at his side. His gaze finally locked on the wooden crate in Richard's arms, and his face became a thundercloud.

An electric jolt of panic hit me. For a heartbeat, the urge to retreat was overwhelming—to flee the hostile flashes and the storm gathering around the man in the center. I was a French widow in a city that wasn't mine, risking everything for a trolley.

Mrs. Klussmann stood beside me, a pillar of strength in the chaos. She'd risked her standing for a cause she believed in. The women behind her stood tall and proud. My fears felt trivial against the weight of their conviction.

I reached into the crate Richard held, my fingers closing around the cold, heavy neck of a magnum. I pulled it free and marched straight toward the mayor, wielding the Bollinger like a weapon forged of glass and audacity.

The press line shifted, cameras swinging toward me as I stepped into the strobe-lit circle. The mayor's jaw tightened. He looked at the bottle, then at me, his eyes darting to the reporters capturing his every twitch. He was trapped in the spotlight.

"A celebration, Mr. Mayor?" I didn't wait for an answer. I held the magnum out, the gold foil glinting. "A vintage this historic deserves to be shared. Surely you have glasses for such an occasion?"

His face went taut, a muscle jumping in his cheek. He

knew the lenses were watching for any sign of rudeness toward a lady—especially one standing with the wives of his biggest donors. He turned to a nearby aide, his voice a strained rasp. "Get the glasses from the restaurant. Now."

While we waited, I unfurled the foil and eased the corks out. The women stepped forward, silks and furs rustling as they claimed the heavy glass—unflinching and ready.

"Serve it with a smile and look them in the eye," I instructed them. "Let the men feel the conviction of your cause before they taste it."

The aide returned with a tray of gleaming crystal. I took the first glass, filled it until the foam threatened the rim, and handed it to the mayor. The other women followed my lead, moving through the monochrome assembly of men, pouring Bollinger with the grace of high-society hostesses and the intent of executioners.

I lifted my own glass.

"Mr. Mayor, a toast to your future leadership. San Francisco rivals Paris in its icons—the symbols that keep the world fascinated." I took a slow sip, holding his gaze over the rim. "It takes a great man to preserve the treasures that define a city. Such a man ensures his place in history forever."

I stepped closer, the champagne bubbling over the rim of his glass. "On that note, these women of the Citizens' Committee assure you that their support—and their votes—are yours, provided you preserve the soul of this city." I turned to Friedel with a smile. "And now, I introduce a woman who embodies that spirit: Mrs. Friedel Klussmann."

Her quiet intensity outshone the flashbulbs. "Good evening, Mr. Mayor." She gazed at the politicians, her voice calm. "You have called the cable cars antiques and a burden. But these are the heartbeat of San Francisco. The clanging bell, the rhythmic hum of the cable—that is the music of our streets."

The reporters pivoted, their flashbulbs deserting the mayor to fix on the woman in the humble overcoat.

"Sir, our past is not a burden; it is our foundation. We rode down here tonight to remind you that the soul of this city is worth preserving. How can a city that discards its traditions truly move forward?"

The mayor stood frozen, the glass in his hand trembling just enough to make the golden liquid catch the light. He looked at the press, then at the women—his own social circle turned revolutionaries—and finally at me. He had no moves left. With a tight, jerky nod, he brought the glass to his lips and took a sip.

Richard leaned in, his voice a low vibration. "He can't win this. He's been outplayed."

The mayor's face transformed, the anger melting into the weary mask of defeat. I raised my glass to Mrs. Klussmann. While I moved through the world with a magnum, she wielded her passion with quiet, lethal conviction.

In this shared victory, I knew I had found a kindred spirit. Behind us, the rhythmic clang of a departing cable car echoed through the canyons of the Financial District. It was the sound of a city's heart continuing to beat—and the sound of a vintage that would never be forgotten.

Bollinger had found its audience. A bold signature for the courageous.

I retired to my suite, the rhythmic hum of the cable cars still vibrating in my bones like a persistent bass note. Outside, the fog was rolling in, blurring the lights of the bay into soft, glowing orbs, but my mind remained on the pavement of Battery Street, illuminated by the violent white of the flashbulbs.

I needed to tell James. I wondered if my letters had reached him yet, or if they were still adrift in a mailbag somewhere over the Atlantic. He understood the weight of history—how it could be both an anchor and a sail—and he would appreciate the audacity of the fight I'd just witnessed. It wasn't just the triumph that moved me; it was the kinship. A shared crusade for a living tradition.

I sat at the small mahogany desk and uncapped my pen. The metal was cold against my thumb, the Fairmont stationery crisp beneath my hand. I dipped the nib, the scratch of the point the only sound in the quiet suite as I began to fly across the page.

My Dearest James,
I've just finished the most exhilarating ride of my life—save for our crossing on the Queen Elizabeth, of course ...

27
TOUT VIENT À POINT
À QUI SAIT ATTENDRE
EVERYTHING COMES TO ONE
WHO KNOWS HOW TO WAIT

1972, Aÿ. Thirty meters deep, the Bollinger caves are more than a cellar; they're a sanctuary where time suspends. The air is thick with the ghost of aging oak and the yeasty perfume of wine fermenting on the lees. Electric lanterns cast dancing shadows against the ancient chalk, illuminating the space where the vines above send their rooted fingers deep into the earth.

I stand at the head of the long, worn table, heart drumming. My family enters, eyes wide. For the first time, I've invited the youngest generation to join our tasting team—to witness the early life of our greatest secret. I need them to feel the weight of this silence.

"Welcome to the roots of the house." My voice echoes, sounding more certain than I feel. "Please, be seated."

Guy Adam, our *chef de cave*, offers a sharp nod. He and I have guarded this vintage since the 1969 harvest; we have whispered over these barrels so often he knows the wine's character as intimately as he knows my own mind. He begins to pour, the pale gold liquid catching the lantern light.

I grip my glass, taking note of Yves' ashen complexion. A rattle in his chest sounds like a clock ticking. Pneumonia has taken a cruel turn. Beside him, Claude moves with methodical concentration. Even as President, he approaches the table like a monk approaching an altar. Claire, his wife, watches with a sharp, intelligent intensity. Their son, Arnold, sits between them, notebook ready, earnest at twenty.

Christian holds his glass to the light with a theatrical flourish. He is the charm to Claude's iron. His sons, Etienne and Xavier, flank him like sentries, already learning to wear their father's easy, salesman-like confidence.

"I have been keeping a secret from you all." I lean forward, a grin finally breaking through. "I wanted you here today because you are the first to taste what I've been preparing for my seventy-fifth birthday in two years. This will be the finest wine this house has ever produced."

I lift my glass into a beam of light. "Before us is the 1969 *Vieilles Vignes Françaises*—Old French Vines."

The name feels like a prayer.

Etienne leans forward. "Tante Lily, how did they survive when all of France was devastated?"

"A combination of grace and grit, my boy. High stone walls kept the world—and the louse—at bay. That, and the sheer, stubborn resilience of the ancient stock."

I close my eyes for a second, picturing those two tiny plots as they were in the sun—the vines gnarled, low to the earth, and fiercely stubborn. Like them, I have grown older, but age has brought a concentration of character that youth hasn't yet mastered.

"Look at the color." I tilt the glass, the gold dancing on the chalk walls. "Burnished gold. Now, the nose. Find the pinot noir, layered and rich from the old oak. It should smell of survival."

"Taste the structure," I tell the boys. "Vinous, demanding. You must decide how this power will be balanced by its final dosage."

"It is extraordinary." Christian held his glass to the light. "A true *blanc de noirs*. But it needs a lighter touch, Tante Lily. The allure of a secret garden. Make it accessible."

The crystal hit the table with a sharp clack as Claude set his glass down. "Christian, that's precisely the fashionable nonsense we must resist."

Christian's smile didn't reach his eyes. "It's called progress, Claude. People want a drink, not a chemistry lesson."

"Bollinger is defined by structure, not trends." Claude's voice was cold. "We keep the dosage lean so the depth can evolve. If we soften it with sugar, we're merely making expensive juice."

"What does the dosage matter, anyway?" Arnold looked up from his notebook. "It's just a finishing touch, isn't it?"

Claude swirled the gold liquid, his movements precise. "It is the final signature, Arnold—the small measure of sugar and reserve wine we add after the yeast is gone. It is meant to balance the acid, to act as a bridge. But if you have a heavy hand, you bury the character of the soil under a layer of syrup. Bollinger doesn't hide the harvest; we let it stand on its own."

"But the world wants elegance now." Etienne leans over, mirroring his father's bravado.

Xavier turns his glass slowly, watching the legs of the wine. "Under-dosing makes for a harsh finish. Like an argument with no resolution. Is that the legacy we want?"

"But over-dosing silences the voice of the vine." Claire looks from one to the other, unwavering. "This wine must speak only of the terroir."

Voices rise among them—a sharp friction. I watch them, heart swelling and aching. I chose Claude to lead because he is the anchor, the purist. But Christian is the one who understands how the world is shifting. Now, watching their sons pick up the same swords, I wonder if I've begun a civil war. Given their temperaments, I fear their differences are irreconcilable. There's no vintage in the world balanced enough to bring these two sides together.

I set my glass down. The soft ring of the crystal against the table was a command they all recognized. I waited until the echoes faded and every eye was on mine.

"Your perspectives are noted." My voice was quiet, cutting through the remnants of their argument. "But this wine is a survivor; it does not need to be managed. It needs time. It will be ready for my seventy-fifth, and not a moment before."

They take a final sip, straining to taste the future. As the family begins to disperse, the tension trails behind them like smoke. Only Yves remains, his slender frame slumped over the table.

"You're exhausted, Yves."

He manages a weak smile. "I wouldn't have missed tasting this for the world." He coughs, a dry, rasping sound.

"Your pneumonia is worse. You need a month in bed. No more work."

He lifts his head, a flash of stubbornness in his pale eyes. "We just started pruning."

"The vineyards will survive a month without you. You've tasted the future tonight; now you must ensure you're here to see it bottled." I squeeze his shoulder. "This is not a request. Go home."

He sighs, heavy with resignation. "Very well." He struggles to stand, his movements stiff and slow as he leaves.

"That's my boy," I murmur. But he's no longer a boy. He's a decade younger than I am, his own vintage weathering.

The chairs sit empty, shadows closing over the table. I've given Claude the title, but the unity of this house is still a ghost haunting these halls. I have one more blend to master before my work is done—the family itself.

28

LE HASARD FAIT
BIEN LES CHOSES
CHANCE DOES THINGS WELL

Dec. 1947, Los Angeles. The green marble fireplace in the bar was pure golden brilliance, the flames hungry as they licked at the heavy logs. I watched the bubbles rise in my glass, listening to the snap and pop of fragrant madrone wood. It had been another triumphant stop, but as I slipped my heels off under the table, the relief was sharp enough to make my eyes water. At forty-eight, my body had ceased politely suggesting I rest; it was now staging a full-scale revolt in every joint and tendon. I just hoped our efforts meant something lasting for the House.

I looked at the bar—a riot of Beverly Hills excess. Gilded bells, gold-flocked poinsettias, and glittering tinsel draped a tree that towered toward the ceiling, glowing with strings of bright, electric lights. It was a world away from the simple pine boughs and beeswax candles we favored in Aÿ.

Richard Blum had already gone up to his room to place his call. It was the middle of Hanukkah, and I knew he was counting the minutes until he could hear the voices of his pregnant wife and their toddler. He had spent the last month pulling off miracles, state after state; the least I could do was grant him a few hours of peace while I sat with my thoughts.

The tour played back in my mind like a newsreel. How wonderfully naïve I had been! America wasn't a country; it was a continent of nations. Each one had its own language, its own rhythm.

In New York, they had treated our champagne like a business deal—fast, efficient, a toast to a contract signed in a skyscraper. Then we went to Boston, where the air smelled of old books and Atlantic salt, and they seemed convinced it was something to be served with afternoon tea and history lessons. I nearly had to shake my finger at them. Chicago was a brash, muscular place that smelled of the stockyards and cold lake wind; there, the pop of the cork sounded like a hard-earned reward. And San Francisco? The Gold Coast and the fog made the champagne feel like a secret shared among pirates.

And now, Los Angeles. A world where they drink champagne like water and drama is the only currency. I thought of the deals signed in booths at the Brown Derby and the gossiping crowds at the Mocambo. It was astounding. It was exhausting.

My eyes wandered to a woman seated alone in a secluded alcove. My heart gave a sudden, sharp rap against my ribs. In her hand was a script, the title in bold, black letters: **JOAN OF ARC**.

I knew that profile—the high, clean cheekbones and the quiet, luminous intensity that had captivated the world. It was Ingrid Bergman.

I raised a hand to catch the waiter's attention.

"Would you please bring that woman a bottle of Bollinger?" I lowered my voice, my eyes never leaving her. "From me."

"Of course, Madame."

I watched him go, my pulse quickening. Miss Bergman must be reading for the part of Joan—the girl from the Lorraine fields, the warrior of France, my own patron saint. In this temple of Hollywood glitz, the coincidence seemed like a message. I couldn't let the moment pass.

Across the room, the waiter placed the ice bucket beside her. He made a subtle gesture toward my table. Ingrid's gaze met mine. She gave a small, surprised smile and a nod of thanks.

The pull of fate—or perhaps the champagne—was too strong. My heels were back on, the pain ignored. I approached the alcove with the same measured stride I used when walking the vineyards.

"Excuse me, Madame Bergman? I am Lily Bollinger. I hope you'll accept this with my compliments. I adored your performance in *Casablanca*. So heartbreaking and brave."

Ingrid looked up, her brow furrowed for a split second before her expression brightened into a look of genuine shock.

"Bollinger?" Her eyes widened. "*The* Madame Bollinger?"

"I am here on business, touring the country." I smiled, warmed by her recognition.

She actually blushed, a delicate pink rising on her cheeks. She looked down at the script, then back at me. "So, as a French woman, you must be familiar with Joan of Arc?"

"Obsessed, actually. She is the spirit of France. I'm rather partial to her fire."

Bergman's expression softened. She gestured to the empty chair with a graceful hand. "Please, would you join me for a glass?"

I sat, the plush velvet catching me. The waiter appeared instantly, his movements silent as he poured. We sat in silence for a moment, the jazz from the piano drifting between us. She looked smaller in person, her face stripped of the studio's soft-focus lighting, revealing a deep, authentic fatigue that mirrored my own. Two women, miles from home, working in a world that never stopped watching.

"To Joan of Arc," I said, lifting the crystal.

"To Joan." She took a sip, then looked back at the script, her fingers tracing the edge of the paper. "It is a challenging role. I'm struggling to understand her. Was she truly touched by God, or was she just ... a fanatic?" She looked at me, her eyes searching, as if I held a piece of the puzzle. "Does anyone really hear God's voice, Madame? Or is it just the echo of their own desires?"

I watched a single bubble travel the length of my glass. "I think we hear his voice all the time. We just don't always listen. He speaks through our passions, our instincts—that voice inside that tells us what is true. Joan's truth was her own. She had the audacity to follow it when the world told her to be silent. That's what made her extraordinary."

Bergman nodded slowly. "So, you believe she heard her own truth?"

"I believe she was a girl who dared to challenge kings because she believed in something bigger than herself. That takes courage, whether the inspiration is divine or simply from the depths of the soul. It is the ability to see the world not as it is, but as it could be."

Bergman's eyes opened wide. The intellectual hunger in her look was startling; a woman who wanted to be more than just a beautiful face on a screen. "Yes. The vision. That is what I am trying to capture. But it feels elusive. Like trying to grasp smoke."

"Perhaps it isn't about the smoke, but the fire it came from." I rubbed my fingers along the stem of my glass, feeling the cold condensation. "What fueled her? Faith? Ambition?

The need to be heard? A complex character has many layers, Ingrid. Just like a vintage that has survived a hard frost."

She took a long sip, her eyes never leaving mine. "Your champagne has a fiery spirit. It has a voice. A conviction." A smile finally crinkled the corners of her eyes. "It is full of the same fire you spoke of. The fire that fueled Joan."

I raised my glass one last time. "To the fire."

"To the fire," she echoed.

I took a final, contemplative sip, the bubbles dancing against the roof of my mouth. I could see the wheels turning behind her eyes, the script no longer a burden but a challenge. My work here was done. I set my glass down with a definitive click.

"I have taken enough of your time, Ingrid. You have a saint to find, and I have a tour to finish."

She started to protest, then smiled, a look of genuine gratitude softening her features. "Thank you, Madame Bollinger. For the wine, yes—but mostly for the fire."

I rose to my feet, ignoring the sharp protest of my tired arches. When I reached the edge of the alcove, I stole one last glance. She was already hunched over the script, her pen moving with a new energy, slashing across the page as if she'd finally found the pulse of the girl from Lorraine.

I'd come to America to sell a label. To prove that Bollinger still had a place in this loud, new world. But in the hush of this alcove, I'd rediscovered the heartbeat of the House.

If Bollinger bubbles could inspire the world's most famous actress to find her inspiration, then they were enough to sustain me through what lay waiting at home: the rubble of the bombed cellars, the empty racks where our vintage had been plundered, and the ache of vineyards still waiting for the men who wouldn't return from the front.

This was the spark I would carry back to the damp, quiet caves of Aÿ to light my own way forward.

The thrill still buzzed through my veins when I returned to my suite. Once again, I felt the urge to write to James. I opened the desk drawer and reached for the heavy, cream-colored Beverly Hills Hotel stationery, but a sudden, cool wave of doubt washed over me.

I'd been writing to him in my mind as if he were a confidant, pouring out my soul and the strange, electric experiences of this journey. But what if I'd read too much into our brief encounter? What if that connection meant nothing at all to him—simply a pleasant diversion on a long voyage?

I looked at the blank page, then gently closed the drawer. My imagination had truly run away with me, fueled by California sunshine and expensive bubbles. James would live on in my memory, a lovely interlude on the ocean, undisturbed by the reality of the post-war world. I leaned back on the plush bed and smiled to myself.

Yes. It could certainly be a movie.

29
APRÈS LA PLUIE, LE BEAU TEMPS
AFTER THE RAIN, THE BEAUTIFUL WEATHER

1972, Aÿ. Inside Église Saint-Brice, the air was dense with the scent of lilies and myrrh—a cloying sweetness clinging to the damp stone. It was the perfume of grief, suffocating and heavy, layering over the scent of old wool and the sharp, expensive perfumes of the mourners. Sunlight, fractured by the stained-glass windows, painted the silent assembly in a shattered mosaic of jewel tones, but the gloom was absolute.

Yves. Gone. An impossible truth. Just yesterday, it seemed, his voice rang through the vineyards, his calloused hands gently caressing the rootstock. Now, I traced the polished wood of his coffin, cold and lifeless beneath my fingertips.

The illness had been a slow, agonizing unraveling. Each day, a piece of him slipped away, stolen by the cough that took his breath, then his voice. Even weakened, he'd insisted on overseeing the pruning, his hands guiding the shears with practiced precision despite their trembling.

"There's too much to do, Tante Lily." His faint, brave smile still reaching for mine. "The vines need me."

He died in May, just as the vineyards exploded with life. It was a bitter thing to see the leaves so vibrant and green while the man who coaxed them from the earth lay still. The silence he left behind was louder than the church bells. And now, this gaping hole in our family—in Bollinger itself.

Christian stood beside me, his face etched with a grief that mirrored my own. To see my strong nephew so utterly exposed tore at my heart. He and Yves had been an unlikely pair, bonded by their shared devotion to the House. Yves, with his quiet wisdom, had tempered Christian's relentless drive, reminding him that the cultivation of exceptional champagne cannot be rushed.

Christian stepped forward to deliver the eulogy. His voice, usually so confident and booming, was subdued. He spoke of Yves's quiet strength and his devotion to the land.

"He taught me so much." Christian pressed a fist to his mouth; a raw sound stifled in his throat. "About patience, about respect for the soil, about the true meaning of family. Yves was more than a vineyard foreman." He finally continued, his voice cracking. "He was the hands of Bollinger, the keeper of our traditions, a guardian of the land."

He faltered, his broad shoulders quaking. He turned away from the congregation, burying his face in his hands. A collective gasp rippled through the mourners. Christian's wife, Marie-Helene, rushed to his side, her arms encircling him.

My gaze drifted to the window, where the vibrant green of the new vines thrived beyond the stone walls, oblivious to the tragedy within. The harvest loomed—a daunting task without Yves. Who would guide the *vendangeurs* now?

But as I looked at the faces of the mourners, united in grief but also shared determination, I knew we would find a way. I would be there; I would guide them and support them, just as I always had.

The church bells began to toll, their somber melody a reminder of life's fragility. Your dedication, my dear Yves, your quiet strength, your love for these vines, will forever be etched in the heart of Bollinger.

As the mourners began to disperse, I felt a hand on my shoulder. It was Cyril Ray, his face drawn with a sadness that surprised me. I immediately stiffened, the warmth of the church draining away.

"Cyril." I pulled away from his touch. "Must you intrude even here? This is not material for your journalistic curiosity. This is private."

Cyril flinches. "Lily, I came to pay my respects. Yves was—"

"He was ours." My voice was a furious whisper. "He was ours, not a footnote for your book. Which was supposed to be published by now."

"It got held up in proofing, I'm afraid. It goes to the printer anytime now."

"Well, thank goodness for that." I brushed past him, out the door, and into the light, moving swiftly away from the heaviness of the church.

But Cyril caught up with me. "My presence here is an intrusion, and I apologize. But when I look at these hills, Lily —when I see that old rootstock untouched by the louse, the vines that Yves and his father guarded—I don't see mere crops. I see the continuity of generations."

His words, poetic yet utterly real, pierced my guard. He didn't just understand what Yves did; he understood why it mattered.

The cold knot of irritation loosened in my chest. "That means a great deal."

The May breeze carried the scent of damp earth and burgeoning vines as we walked back toward the house. Cyril offered his arm, a gesture that was strangely comforting.

"It must be difficult to lose someone so vital to Bollinger," he said softly.

"Yves was family." A sudden lump formed in my throat. "And, he understood the vineyards in a way no one else ever could."

Cyril's gaze swept across the rolling landscape. "When I first visited, Yves was my guide. He explained the nuances of each plot, the history etched into every vine. It's remarkable that we were treading the ground where his ancestors had been making wine for centuries, along with the Bollingers."

"Indeed," I agreed. "We carry a heavy responsibility to uphold that legacy."

"I've always been fascinated by the names of your vineyards. *Côte aux Enfants*, *Pisse-Renard* ... Where on earth did those names come from?"

"They are centuries old, Cyril." The corners of my mouth twitched. "Each one tells a story. *Pisse-Renard*, for instance, translates to 'fox's pee.'" I managed a smile despite my grief. "Apparently, the grapes grown there had a rather ... distinctive aroma in those days."

"And who will be the next director of the vineyards?"

"It will be Jacques Bouzy, Yves's assistant." I met his gaze. "He has learned much from Yves; he has that same instinctive, bone-deep understanding of the soil."

Cyril nodded. "Yves would be pleased."

As we reached the house, a quiet resolve settled over me. Despite the loss, the sight of the vines affirmed that Bollinger would endure beyond us all.

Cyril paused, his gaze lingering one last time on the horizon of vines before he adjusted the collar of his coat against the breeze. "The book launch is scheduled next month in London. I do hope you'll be able to come. It wouldn't be the same without you."

A wry smile touched my lips. "I suppose someone has to make sure you got all the facts right."

30

NE PAS VENDRE SON ÂME AU DIABLE

NOT TO SELL ONE'S SOUL TO THE DEVIL

1948, Havana. It had been a long six-week tour, but Richard Blum had saved the most exotic for last: Havana! His enthusiasm was cut short by a telegram: his wife was delivering their second child. I insisted I could handle this final destination alone, and he finally agreed to take the next plane home from Miami. Family comes first.

I boarded the *SS Florida* for Cuba. The sleek ocean liner cut through the turquoise Caribbean toward Havana, a city with a reputation for danger lurking beneath a veneer of glamour. As I disembarked, the humid air, thick with the scent of salt, tobacco, and overripe fruit, pressed in on me. My heart longed for the green country air of Aÿ.

A black Cadillac loomed at the end of the pier. It was long, menacing, and entirely foreign to me. Its tinted windows shaded my host, Señor Alejandro Menendez, the man Richard Blum had informed me controlled Cuba's liquor trade. Menendez was a *jefe*, a boss whispered about with fear in Havana's smoky backrooms.

The driver held the door, but I wasn't prepared for the

man who stepped onto the gravel. Alejandro Menendez emerged with a heavy, unhurried grace that made the lazy dockworkers look frantic by comparison. His white linen suit was a blinding searchlight against the rusted backdrop of the harbor—the attire of a man who owned the air everyone else was breathing. An unlit cigar rested in the corner of his mouth like a deliberate accessory. Gold links caught the sun in the hollow of his throat, bright against skin the color of polished mahogany: dark, dense, and seemingly smooth to the touch.

"Madame Bollinger. Welcome to Havana." The voice was a low rasp, steady and cool. "It is an honor to host the woman who defied the Nazis to keep the champagne flowing."

He took my hand. His grip was firm pressure that didn't let go quite when it should have.

"My agent is prone to hyperbole." My laugh sounded thin in the humid air. "The goal wasn't to be a legend, Mr. Menendez. It was simply to ensure there was still a cellar left when the war ended."

The driver, a tall man whose eyes never left the street, quickly opened the rear door. Menendez made a subtle gesture, indicating I should enter first. Once I was seated on the wide, cool leather, he slid in beside me. The door clicked shut, sealing us in the insulated darkness. Without a word, the driver eased the heavy Cadillac away from the pier, merging silently into the humid throng of the city.

"Blum told me you didn't simply save your brand from the Nazis." His smile flashed white in the darkness of the car. "But that you outwitted the *Boche*, a true act of defiance. You sabotaged their orders, hid your best vintages in the walls of your cellar, and even stole ration cards to feed your workers. He claimed you are a master of strategy—a woman who knows how to succeed by any means necessary."

My cheeks burned with a sudden heat that had nothing to

do with the sun. "I did what was necessary to survive. Nothing more, I assure you." Richard Blum's warnings echoed in the back of my mind—that women in Havana were afforded no respect. He'd crafted this myth of the 'Heroine of the Resistance' as a shield, a currency of power he knew Menendez could respect.

The massive Cadillac glided through the city, a silver-trimmed predator through a colorful chaos. Vendors sang their wares above the low thrum of the engine, the air thick with the competing smells of rum, exhaust, and sweet, overripe guava.

"You see, Madame?" The low rumble of his voice held the heavy, breathless weight of the air before a hurricane. "They call Havana the Paris of the Caribbean, but that is a lie. This city is not about art or romance; it is about a very simple thing: desire. Americans come here hungry for a taste of freedom from their own rules. They want to gamble, to dance the mambo, to drink all night. We give them what they crave. This is a city built on a simple promise: for a price, anything is possible."

He leaned closer, smelling of bay rum and cured tobacco.

"Your champagne, Madame, it is the purest form of that promise. It is the toast to power. We will not just sell champagne; we will sell a dream."

A chill snaked down my spine as the Cadillac cut through the shantytowns—a blur of pleading eyes and derelict shacks. The collision of excess and squalor hit me with the force of the humid air, the scent of his expensive cologne suddenly cloying, like perfume on a corpse.

My champagne—the drink of tradition and survival—was being twisted into an ugly indulgence for his corrupt world. In France, our houses supported the hospitals, the schools, and the people. Our stability was rooted in the chalk and the earth.

This place, by contrast, smelled putrid with the scent of stagnant power—a structure rotting from the inside out.

I dressed for the evening with a forced truce: I was here for business, not to pass judgment. When I reached the top of the grand marble staircase, Menendez was already waiting in the lobby. My Jacques Heim dress of deep emerald silk, the skirt cascading behind me with a languid grace.

He looked pristine in a midnight-blue silk dinner jacket—a custom creation he wore without a hint of perspiration in the rising humidity. He turned as I reached the final step, his smile a slow, deliberate unveiling of power. His gaze traveled from the hem of my silk to the neckline before finally meeting my eyes.

"Madame Bollinger. The emerald is a statement. Green is the color of money and, in this city, the color of envy. It suits a woman who knows what she wants."

A phantom chill touched my neck, but I held my ground. He took my arm and led me toward the Comedor de Aguiar. The space was a breathtaking display of Spanish colonial grandeur—hand-carved mahogany and vast arched windows framing a black sea—yet it was overlaid with a frantic, electric wealth. In Paris, luxury is whispered; here, it screamed. The lighting was fierce, casting a hard glow on every surface as if to ensure no diamond or bribe went unnoticed.

A live band played a jazzy *son cubano*, its rhythm pulsing with a primal ferocity. Menendez led us to a prominent table near the center.

The staff's reaction was immediate. The maître d' and the manager greeted him with overblown compliments and fixed, darting eyes. Their fear was a physical thing—an invisible weapon Menendez wielded without effort. My stomach tightened as the freshly shaken daiquiris arrived, the large coupe glasses adorned with orchids.

"You and I are not so different, Madame. We both found a way to thrive when all seemed lost. I control the joy in this city, and you control Mother Nature to do your bidding."

"The difference, Menendez, is that Mother Nature does not surrender quite as easily as your citizens seem to."

The rum was already reaching my head. I expected a flash of temper, but his laugh expanded into a full, genuine rumble.

"Ah, your tongue is as sharp as your mind, Madame Bollinger." He wiped his eyes with a linen napkin. "This city runs on a currency of dreams. We give them what they cannot find anywhere else."

He ordered a feast: succulent lobster, *lechon asado*, and platters of black beans, all paired with Bollinger—a not-so-subtle reminder of the market he could deliver on a golden platter.

As the evening wore on, Menendez held court. American gangsters and Cuban politicians filtered in to pay their respects. Each offered a handshake of fealty, their eyes fixed on him with a deference that bordered on the religious. I wouldn't have been surprised if they'd knelt to kiss the heavy sapphire on his hand.

In this country, Menendez was the emperor. My champagne was to be the latest jewel in his crown.

The business was conducted the next day at his hacienda on the outskirts of the city. We drove down a winding, unpaved road, leaving the city's noise behind, only to be swallowed by a different, more ominous silence. Thickets of palmetto and wild sugarcane choked the roadside, the air growing hotter and more restrictive with every mile. The white-washed walls of the estate gleamed in the sun like a bleached skull. Inside, the scent of wet earth and the sickly-sweet perfume of tuberoses reeked like a funeral shroud.

Menendez led me through an immense mahogany door into a private study. The air inside was sealed and unnaturally cool, heavy with the scent of aged leather and the stagnant remnants of cigar smoke. A young man in a starched white linen jacket placed a glass of iced limeade on the corner of the desk. He bowed without meeting my eyes and melted into the shadows behind the door.

"Please, Madame, take a seat. Let's talk about champagne."

Menendez rounded the desk and sat on the front corner, placing his bulk too close. My skin prickled. Richard Blum had spent months sweating over the logistics of this trip, handing me his hard-won contacts like a sacred trust. I couldn't fail him—not when he had staked his own reputation on my arrival.

"Your operation, Madame Bollinger, is exquisite, but it is vulnerable. I've been told you have aging reserve champagnes that are precious but desperately strain your cash flow. You need to buy more vineyards to meet post-war demand, and you're researching new bottling equipment—the latest German model. I know the cost down to the last franc."

He was speaking of my company's secrets as if they were his own. The violation was as invasive as the jungle outside; this was no negotiation. It was a calculated coup.

"But you need not worry about all those expenses any longer. My orders will more than cover your vineyard expansion, that new equipment, and the labor you need."

He smiled, teeth rimmed in a permanent tobacco stain, and pushed a massive leather-bound book toward me.

"I deal in volume, Madame. Take a look. These are the veins of my empire: ledgers detailing the city's vast liquor imports—a spiderweb of distribution networks I command."

He leaned over me, his eyes narrowing.

"I will make you a very wealthy woman, Madame Bollinger. But to do that, you must trust me completely."

He took his time lighting a cigar, letting the sweet-heavy smoke rise to the ceiling fan. The delay was a show of absolute control.

"I will be the sole importer of Bollinger for the entire Caribbean. We will do this directly, you and me. We will not need your agent, Mr. Blum. I will handle all the business, and we will split the profits he would have taken. A substantial discount, of course, for the guarantee of such a high volume of sales."

The offer was a masterstroke of predatory business: wealth, security, and absolute market dominance. But the price was Richard's head on a platter. He had opened these doors for me; I would not be the one to lock him out of them. A sour, acidic knot tightened in my gut.

"Señor Menendez, with all due respect, I don't think this will work out. My brand is not for sale in this manner."

The smile vanished. His voice became a blade.

"You're being a romantic, when business requires cold calculation. I expected more backbone, more savvy business sense from a woman of your reputation. It's just business, Madame."

"No, Señor Menendez. I am declining."

His eyes turned to flat black stone. He gestured toward the two men in linen suits standing by the door, guns holstered at their sides.

"That would be most unwise to decline, Madame. You did what was necessary to survive the Nazis. You will do what is necessary here, too."

He leaned in, his foul, cloying cologne a final invasion of my space. Then he sat back, folding his hands in his lap with the chilling poise of a predator who knows his prey has nowhere to run.

"You have until morning to reconsider. I am confident you will make the right decision for the benefit of all parties. My driver will take you back to your hotel."

I stood and walked out without looking back. I did not need until morning; I needed to be off this island before he realized I wasn't coming back to the table.

At the hotel, the humid air was a physical weight against my chest. I checked the small gold watch on my wrist: 5:15 p.m. The *SS Florida* was scheduled to weigh anchor at 7:00 p.m. for the overnight crossing to Miami. It was the last departure of the day. If I missed it, I would be a sitting duck in this hotel room when Menendez's "morning" arrived.

I worked with cold, furious precision, throwing clothing and paperwork into my trunks. Every second was a second Menendez could use to close the net. I paid the porter triple his fee to load the luggage into a waiting cab, my heart hammering a frantic rhythm against my ribs.

"Terminal Sierra Maestra," I told the driver. I shoved a wad of pesos into his hand. "The *SS Florida* leaves at seven. If I make it, there is more for you. Drive."

The cab lurched into the evening traffic. I kept my eyes on the rearview mirror, watching for any black sedan that lingered too long behind us. Richard had worked too hard for this, had trusted me too deeply, for me to let his legacy—and mine—be swallowed by a predator in a starched linen suit.

I had ninety minutes to disappear, or Menendez would ensure I never left at all.

31
CHAPEAU!
HAT!

1972, London. "Why the cloak and daggers, Christian?" I spear the Lalique ornament deep into the sable and silver sweep of my hair, the metal grazing my scalp. The sting necessary to keep the beehive twist from escaping. We've spent the morning calling on demanding London clients, stretching my French manners thin as a summer crepe. Christian promised this outing was a necessary reprieve, but the way he's driving suggests something far more electric.

"Now, Tante Lily." His voice rises above the robust growl of his Ferrari Daytona. "If I told you, it would spoil the surprise." Hands gripping the leather steering wheel, he glances sideways with a naughty glint behind his oversized YSL frames. He muscles the Ferrari through the soot-stained streets with terrifying speed. A frantic pulse pummels my throat. Christian has a way of making even a detour feel like a clandestine operation.

We turn off the main road, following a high perimeter wall of faded brick. Christian screeches to a halt before a formidable black metal gate. A uniformed guard checks the clipboard for his name, then pushes a heavy lever, and the gate swings open with a screech. Christian points to a weather-beaten sign against the manicured grass: **PINEWOOD STUDIOS**.

My breath catches, the morning's meetings forgotten. This is the inner sanctum—the birthplace of the James Bond films. A sudden, sharp heat attacks my chest. This is the world I escape to most nights in the bath. A world of suave, high-stakes daring where the risks are absolute, and charm is a weapon.

"You're serious? We're actually going in?"

"You've met the man, but you haven't met the mission. It's time you see how the flesh and blood becomes the legend."

I manage the low-slung exit with concentrated grace much more suited to the dignified height of a Bentley, and stand to find Christian hauling a steel cooler from the boot.

"What on earth is that for?"

"Refreshments." He shuts the lid with an expensive thud, meeting my gaze with a glint of manic energy. "I haven't seen Cubby since Monte Carlo, but I couldn't stop thinking about our favorite spy. Why on earth would he be drinking martinis when he could be drinking Bollinger?"

A conspiratorial smile tugs at my lips. This was no accident; it's been Christian's plan all along.

"Is Cubby Broccoli expecting us?"

Christian doesn't answer immediately; instead, he lifts the cooler, the ice rattling inside. "Not today, but I thought James might be getting thirsty. Saving the world always makes one thirsty, doesn't it? Pays to be prepared."

"Then we'd better not keep James waiting. Move, Christian —before the ice melts." I lead the way, my heels clicking a sharp rhythm against the asphalt. At the massive stage door, I catch the iron handle and pull. The door is heavy, a barrier between the mundane and the miraculous. I hold it wide, inviting my nephew to carry our prize inside.

Christian guides me through the labyrinthine sets of the studio. The atmosphere buzzes with frenetic energy, a mix of creativity and urgency that's intoxicating. Cameras whir and click, their shutters snapping like a thousand crickets in the vineyards. Lights flash, stabbing at my vision. People dash through the glare, their voices rising in creative chaos. The scent of strong coffee stings my nostrils and mingles with the faint aroma of makeup and the fragrance of expensive perfume, a heady mix that speaks of long hours and high stakes.

We find the viewing platform overlooking the set, where a scene of high drama unfolds. The set is a meticulously crafted replica of a Louisiana bayou. It's astonishing how completely they fabricate reality. The air carries the clammy scent of damp, decaying earth and a metallic note from the fake swamp water. An insidious chill seeps through my silk stockings, making the fabric cling uncomfortably to my calves. Below us, the murky water reflects the blinding arc lights like glass, interrupted by a slick mat of bright-green algae. A gnarled cypress rises from the false swamp, heavy with Spanish moss hanging in weeping curtains. The atmosphere presses against my chest, and I'm transported to the swamps of Louisiana.

Monsieur Broccoli sits in the producer's chair, his attention locked on the actors. A powerhouse of a man in a navy blazer with gleaming brass buttons, a patterned cravat peeking from his open collar, and trousers that hold a razor-sharp crease. Loafers, no socks. He twists a gold signet ring on his pinky, one eye on the monitor, the other on the set. He doesn't so much as blink.

Jane Seymour is bound to a stake with thick, fraying ropes that look slick with moisture. She wears a white, flowing chemise that clings to her porcelain skin. The low neckline and the loose, innocent waves of her hair enhance her vulnerability. Near her bare feet, a swarm of dark, patterned snakes is coiled, their sinuous bodies writhing together and their forked tongues flicking silently in the humidity.

Surrounded by voodoo drummers, their faces hidden behind grotesque wooden masks, the air thickens with a chilling chant. The rhythm quickens, a desperate pulse thumping against my eardrums until the studio's hum vanishes. The raw, rhythmic surge bypasses thought. A cold dread tightens my chest. The sight of those monstrous masks closing in on her helpless beauty sends a shiver across my skin that no logic can soothe. This isn't London. This isn't cinema. It is primal terror.

A high screech permeates the air, the banshee wail of a tormented soul. From the shadows, a larger, more horrifying figure steps forward. His mask is a weathered, black leather monstrosity with empty eyeholes that stare directly into Jane's face. His breathing is a wet, raspy noise audible even from the viewing platform.

He carries a massive, curved machete. The blade is dark, pitted steel that reflects the arc lights in a greasy streak. With a furious, fluid motion, he slashes the air, a heavy–*SSHH-WHIP*–and lets out a fierce, guttural yell. His body coils to strike as he raises the gleaming blade high, bringing it down in a swift, horrifying arc directly toward Miss Seymour's exposed neck.

A violent constriction seizes my throat, and a sickening shudder runs down my spine. The faint, acrid scent of hot metal and sulfur hits me, and the world blurs into a haze of shadow and steel. My hand snaps out, gripping the railing until the iron bites into my palm and my knuckles ache white.

The air explodes from my lungs before I can catch it. Raw and jagged, my voice tears through the silence of the set: "No! Don't you dare. Stop this right now!"

All heads twist in my direction. The director yells, "Cut!"

Christian rushes to my side, his voice low and urgent. "Tante Lily, what in God's name? Are you alright?"

Cubby Broccoli whirls around, pointing a stiff finger up toward me. His voice cuts through the studio noise with cold authority. "Madame, this is cinema! We're staging a scene, not committing a crime! That outburst just cost us a small fortune." He holds my eyes with startling hostility. "Get control of yourself. If you interrupt my set again, you're on the stake for the next shot."

A hysterical laugh bubbles up in my throat, and I jam my fist against my mouth to stifle the sound.

Broccoli gives the crew a sharp, single clap of his hands and snaps attention back to the set. "Alright, everyone. From the top."

Christian squeezes my hand till it hurts, his expression both concerned and mortified. "We should leave."

I swallow my pride. "Not on your life. Roger Moore is standing in the wings, ready to go on set. I didn't come all this way for an early exit." I step back to the viewing platform railing and grasp the cold steel until my knuckles ache.

The filming resumes. I hardly dare to exhale, my eyes searching for the artifice—the hidden wires, the safety nets. I tell myself the tears on Jane's face are a calculation, a performance designed to pull at the gut.

Then, Roger Moore slams into the frame. He is all crisp tailoring and cold fury, his Walther PPK spitting rhythmic flashes of fire that crack against the studio walls. As Bond, he moves with a stylized grace, disarming one villain with a swift kick before dropping another with a single shot. He dispatches the remaining attackers effortlessly, leaving them crumpled in the shallow, fake swamp water. With the danger neutralized, he reaches the stake. A single, clean slice of his knife severs Jane's bonds, and he scoops her into his arms, carrying her toward the shadows.

The knot in my stomach thaws into a giddy, reckless euphoria. I find myself gripping Christian's arm, my heart hammering a rapid, adrenaline-soaked rhythm against my ribs. *This* is the glamour Christian promised.

"Cut!" the director bellows.

The lights blaze to full power, obliterating the jungle gloom in a harsh, yellow wash. The crew swarms. Technicians haul heavy, black cables across the floor while grips tear down the foliage, yanking away the Spanish moss in great, dusty handfuls.

"It's over," I whisper. The magic has evaporated, leaving only the smell of sawdust and stale coffee.

Christian squeezes my arm, his voice a low, knowing murmur. "They're not quitting, Tante Lily. They're building the next world."

Before my eyes, the set transforms. A heavy drone starts as pumps siphon away the murky water, leaving the tank floor glistening and bare. Carpenters move with clockwork precision, unbolting the gnarled cypress trees and folding the massive scenic flats back like giant cardboard screens. The jungle is stripped away to its skeleton—raw plywood and scaffolding.

Then, as if by a magician's sleight of hand, a luxury hotel suite slides into place. Gilt-edged furniture and plush velvet chairs appear where the snakes had been writhing moments before.

"From a disgusting swamp to a five-star suite in under ten minutes." I swipe my hands clean, the last of the adrenaline fading. "That, Christian, is the only acceptable timetable for a home renovation."

Christian throws back his head and laughs. The tension leaves his shoulders. "Be sure to mention that to your contractor when we get back home."

It seems as if he's forgiven my involuntary scream. The heat of the embarrassment leaves my face, and I'm back in my own skin—no longer the old woman who lost control in a Bond movie. All we need now is a glass of champagne for a full recovery. Seeing Cubby walking toward us, I just may get the chance.

Cubby Broccoli's scowl vanishes as he recognizes Christian. He does a double take, his face breaking into a wide grin as he reaches out for a vigorous handshake. "Good God, Christian! I should have known it was you creating all the ruckus up here."

My cheeks color, but I hold my ground. "Actually I'm the culprit." A slight curtsy accompanies my words. "But Christian promised me quite the spectacle, and you certainly haven't disappointed."

Cubby catches my hand, his grip reassuring. "No worries, Madame. The next take was better anyway." He nods toward the cooler in Christian's hand. "A little wrap party incentive?"

Christian slides the cooler over, a sharp glint in his eye. "Depends on how many takes Roger needs to get it right."

Cubby flips the lid. The gold foil catches the studio lights. Cubby wags a finger at Christian with a knowing grin. "I like your style, Christian. Why not?" He signals a prop boy and points toward the set.

On the floor, the mess of cables and grit vanishes the moment the cameras pivot. The set becomes a lush lie of velvet and wood. Roger Moore doesn't just wear the tuxedo; he inhabits it. He lifts the receiver, that effortless Bond mask clicking into place.

"Bollinger '69, please," he says into the prop. "Well chilled."

I gasp silently, the name *Bollinger* hitting me like a mallet. Spoken with that accent, in this setting, it sounds like a decree of destiny. The full, ridiculous weight of what Christian has orchestrated settles over me. My hands tremble—a mix of delayed shock and pure, sharp elation. This isn't just a film; it is a global proclamation.

I reach out and squeeze Christian's hand, my grip tight and wordless. He meets my gaze, his eyes bright with the shared knowledge of what he has accomplished here. In this one line of dialogue, he has anchored our legacy to an icon.

We watch as the ice bucket is delivered to the suite. Roger Moore accepts the bottle with practiced ease, his eyes holding the camera as he eases the cork. No vulgar explosion, only a refined hiss that commands the room. He pours a steady stream of gold into the flute, the bubbles catching the arc lights like tiny diamonds. He takes a long, deliberate sip in the glow of the hotel lamps.

A fierce, giddy rush surges through me. Suddenly, I see it: all the women in the world watching this scene over and over. They will imagine themselves in that room, momentarily sharing Bond's perfect, reckless world just by tasting that same vintage. It is the ultimate fantasy, captured in a single glass.

Cubby returns as the scene wraps, the open chest in his arms. His grin widening. "What did you think, Madame Bollinger?"

"I'd say it's a match made in heaven." I meet his gaze, the victory cold and sweet.

Christian steps into the beam of the can light. "Why would Bond drink anything but the best and boldest? It's the only vintage that matches the mission."

Cubby's laughter booms through the rafters. "Brilliant. Then Bollinger it is for Bond. From this day forward." He reaches for a bottle, the glass glistening. "Shall we seal the deal?"

"Allow me." I take the bottle from him, a burst of nervous energy fueling me. "You've shown us your magic, Cubby. Now, let me show you ours." This, I understand. This is my kind of drama.

I whip the Lalique pin from my beehive. My hair falls in a heavy wave as the crew begins to converge, drawn by the spectacle. The pin, carved from amber-toned horn and inlaid with black pearl, is cool and heavy—my elegant, personal saber. I track the spike along the bottle seam with precise, swift control.

"Voilà!"

The cork and cage fly off with a sharp, ringing *crack!* A unified cheer erupts as the fine mist sprays into the air, the scent of yeast and triumph sharp against the hot studio lights. A young grip is already there, sliding flutes in to catch the overflow. I lower the bottle, a grin spreading.

"Positively cinematic!" Cubby stares at the clean break in the glass.

A wave of applause washes over me.

Cubby raises his glass. "To Bollinger and Bond!"

"Bollinger and Bond," Christian and the crew echo.

The nectar dances on my tongue, tasting of success and pure, fizzy possibility. I raise my glass toward Christian, my voice low. "Chapeau. Bravo. This stroke of genius was entirely yours."

He quietly clinks his glass against mine—a silent acknowledgment of our shared victory.

32
PLUS D'UNE CORD À SON ARC
MORE THAN ONE STRING TO HIS BOW

1951, Aÿ. The uncharacteristically cool September had vanished, replaced by a heat that turned viciously personal. A sweltering weight settled over the vines, ripening the pinot noir at a suicidal pace. Unless we harvested *tout de suite*, the vintage would bake on the branch, turning our signature acidity into something flabby and spent.

A bead of sweat tracked through the dust on my temple as I worked alongside Yves. The air was thick enough to chew, the dry earth crunching like bone beneath our boots. We were debating which rows to sacrifice to the sun when a low rumble drifted from the direction of Épernay. A monstrous, boxy bus —a metallic beast out of place on our dirt road—lumbered into view.

"*La vache!*" I pulled at the kerchief, pinning back my hair.

The San Francisco delegation. I had spent weeks in America promising these men the refined elegance of Bollinger; now they had arrived to find the Madame covered in the grime of a frantic harvest.

"Don't worry, Tante Lily." Yves sensed the tension in my

shoulders. "The harvest is secured; you go attend to the Americans."

I turned toward the house, but the sight at the *pressoir* stopped me cold. The line of wagons stretched out like a hungry serpent, the grapes already beginning to simmer. If they sat much longer, we would be bottling jam, not champagne. I was trapped between the prestige of our brand and the literal juice of our future.

Christian was near the cellar, leaning against the stone wall and laughing with a maid. At twenty-three, he had already walked away from a silver-spoon career in banking to join us— a move his father viewed as a tragedy and I viewed as a whim. He'd spent a few months at Veuve Clicquot, but Yves claimed teaching him to prune was as productive as training a truffle pig to fly. I was convinced he lacked the patience for the slow, brutal honesty of winemaking.

But right now, he was the only weapon in my arsenal.

"Christian!" I pointed toward the drive. "The Americans are early. Lead them through the vineyards, show them the cellars—tell them anything that sounds expensive. I'll join you in two hours."

A reckless flash lit his eyes. He gave the maid a wink and smoothed his shirt. "Consider them dazzled, Tante Lily."

I didn't have time to wonder if that was a promise or a threat. I plunged toward the press house. Inside, the air was a riot of smells—the sweet, velvety essence of crushed fruit and the earthy tang of skins. I grabbed a cluster of pinot and held it up, my voice cutting through the rhythmic groan of the wooden press.

"*Mes amours*, look at these. Every grape is a child we've left out on a dusty road. If they stay in the sun much longer, they'll burn. Are we going to let our children burn?"

The chatter died instantly.

"Save the children, and there will be chocolate for everyone tonight!"

A chorus of laughter swept the table. The pace shifted from a trot to a gallop, and I joined them, my hands quickly staining crimson. For ninety minutes, I wasn't the head of a house; I was a sorter, a laborer, a defender of the vintage. Only when the wagons were moving and the juice was flowing cold did I sprint to the house. I scrubbed the grit from my nails and slipped into a silk Heims dress. The general was finished in the mud; now, it was time to win the war in the drawing room.

When I pushed open the heavy oak doors, the cool air hit me like a benediction. I expected chaos; instead, I found the delegation rapt.

Christian stood at the center of the room, an open bottle of our 1929 vintage in his hand. The restless, fidgeting boy was gone; in his place was a young man of startling, magnetic confidence.

"Every bubble is a memory." He held his glass to the light so the afternoon sun set the liquid on fire. "My aunt says you can taste the very soul of the work—the vigilance of the dark cellar and the laughter of the harvest—in every tiny bead."

I remained in the doorway, watching him work. He was weaving a myth out of our labor, turning the back-breaking heat I had just escaped into a romantic narrative of passion. He might have hated his father's bank, but he clearly understood the value of an asset.

"Your nephew is a marvel, Madame Bollinger." One of the American ladies twinkled as she took a sip. "He speaks of champagne as if it were a religion."

"Yes, he seems to have found a pulpit that suits him." I met Christian's gaze. He didn't flinch, simply inclining his head with a ghost of a smirk.

A gentleman from the delegation leaned forward. "How do

you maintain such a specific style when the vineyards are so varied?"

I opened my mouth to answer, but Christian beat me to it. "That, sir, is the art of assemblage."

"We begin with pinot noir, the soul of the blend. But the secret lies in our reserve wines—specially selected magnums aged over many years. They are the colors on the palette. My aunt is the master who knows exactly how to layer them to ensure the canvas never changes."

I was floored. Through all the daydreaming, the technical details had actually stuck. He'd learned more than social graces at Clicquot. He had even coaxed Yvonne into divulging the secret ingredient in her fig jam—a feat of diplomacy I had attempted for years without success.

As twilight began to purple the sky and the bus rumbled away, I watched from the window. Christian was already loosening his tie, the steadiness of the afternoon evaporating as he checked his reflection in a silver tray.

The wild card was back, but the game had changed. I had been looking for the slow endurance of a farmer in him and found nothing. Perhaps I was looking for the wrong virtues. The House needed soil and sweat, but it also needed a tongue that could turn a harvest into a legend.

Christian was a disaster with a pruning knife, but he had conquered the room with a velocity a more plodding man could never achieve. I was ready to offer a word of rare praise—until he reached for the bottle and poured himself a final, unearned glass without asking.

The praise died in my throat. I wouldn't be handing him the keys to the cellar just yet, but the door was open. I would watch him to see if today's performance was a transformation or merely another well-timed act.

33
C'EST LA FIN DES HARICOTS
IT IS THE END OF THE BEANS

1972, London. The two years of invasive scrutiny finally culminate today, and I can't be more thrilled. I am here at Cyril's personal invitation for the launch of his book at Harrods—the largest bookstore in London and the only stage grand enough for the legacy of Bollinger. I'm happy for Cyril; he has labored over these pages with the intensity of a cellar master, and he deserves this day of recognition.

I chose my finest Jacques Heim, a suit of timeless navy wool that speaks of authority without shouting. To play the part, I wear my pearls and the Lalique pin in my beehive. On my left wrist, I wear the Bulova watch Jacques gave me. I haven't had time to get it fixed, but today its weight is a comfort.

I step into the roaring nexus of Harrods, where the overabundance of exotic perfumes battles with the powerful aroma of old money. To my left, the book department is an exercise in meticulous prestige—dark, burnished mahogany shelves designed to make a man feel instantly educated. To my right, the wine and spirits hall glitters with pure, unadulterated indulgence, a wonderland of green glass and gold foil.

Down the main aisle, they've established Cyril's long signing table beside a glistening bar serving Bollinger by the glass, the bubbles catching the light like tiny diamonds. The line snakes toward the entrance, a celebratory mob that has come to see the man who turned our lives into literature. Cyril Ray, the celebrity, holds court; Bollinger, the brand, pays the bills.

"Tante Lily, it's phenomenal!" Christian's voice cuts through the elegant hum as he thrusts the book into my hands. His grin is infectious. "They can't print them fast enough. Harrods, Waterstones—everyone is clamoring for it! You're the toast of London, darling!"

I take the book, feeling a surge of warmth. It is a handsome burgundy volume, foil-stamped with *BOLLINGER: Tradition of a Champagne Family*. The dust jacket smells sharply of new ink—the scent of a legacy secured. But as I look at the cover, my smile falters. It features our Manor House—looking elegant and grand, a beautiful architectural portrait—rather than the sprawling vineyards or the people who toil in them. I had given him the soul of the estate; he chose the masonry.

Christian is stolen away by a reporter, and I retreat to a corner display banquette behind a massive velvet curtain to finally savor the fruit of our partnership. I crack the spine, the crisp snap sounding like a promise.

My excitement lasts only a moment as I scan the chapters.

My eyes latch onto the chapter title: *Madame Jacques*. After thirty-one years of commanding the firm, navigating the Occupation and global expansion, I find my slim chapter tucked behind the shadow of my husband and his family. I fumble through the pages, skip-reading with a growing sense of vertigo as the words on the page turn hostile.

"A childless widow at forty-two—and the childlessness, as we shall see, was to shape her character ... "

The air in the alcove grows cold. I had spoken to him of the quiet house, believing I was talking to a friend who understood the sacrifice. Instead, he played the taxidermist, gutting the spirit of my life and stuffing the remains with his own assumptions. He pinned me to the page like a captured insect, defining the woman I am solely by the children I never had.

I force myself further, searching for the partner I thought I knew. *"... nothing much else cropped up in her long, unhurried day but a consultation with the cook."*

I turn the page, another insult. The trivialization of my hobbies. *"... or perhaps she might occupy herself with her stamp collection, the quiet pastime of a woman with few other distractions."*

Distractions? I stare at the words until they blur. Had he not seen me in the gray light of dawn, patrolling the frost-bitten vines while the rest of the world slept? Had he not sat in my office while I charted global shipping routes or stood in the damp chill of the cellars while I trained my nephews to respect the sediment as much as the sparkle? He had witnessed my exhaustion, the calluses on my hands, the frantic pace of harvest ... He had looked at a lifetime of industry and seen only a vacant afternoon.

But then, the final stroke: *"Madame Bollinger's face is expressionless—even dour, as befits her Scottish ancestry."*

He isn't just describing my temperament; he is calling me ugly. He's studied the lines of my face, lines earned from decades of grit and laughter, and dismissed them as a joyless, plain mask. To him, I am not a woman of depth; I am a severe, unlovely artifact of my heritage.

Everything I thought we were building together—the shared wine, the late-night stories, the mutual respect—was pulled out from under me like a cheap carpet. I was no longer standing in the warmth of a friendship; I was standing on the bare, cold floor of a clinical observation. He hadn't been admiring the "proprietor"; he had been pitying the "widow."

I shove the book under my arm and rip the curtain aside.

"I've been looking all over for you," Christian says, reaching for my arm as I emerge. "Peggy Guggenheim is here—"

"Darling, that's wonderful. But I must catch the next flight home." I spot Cyril nearby, his arms already open for a self-congratulatory embrace. I move first, seizing his elbow with the cold precision of a vine cutter and steering him toward a secluded alcove. My fingers are a vice on his sleeve.

"Something troubling you, Lily, dear?" He raises an eyebrow, a flicker of malice in his eyes that I had been too blinded by friendship to see.

"A 'dour-faced Scotswoman'?" My voice is low, vibrating with the weight of two years of wasted trust. "Is that what my cooperation bought the house, Cyril? A caricature defined by what I *lack*?"

"Surely you jest, Lily. I merely painted an honest portrait. The absence of children undeniably shaped your priorities. It's the truth."

"If it is the truth, it is a remarkably lazy one. You spent two years at my table and concluded that my face is expressionless. Perhaps, Cyril, I simply found nothing you said particularly worth reacting to."

He stiffens, his smug smile faltering for the first time.

"I gave you my time—the most precious asset I have—to cement Bollinger as a leader. Instead, you've characterized me as a relic. "You've used our friendship to diminish the very legacy I trusted you to uphold."

"I had no idea you would feel this way. I thought you were immune to criticism."

"I am a businesswoman, Cyril. Not a statue you can chip away at for your own amusement."

At that moment, his publisher approaches, radiating bonhomie. "Madame Bollinger! Wonderful news. We're scheduling a book tour. Just the two of you, charming the provinces!"

My expression cools to a sub-zero stare. "I'm afraid a tour is out of the question. As Mr. Ray has so eloquently noted, I am a woman of simple, country habits. I wouldn't want my dour presence to dampen the festive atmosphere of your sales figures."

I gesture toward Christian, who is watching from the periphery. "Take my nephew instead. He possesses the natural charm you find so lacking in me, and he is far better suited to the theater of a book tour."

I turn back to Cyril one last time, my eyes raking over his towers of signed books. "You can keep your book, Cyril. After all, I have my stamp collection to attend to."

I don't wait for his mouth to close. I simply turn and walk toward the exit, my heels clicking a sharp, rhythmic tempo against the Harrods floor.

Oh bother. Didn't I give that stamp collection to my great-niece? I wonder, my stride never faltering as I reach the heavy glass doors. *Such a pity. Then I'll just have to trundle off to the spa. Yes. That's what I'll do with all the spare time I didn't know I had.*

Cyril Ray's wildly successful book sits on the corner of my desk, untouched for months. I open it again, my fingers tracing the familiar lines as the sun drops below the horizon.

He actually captured the essence of Bollinger with remarkable precision. The rolling hills and the chalky slopes spring to life; I can almost smell the rich, earthy scent of damp soil and blossoming vines. He even brought my beloved Jacques back to life—the dashing airman and sportsman. Jacques would have loved this book. He would have clapped Cyril on the back and declared it a masterpiece.

But Cyril took my desire to keep Jacques's spirit alive and twisted it into a pathetic portrait of a childless widow. My fingers claw into the hard cover. I will not be defined by his words.

Yet, I must acknowledge his insight. He accurately portrayed the crucial talents of Claude, Christian, and Yves. He's made us legendary. A flicker of pride warms the chill of betrayal; Bollinger will be on the lips of every connoisseur in Europe and America. So what if my ego is bruised? The reputation of the House is worth the price of my fury.

34

RETROUVER SON ÂME SŒUR
TO REDISCOVER ONE'S SOUL MATE

1953, Bagnoles-de-l'Orne, France. The harvest had drained me to the core. This was the escape—a chance to settle the nerves and recover my strength before the cycle of work began all over again. As the train neared the town, I closed the new James Bond book I'd purchased in Paris, *Casino Royale*. The landscape shifted, revealing a beauty that was both fierce and fragile. Forests, their leaves blazing with autumnal defiance, swept over the hills. A glimpse of the lake, a shimmering jewel nestled amongst the trees, its surface reflecting the heavens, promised the sanctuary I sought.

The Grand Hôtel, a magnificent monument to *Belle Époque* extravagance, loomed before me. Stepping inside, I was enveloped in a world of gleaming marble floors and sparkling chandeliers. A far cry from the boisterous camaraderie of the harvest, a world of quiet sophistication that whispered promises of renewal.

A bellhop escorted me to my room, a haven of tranquility overlooking the lake, bathed in the soft light of the late afternoon. Here, there was no hint of the harvest, no reminder of the relentless pressure to produce and maintain the legacy.

I paced the plush carpet of the suite, fingers pressed hard against my throbbing temples. Problems, improvements, new methods—the ghosts of the vineyard followed me even here.

I caught my reflection in the gilded mirror: Lily Bollinger, the indomitable matriarch. I reached back, pulling the pins from my hair until the heavy coil tumbled down. The spa would wash away the grit of the harvest, but only I could shed the rest. This week, there would be no business. Only the woman who loved a reckless gamble.

I ventured to the spa. Attendants in crisp white uniforms, their smiles as soothing as the soft music—a faint, flowing melody of piano and strings piped in from a discreet turntable—offered herbal teas and chilled water, their every gesture an invitation to surrender to serenity.

I stepped down into the sunken tub. The dark mud swallowed me, warm and heavy. It smelled of ancient rain and deep roots—the same primal scent that rose from the Aÿ vineyards after a storm. For years, I had commanded the soil; now, I simply let it hold me.

Submerged, weighted, and warm, I let the steam blur the room until I was back on the deck of the Queen Elizabeth. Commodore James. A rare spark—intellect meeting intellect. I had risked three letters. Then, I had counted the days until the counting became a hum of static. That silence had a gravity the mud couldn't match.

Eleven years since Jacques. Maybe the soil was the only thing that would ever claim me.

"Enough." The word splashed in the quiet room. "I will not spend this precious time wallowing."

I looked down at the thick, dark sludge coating my arms. It was absurd. A giggle burbled up, then a full-blown laugh that bounced off the tiled walls.

"My God, I *am* wallowing!"

For weeks, I'd been trudging through the clay of the vineyards, and here I was paying for the privilege. My hand found the bell, the sharp ring cutting through my own laughter.

The bell's chime lingered in the air, a bright, metallic punctuation to my laughter. Within moments, the attendant appeared—a quiet shadow behind the frosted glass—before entering with a soft, deferential nod.

The transition from the mud was a slow, deliberate ritual. She assisted me from the sunken tub, the dark sludge sliding off my skin in heavy ribbons. I stood under the rhythmic pulse of a warm needle-shower, watching the dark swirls circle the drain. It was as if I were watching the last vestiges of the Aÿ soil, and the burdens that came with it, finally release their grip.

Wrapped in a robe of plush, white toweling, like a cloud against my sensitized skin, I was led down a quiet corridor. The air here shifted, losing the scent of wet earth and taking on a crisp, mineral quality.

Then, the thermal waters.

The heavy doors opened to reveal a mesmerizing expanse of turquoise and shifting steam. I paused at the marble lip of the pool, letting the robe slip away. As I sank into the mineral-rich heat, feeling the water claim the weight of my limbs, the tension didn't just leave; it dissolved, unspooling from my spine until I was suspended in the blue.

"Madame Bollinger."

The attendant's voice was a soft vibration against the tile. "You are now immersed in the Grand Source. It flows from the heart of the earth at a precise 24.3 degrees Celsius." She offered a knowing smile. "The legend says these waters rejuvenate the body and even grant a kind of eternal life."

I let my head fall back against the towel. The peace spread through me like a vintage Bollinger—the bubbles replaced by the water's heavy caress. But eternal life? The thought was frankly exhausting. If a life had no end, where would one find the edge? Where was the necessary tension that forced a soul toward excellence?

No, the miracle was the precision. 24.3 degrees. That was consistency—a promise kept by the earth. I didn't crave eternity; I craved a life lived with such fullness that every vintage was treated as the last.

By the time I reached the massage table, I was as pliable as a vine tendril in the spring sun. Strong, sure hands kneaded the final, stubborn knots from my shoulders. I lay cocooned in heavy, soft towels, the scent of lavender and cedarwood rising in the warm air. My anxieties seemed to liquefy, carried away on a silent current.

The "Matriarch" was a heavy cloak I had left in the mud. Here, beneath the towels, the armor was gone.

There was only me.

What did I want? I didn't reach for an answer, not yet. I simply let the question hang in the air, as fragile and shimmering as the steam rising from the Source. I was a blank page, waiting for the first ink.

That evening, I chose the black silk—something new that clung to my skin, unapologetically bold. So different than anything I'd owned before. A garment for a woman who was ready to gamble.

The casino was a humid swirl of perfume, cigar smoke, and the golden glow of crystal chandeliers. The metallic clatter of chips and the hushed, rhythmic slap of cards created a frantic pulse that vibrated through the air, the heartbeat of chance. Here, there was no legacy to uphold, only the next hand.

I headed for the Baccarat table and scanned the players. My breath hitched.

James.

Commodore James McCullough. His silver hair gleamed like moonlight under the casino lights, his profile as sharp and familiar as a recurring dream. My heart gave a wild, sudden flutter. The laugh lines were deeper now, his features softened by a decade of sea salt and sun, but his eyes were the same—a brilliant, mischievous blue that held an ocean of wisdom.

As he met my gaze, a slow, incredulous smile spread across his face. He rose, leaving his chips where they lay, and moved around the table to sit directly across from me.

"Lily?" His voice was a low, warm rumble. "Is that truly you?"

"James." The name was a breathless whisper. The surprise was intoxicating and impossible. "What on earth are you doing here?"

"Don't you remember telling me about your special retreat?" He leaned in, his eyes sparking with fire. "I've been thinking about coming here ever since. The forests, the silence ... so different from the open sea. But what about you? Isn't it harvest time?"

"The harvest is over," I said. "This is my escape."

A waiter paused beside us with a tray of half-full flutes. "Champagne, Madame? Monsieur?"

I glanced at James, a mischievous impulse taking hold. I

was already throwing caution to the wind; why stop now? "Maybe martinis are in order?"

James's eyebrows raised in approval. "An inspired suggestion. And how do you take yours? Gin or vodka? With a twist?"

I turned to the waiter. "A Vesper, please. Three measures of gin, one of vodka, half a measure of Kina Lillet. Shaken until ice-cold."

James let out a soft, amused whistle. "Bring us two. The only thing more dangerous than that drink, I suspect, is the woman who orders it."

As the waiter departed, James's eyes never left mine. "A Vesper," he chuckled. "Where did you hear of such a thing?"

"Catching up on my reading during the train ride from Paris. A rather thrilling new novel. Ian Fleming's *Casino Royale*."

The waiter returned just as the dealer pushed the cards toward us, setting two brimming, sweating glasses on the table. The drinks glowed a pale, milky gold.

"Your Vesper Martinis, Madame." He set them down with a slight, stiff bow—the silent protest. "Severely shaken, as you insisted."

An irrepressible giggle burbled up from within me. "It seems I'm very specific about my poison tonight."

James lifted his glass, his eyes holding mine over the rim. "To danger."

I touched my glass to his with a sharp *clink*. "To adventure." I took a long, bracing sip. The Vesper was intense—a cool, crystalline shock of fire that settled my nerves and made my blood fizz.

The dealer called for bets. James placed his chips on the banker. I put a large sum on the player.

"Still a risk-taker, I see," he winked.

"The odds are only one part of the equation, James. The secret is to trust your instincts."

The cards fell. I won the first hand, my pile of chips growing. Then the next. And the one after that. My luck was extraordinary, but it was more than the cards; it was the rare feeling of being completely in sync with the moment, the game, and the man across the table. I was winning more than money; I was winning back the woman I'd thought lost to the vines.

Finally, I swept my winnings into a large pile. "That's enough for one night."

He smiled, a glint of admiration in his eyes. "Thank goodness. I was beginning to worry I'd have to sign over my yacht to pay my debt."

I looked at the chips, then back at him, my pulse still humming from the win. "It seems only right that the victor provides the feast. I'm buying dinner, James."

He rose and offered his arm. "I'd be a fool to refuse a lady with such a hot hand. But this time, no piracy."

"No promises," I quipped, taking his arm. "I've been known to commandeer a ship myself if the company is good enough."

The casino's boisterous clamor faded to a distant hum as we were led to a quiet corner of the dining room. The air here was different, no longer buzzing with the frantic pulse of the tables, but thick with a decade of unspoken thoughts. We were seated in a secluded booth, the plush velvet cocooning us in a sudden, sharp intimacy.

The wine in my glass was a deep, bruised ruby. Candlelight

made James's eyes glint with warmth. The scent of roasted duck and wild herbs rose between us—a rich, earthy cloud. It should have grounded me, yet it acted like a heady vintage, leaving me remarkably light-headed.

James watched me, his gaze steady and kind. A nervous vulnerability crept in, cold and unfamiliar. I was used to being the woman in charge, the one who navigated storms and balanced ledgers, but the Commodore didn't need a "boss lady." The fear that this reunion was a fragile misunderstanding —one that would shatter the moment we spoke—tightened my chest.

I set my fork down. The silver made a dull *thud* against the linen.

"I have to confess something." My voice sounded brittle. "I wrote to you after the voyage. Three times. I never received a reply." The admission hung in the air, raw and aching. I watched his face for any flicker of falseness, any hint of a convenient excuse.

His eyes widened with genuine shock. "Letters? Lily, I never received any letters." He reached across the table and covered my hand with his—a powerful anchor. "I never knew. Truly. I wrote to you in Paris as well, but the envelope came back a month later. *Return to Sender*. I thought you'd changed your mind."

A wave of relief broke over me, so sudden it nearly brought tears. "Paris? Why Paris?"

"I used the address from your passport."

A jagged, crazy realization dawned. "My passport. That's it. I sold the Paris apartment years ago." The words flowed more easily, the pressure in my chest dissolving. "I live in Aÿ now, full-time. At the winery."

So, we hadn't been indifferent. We were simply two ships, lanterns lit, passing each other in a decade of fog. All those years I'd spent wondering why he'd stayed silent, he had been reaching for a door I'd already closed.

James smiled, a slow, understanding curve of his lips. "So you didn't change your mind." He ran his thumb gently across the back of my hand, a rhythmic, soothing heat.

I shook my head, not trusting myself to speak. I hadn't been mistaken, and neither had he. We had formed a connection on that ship that time and distance hadn't managed to dim.

Looking at him now, his face illuminated by the soft, flickering amber of the candle, I understood what I'd been missing. It wasn't a business to expand or a vintage to perfect. It was the absence of this—the easy, quiet intimacy.

The world narrowed down to the warmth of his skin against mine. I wasn't a famous name on a bottle or the keeper of a legacy. I was just Lily, finally stepping out of the fog.

James walked me back to my room, his hand brushing mine—a casual touch that sent a jolt of awareness through me. The hallway seemed impossibly long, the air humming with a question. At my door, he paused, his gaze deep and stormy.

"May I see you tomorrow?"

His voice held the silence captive. The crushing weight of my name and the iron of my duty felt suddenly distant, eclipsed by the terrifying reality of him. My palm pressed into the door's grain, seeking an anchor, but I could only feel the pulse of his presence behind me, drawing me back into his heat. To let go, to choose the thrill over the legacy, was a vertigo-inducing leap. He stayed patient, a steady anchor in the dark, giving me the space to fall.

My hand found the brass key. I slid it into the lock, the metal solid under my fingers. As the door swung open, a whisper of his cologne—sandalwood and salt air—filled my senses. It was the only answer I needed. I looked up at him, the man who had inexplicably found his way back to me.

My lips found his in a kiss that was bold, hungry, and long overdue. I pulled him across the threshold and shut the door. No more fog. No more world. Only desire.

35
EN FAIRE TOUT UN FROMAGE
TO MAKE A WHOLE CHEESE OUT OF IT

1973, Aÿ. This harvest has been a constant wrestle with a petulant sky, by turns sluggish, blazing, and torrential. Claire and I put our correspondence aside in the office to join the women at the sorting tables, a gesture of solidarity for the exhausted crew. The press house is thick with the sweet, feral scent of fermenting grapes. The air feels damp and close, smelling of sulfur and frustration. Electric lamps cast long, sickly yellow rectangles across the concrete floor.

Claire smiles at her husband, Claude, who wears heavy navy coveralls instead of his usual suit. As président, he shouldn't be in the muck, but a difficult harvest demands his presence. He's overseeing their son, Arnold, running the old Coquard press—a cantankerous, cast-iron monster.

A burst of expensive grey wool rips my attention from the tables. Christian strides in, an immaculate Parisian apparition. He signals to his sons, who are checking in truckloads of grapes on clipboards.

"Hard at work I see. Excellent, excellent." He waves both hands, all smiles.

I can't help but smile at the sunshine he brings to the barn, albeit misplaced.

"Good morning, *mes amis*! Lily! Claire, they've got you working in here too?" Christian nods to Claude and Arnold. "Another magnificent harvest for the House, eh?"

A deafening, splitting crack—like a cannonball through timber—shatters his cheer.

Christian's smile vanishes. The crew freezes. The immense central screw of the ancient press jerks sideways, and a massive, ragged fissure rips through the cast-iron drainage table at the base. Thick, reddish-pink juice begins to weep onto the concrete. It isn't just liquid; it is a year of sweat and prayer flowing toward the floor drains. The sound of it splashing against the stone is the sound of a fortune being poured away. Every second it sits, the must oxidizes, turning from vibrant rose to a bruised, useless brown.

The silence is heavier than the broken machine. My urge is to jump in and bark orders, but I hold back. This is Claude's floor.

Claude lunges toward the console, his face bleached of color. "Kill the motor! Kill it!"

The grinding stops.

"Arnold!" Claude grabs his son's arm, staring at the break. "Can you save it? Tell me you can repair it."

Arnold runs a grimy hand over the jagged fracture. "The drainage table is ripped clean through. But I'll try." He hesitates. "We clear the load, use the chain hoist to lift the cage, and weld a steel patch. But even working non-stop, we won't be pressing for two days."

Claude clutches to the flimsy lifeline. "Order the steel now."

Christian disappears into the phone on the wall. I hear the frantic *ting-clack* of the rotary. His voice carries through the receiver, sharp and urgent. "A press? A hydraulic press ... this afternoon?"

He strides back to me, his eyes glittering with success. "I just secured the new pneumatic press from Épernay. Delivery and installation by dusk. We need to clear this section immediately."

Claude advances on him, forcing Christian back against a stack of crates. "You flout my command? I gave the order for repair. I am the président! That machine is an expense we haven't squared!" He jabs a finger at Christian's chest. "You could sink this company with such a reckless move."

"We needed a new press years ago." Christian stabs a finger back. "And don't worry about the ledger; I just doubled the Cunard contract. It'll pay for the press and then some."

The two men stand face-to-face. The only other sound is the relentless *drip, drip, drip* of wasted juice. Marking time.

I stride toward the large open doors, signaling them to follow. We walk fifty yards into the vines in total silence, the squelch of the mud under our boots the only rhythm. Outside, the air is clear, the clusters of grapes glowing with an incandescent beauty.

"We're in a crisis. This is no time for this drama." I meet both their eyes. "The quality of this vintage and our financial health are at stake. You both share a devotion to Bollinger beyond measure, but you must respect the office. Claude is the président. He makes the final decision."

Christian begins an indignant sputter, his face flushed.

I cut him off. "What do you want to do, Claude?"

Claude is incandescent with rage, his coveralls soiled from endless hours of labor. He stares at Christian—the man who just publicly challenged his crown—then looks past me at the barn where his legacy is leaking onto the floor. I imagine him calculating the damage to his pride against the damage to the wine.

"Can you guarantee the Cunard contract will cover the full cost?"

Christian's face is tight. "Absolutely."

Claude takes a deep breath, the steam leaving his body, replaced by a cold, steely resolve. He gives a stiff, pained nod. "We need the new press. I'll have the crew make room."

Victory flashes through Christian's eyes. "Etienne! Xavier! Pull the trucks into the shade!"

Relief washes over me, cold and hollow, chased by a deep, abiding frustration. Claude has saved the vintage, but his dignity was the price. Christian has undercut the président and won, and the victory tastes of ash. They are the future of this house, yet they still don't know how to work together. And we're running out of time.

36

LE MALHEUR DES UNS FAIT LE BONHEUR DES AUTRES

ONE'S MISFORTUNE, ANOTHER'S GAIN

CHRISTMAS EVE, 1958, London. Outside of Courtroom Number One, carolers sang of "Peace on Earth," their voices an innocent contrast to the slaughter occurring within. France was fighting for its very lifeblood. *Bollinger et al. v. Costa Brava Wine Company*—a title that lacked the poetry of the vineyards, yet held the power to uproot them. We were here for one purpose: to stop these Spanish thieves who were systematically stealing our identity. They had the nerve to slap the name "Champagne" onto bottles of cheap, mass-produced Spanish fizz and flood the European markets with it. By doing so, they were robbing us of our name and our history. I intended to make them regret the breath they used to utter the word.

This was not a mere commercial dispute; it was a crusade to prevent the total decimation of our industry. If the courts allowed Spain to hijack our name, "Champagne" would cease to be a place of excellence and become a generic word for bubbles. It was a necessity to teach the world's imitators that our name is not a descriptor to be seized by any peasant with a corking machine.

The sheer audacity of it—trading on centuries of sacrifice and proprietary knowledge—ignited a cold, steady fury in my gut. If we lost, the legal floodgates would burst. Every country on earth would bottle its local swill and sell it under our banner, poisoning our reputation and draining our economy. The slow perfection of our blends, the specific chalk and clay of the Marne that gave our wines their soul—all of it would be rendered meaningless. It was the murder of a legacy by a thousand legal cuts.

The bare bulbs hanging from the high ceiling cast a sickly yellow pallor over the proceedings. The air was thick and stagnant, heavy with the stench of unwashed wool, sweat, and stale tobacco. Beside me, Mr. Keeling sat with a detached British composure that I found increasingly tiresome. One pays a barrister an exorbitant fee precisely to avoid the burden of his personality; I found his lack of fire nearly as offensive as the Spanish wine.

"Nervous, Madame Bollinger?"

"Concerned, Mr. Keeling. One is always concerned when the fate of a civilization is left in the hands of men who likely believe bubbles are a sign of carbonation rather than a gift from God."

Keeling offered a tight-lipped smile, his gaze fixed on his notes, his fountain pen poised like a weapon he didn't know how to wield. "A matter of principle, then. And we have a strong case."

"We have a factual case, Mr. Keeling. Whether these jurors have the soul to understand it is another matter." I turned my gaze to the jury—tradesmen, clerks, shopkeepers. I weighed them and found them wanting. They sat there in their off-the-rack suits, blinking at the mahogany. Asking them to judge the sanctity of the Marne was like asking a cobbler to assess a

Cartier necklace. They saw a bottle; they did not see the centuries of blood and chalk it took to fill it.

I leaned over to Keeling, letting my nerves run away with my mouth. "If this court allows Spain to sell their fizz under our name, I shall begin bottling the Thames and selling it as Holy Water. The fraud would be identical—and the water likely more palatable than what Costa Brava is peddling."

Keeling cleared his throat, a sound like dry parchment rustling in a drafty room. "Let us hope it doesn't come to that, Madame."

As he rose to speak, the legal machinery began to grind. His words turned our heritage into a leaden recitation of the Merchandise Marks Act. He hammered on about "geographical indications" and "trade descriptions," reducing the very lifeblood of France to a series of dry clauses. He spoke of law where he should have spoken of soul; he argued over labels when he should have been defending the very dirt of our vineyards. Watching him was like watching a man try to describe a sunset by reading a weather report.

The jurors' eyes glazed over. To them, this was a tedious squabble over a capital letter: *Champagne* versus *champagne*. They saw a word; I saw a border. They heard a legal technicality; I heard the death knell of my home. They didn't see the theft of a birthright, nor did they care that centuries of French history were being stripped for parts to decorate a cheap Spanish bottle.

When the judge finally dismissed them to deliberate, a cold sludge crept through my veins—a premonition of disaster that tasted like rust. I stood, refusing to show the tremor of dread that threatened my composure, and looked toward the exit. The Spanish contingent was already moving, whispering amongst themselves with a greasy sort of confidence.

The wait for the verdict was agonizing. The carolers had gone home, and the snow had turned to sleet—gray, biting, and smelling of wet soot. Finally, the door swung open. The jury filed back in, their faces grim, their eyes averted. The foreman, a portly man with a walrus mustache, cleared his throat.

"In the matter of *Bollinger et al. versus the Costa Brava Wine Company*, we find the defendant—Not guilty."

The verdict hung in the silence, suffocating. I had failed to protect Bollinger. The names of the fallen Houses looped through my mind like a eulogy: Krug, Roederer, Taittinger. I had promised them leadership; I had given them a funeral. To these jurors, the label was a detail, a mere dispute of trade. They saw a bottle of Spanish wine; they didn't see the bloodlines being erased.

The judge banged his gavel, the sound a final, crushing blow. "The jury has ruled that the description, while perhaps misleading, does not constitute a crime under the Merchandise Marks Act. Furthermore, the plaintiffs are hereby ordered to pay all court costs, including those of the defendant. The case is dismissed."

A cheer, raucous and triumphant, erupted from the Spanish representatives. To add insult to injury, we, the eleven grand champagne houses I represented, were now liable for the legal fees of the very thieves who sought to undermine us. The injustice of it crushed me like the old wine press squeezing the last drop from the grapes.

"Well, there you have it, Madame Bollinger." Keeling began gathering his papers with maddening British efficiency. "A disappointing setback, to be sure. We must now focus on the appeal, which will, of course, necessitate a substantial increase in my retainer—"

"This ... this is no setback, Mr. Keeling." My voice caught, a traitorous tremor in my throat. I pulled on my coat, my spine forcing itself into a rigid line. "It is a ... it is a travesty. It seems England's law cares more for a fraudulent label than for the integrity of history itself."

"I presented the legal facts with every professional competence, Madame. I did all that could be done with the legislation at hand." He gave a smug, tiny shake of his head.

My voice dropped to a lethal whisper to mask the shake in my hands. "Mr. Keeling, you treated the birthright of Champagne as a clerical error. You allowed a cheap lie to defeat the absolute truth, and you expect to be rewarded for the privilege. Your failure is as profound as your fee is obscene."

I did not wait for his answer. I turned my back and walked out.

The heavy doors swung shut, failing to muffle the laughter of the Spanish contingent. As I passed, their slicked-back grins cut like glass. My mind was already at the telegraph office, composing the eulogy for the Houses—the families who lived in the chalk dust of their own cellars. How do I tell them the world has declared our soul common property? That the soil under their fingernails is no longer theirs to name?

Pools of streetlamps illuminated the empty pavement. Ah, yes. It was Christmas. No taxis anywhere. The sleet turned into a biting, sideways rain that soaked through my wool coat in seconds. I wrapped my scarf tight, head down, fighting for every step toward the hotel. Each slip on the icy sidewalk sent a jolt of panic through me.

Ahead, a beacon. A small Catholic church, its heavy oak door propped open, spilling warm, golden light onto the wet stone. The swell of an organ—a powerful Christmas hymn—pulled me toward the threshold.

I slipped inside, finding a pew near the back. Hundreds of candles flickered in the sanctuary, their glow so unlike the sickly, institutional bulbs of the courtroom. The air was thick with pine and frankincense. As the choir began the "Gloria in Excelsis Deo," I let the loss crash over me—the faces of the families at Bollinger, Moët & Chandon, Clicquot, Krug. Names that had stood for centuries, now reduced to a list of losers on a law clerk's desk.

I put my head in my hands, bowed and silent, letting the sharp disappointment run through my veins until it was spent. But as the priest's rhythmic Latin filled the space, the despair began to shift. The organ music, voices and sacred incense were reminders: some things ... true things ... endured.

The *Champanoise* had outlasted two World Wars. We had baffled the Nazis at our cellar doors with false walls and hidden bottles. We would certainly not allow our heritage to be murdered by a Spanish counterfeiter and a dull British jury. They'd won a battle, but the war for the soul of Champagne was just beginning.

I rose from the pew. The cold knot in my stomach was gone, replaced by a clarity as sharp as crystal.

1960: The Chancery Division, High Court of Justice. The atmosphere was airless, heavy with dusty leather and cold parchment. I sat flanked by Robert-Jean de Vogüé and Victor Lanson, while behind us, the benches were crowded with the quiet, rigid presence of the other Houses—Krug, Chandon, Bollinger's cousins and rivals alike.

Their presence a mighty shield. Two years ago, we had stood in a drafty Magistrates' Court, gambling our future on a criminal jury. We had lost the bet because we tried to prove the Spanish were criminals. It was a mistake.

We'd changed our strategy, abandoning the criminal docks for the Chancery Division. We weren't here to talk about punishment; we were here to talk about ownership. By invoking the civil law of "Passing Off," we were asking the judge to acknowledge that Champagne wasn't a generic word —it was property. It belonged to us alone.

I watched the clock, my jaw tight. If we lost this injunction, our name would become a generic label for any cheap fizz, and the vineyards would wither. Closing my eyes, I reached for the feel of the *crayères* of Aÿ beneath my feet—I needed that grounding, if only in my mind.

Justice Danckwerts looked down from the bench. "On the face," he began, his voice gaining resonance, "the name 'Spanish Champagne' is meant to cash in on the reputation of Champagne. A more wicked piece of propaganda would be difficult to imagine. 'Spanish Champagne' patently and deceptively sets out to pass off the defendant's product."

Lanson's fingers dug into the wool of my sleeve—a silent grip of iron.

The injunction was granted. Costa Brava was restrained immediately. Every label was to be changed within forty-eight hours, without appeal.

The tension of two years exploded in a single, shuddering breath. The cold dread of 1958 vanished, replaced by a warmth that flooded my face. De Vogüé's grip tightened on my shoulder, not as a patron, but as a peer.

Mr. Wilberforce approached, tucking his papers into his briefcase with a look of quiet triumph. "A historic day, Madame Bollinger. I trust the result is to your satisfaction?"

I smoothed my gloves and stood, my spine unfurling. "More than satisfaction, Monsieur. Today, you didn't just win a case; you ensured that when the world reaches for Champagne, they are holding our history, not a lie." I looked at de Vogüé and the row of titans behind him. "But I believe we've all had quite enough legalese and hard chairs for one lifetime. Gentlemen, the Connaught has a cellar that has been waiting for our celebration. Shall we?"

I gathered my competitors—my friends—and we marched out together into the London dusk. United. Triumphant. A phalanx of twelve who had won for all the Houses of Champagne, big and small.

The wine cellar of the Connaught was a cathedral of cobwebs and iron-latticed bins, a subterranean sanctuary that smelled of damp earth and resting vintage. I'd bypassed the velvet-draped dining room for this—a long, candlelit table of dark oak set deep in the guts of the hotel, where the city's noise was muffled by six feet of brick and three centuries of history.

I sat at the head of the table. To my right sat Robert-Jean de Vogüé of Moët, and to my left, Victor Lanson. Further down, the candlelight caught the sharp features of Paul Krug and the aristocratic profile of Count Frederic Chandon. Mr. Wilberforce sat among us, looking like a man who had successfully negotiated a peace treaty between ancient kingdoms.

These were the men who usually fought me for every acre of vines and every bottle of export. But tonight, there were no rivals. We were the Twelve Houses, a guild forged in the fires of a two-year siege.

"To think," Krug's deep voice echoed off the arched ceiling. "We almost lost the name forever. If we hadn't pivoted, we would have settled for a mere label change and a fine in fifty-eight." He looked down the table at me, his glass unraised for a moment. "We owed it to the soil to be more stubborn."

The sommelier poured the Bollinger first. As the fine, persistent beads of light rose in my glass, the room fell into a respectful hush.

Robert-Jean stood, his tall frame casting a long shadow against the bins of Bordeaux and Port. "We've always called ourselves the *Grandes Marques*." His voice resonated in the cool air. "But tonight, we are the protectors of the Marne." He raised his glass toward me. "To Lily for leading the charge."

"*À votre santé!*" Crystal clinked like a toast of swords. These men—survivors of wars, German Occupation, and the slow grind of history—no longer saw Jacques's widow. They saw an equal.

I held my glass high, meeting their eyes one by one. "Here's to the fact that now our grandchildren will inherit a name that actually means something."

As they leaned in to clink my glass, I took a long, exquisite sip. The wine was cold, sharp, and brilliantly clear. The taste of ownership was absolute.

Champagne wasn't just a beverage anymore. It was a territory. And we were its sovereign rulers.

37
IL N'Y A PAS DE
ROSE SANS ÉPINES
THERE IS NO ROSE WITHOUT THORNS

1973, Bagnoles-de-l'Orne. The scent hits me the moment I step off the train—sharp pine and the cold, mineral breath of damp earth. For ten years, this week in Normandy has been my only act of subversion. No guilt, no responsibilities, no burdens. Just James.

But the platform is empty.

His daughter needed him in Somerset. Something about teenagers—a reasonable, domestic excuse that makes my blood run cold with jilted irritation. I'm seventy-three years old, yet my chest tightens with the petulance of a girl stood up at a dance. I've traveled all this way for a ritual he's allowed to be broken by the very real world we promised to leave behind.

I stand there, clutching my suitcase, realizing that without him, the silence of this town isn't a refuge. It's an insult.

I check into the Grand Hôtel, its grandeur a comfort to me. But the first day, I'm restless. The carefree nature of our meetings is now weighed down by thirty years of business, family duty, and the nagging certainty of aging.

The silence of my suite overlooking the lake amplifies my

regrets. I decide it's for the best that he isn't here; our lives are simply too complicated to indulge this fantasy any longer. If I can't change something that's over and done, I can move on.

By the time evening arrives, the old hunger for adventure wins out. Tonight, I crave the thrill of the tables. I trade my sensible attire for a daringly low-cut emerald-green gown—the color of my beloved vineyards. A touch of rouge, a dab of perfume, and the transformation is complete.

Making my way through the gilded halls, the Baccarat tables beckon. The green felt is a battlefield where fortunes are won and lost. The clatter of chips, the murmur of voices, the swirling tones of a lounge piano playing Bacharach—it all ignites a spark.

And there he is. My James.

My heart gives a sharp, breathless thump. His hair is a silver crown now, but his eyes still hold that same mischievous glint. He is a vintage that has only improved with age, a rare blend of sophistication and masculinity.

My voice, a silken whisper, cuts through the clatter of chips. "I believe we have a score to settle."

James looks up, a slow smile spreading across his face. "Are you sure you are up to the gamble?"

"Only if there's something worth winning." I slide into the chair, my leg brushing against his. A deliberate spark of electricity.

He inches closer, his scent a mix of sandalwood and expensive gin. "Care to raise the stakes, Lily darling?"

"Don't tempt me."

The game is a push-and-pull of veiled intentions. He plays

with a cool confidence, his movements precise. I counter with calculated boldness, my instincts honed to a razor's edge. As the night wears on, the crowd thins until we are the last two players remaining—a private performance under the watchful gaze of the croupier.

The tension tightens. James slides a mountain of plaques into the center. "Banco."

The air in the room seems to vanish. It's a challenge—an all-or-nothing move. I don't blink. I match his bet with a steady hand. The croupier deals the cards with agonizing slowness. James looks at his hand, his expression a mask of inscrutability.

I peel back the corner of my cards. A five and a four. A Natural Nine. I lay them down with a flourish. "Le Grand Tableau."

James meets my gaze with a gleam of pure admiration replacing his poker face. He pushes the massive stack of chips toward me. "Well played. You haven't lost your touch."

"Hopefully, neither have you." I let the victory lace my voice. "But I believe I've earned the right to name our next adventure."

He leans closer, his voice dropping to a low vibrato. "And what would that be?"

"A moonlit swim in the Grand Source." My lips brush his ear. "Did you know the waters hold a steady 24.3 degrees?"

He chuckles, the sound deep and resonant. "But did you know the Bagnoles waters are believed to give eternal life?"

I take his hand, kissing his knuckles while holding his gaze. "Why not give it a try?"

"Lead the way, Lily."

The Grand Source is a subterranean cathedral of steam and shadows. At this hour, the bathers have long since retreated, leaving the thermal waters to simmer in a silence broken only by the rhythmic drip of condensation.

I shed the emerald gown, letting it pool on the stone tiles like a discarded skin. Stepping into the water is a shock of a different kind—not the cold snap of the Marne, but a heavy, enveloping warmth that feels like returning to the womb. 24.3 degrees. The exact temperature of a life lived without armor.

James follows, his silhouette a silver-edged ghost in the moonlight filtering through the high clerestory windows. When he reaches me, the water between us shimmers, a liquid conductor for the electricity humming between us.

He doesn't say a word. Doesn't have to. He pulls me into the circle of his arms, the buoyancy of the spring water making us weightless, as if the gravity of our seventy-odd years has been suspended. My head rests in the hollow of his shoulder, the scent of the minerals mixing with the lingering sandalwood on his skin.

"Eternal life." I breathe the words against his neck.

"Is that what you want, Lily?" His voice is a low vibration, humming through his chest and into mine.

"I want tonight to last a century," I admit, the honesty of it startling. In the gilded halls at home, I am a matriarch, a titan of industry. Here, stripped bare and suspended in the dark pool, I am just a woman who's spent thirty years longing for a man she only sees here. Right here. Right now.

He lifts my chin, his thumb tracing the curve of my lip. The moonlight catches the water droplets on his lashes, making them sparkle. When he kisses me, it isn't the polite peck of occasional lovers. It is deep, restorative, and terrifyingly sure.

We drift there for hours, the steam rising around us like a veil, blurring the lines between the water and the air, between the past and the present. It is a Technicolor dream in shades of blue and silver. By the time we finally emerge, shivering slightly as the cool night air hits our damp skin, a shift has occurred. The rules haven't just been bent; they've been dissolved in the Grand Source.

We spend the next day together, savoring the tranquility of Bagnoles-de-l'Orne, but something has changed. Deepened. It's as if the world has been dialed into a sharper, more brilliant frequency. We wander deep into the forest, the air thick with damp pine and wild cyclamen, our steps muffled by moss and earth. I find myself reaching out to caress the line of his jaw, wondering—for the first time with real fear—how I ever manage to leave him.

Beside a running stream, we find a pristine ribbon of sand and spread our feast. I feed him grapes from the market, their skins snapping to reveal a cool, honeyed sweetness. The *Camembert de Normandie* is a molten, golden treasure. He slices into a *Pâté en Croûte*, the pastry crisp and the center rich with truffle and seasoned duck. We share it on torn pieces of a sourdough baguette, followed by a *Cidre Bouché*. The cider is cold and effervescent, hitting the back of my throat like drinking liquid starlight.

I lay back in his lap, the sunlight filtering through the canopy in shimmering coins of light. As he combs his fingers through my hair, he looks down, his expression searching.

"What is happening here, Lily? Why is today so different?"

"Because I thought you weren't coming." I pull him closer, my voice barely a whisper. "I realized I couldn't bear to be here without you. Then you appeared, and time started again."

The air vibrates with the impossible weight of that admission. His silence says it all; this doesn't fit his life, his family. But I needed him to know.

Without a word, James leans down, his arms surrounding me with a strength that defies the years. He lifts me as if I am the most precious thing he has ever held, carrying me back toward the hotel, to his room—Number 243. The Grand Suite, its name a tribute to the precise 24.3 degrees of the Grand Source spring where we were baptized the night before.

The world outside ceases to exist. There is only the heat of our skin, the scent of sandalwood, and the terrifying, beautiful realization that we aren't just indulging in a yearly ritual. We are creating a future I'm no longer willing to give up.

The next morning, I wake up in his suite. The windows offer a view of the lake, where the rising sun paints the glossy surface with an apricot glow.

The air in the room is sweet with the lingering scent of our intimacy. James lies beside me, his silver hair a halo against the crisp white sheets, a single, deep line etched between his brows. Not a young man, anymore, but a testament to the enduring allure of experience and sophistication. In his late seventies, I imagine, and I wonder with a sudden, sharp pang, how many mornings like this we will still share.

I slip out of bed, my feet finding the cool wood floor. Stepping onto the balcony, I gaze out at the breathtaking panorama, the world spread out before me like a tapestry woven from forest, sky, and steam rising from the thermal baths. A wave of contentment washes over me, a sense of peace that has eluded me.

But the blending of last fall's vintages begins next week, and it is crucial that I'm there to oversee it with Claude and Christian. They're waiting for me.

James joins me on the balcony, his arms encircling me from behind, his wool robe a comforting weight. "What are you thinking, Lily?" His lips brush the edge of my ear, sending a slow shiver down my neck.

"I'm thinking about ..." A sigh escapes my lips, hating to tell the truth. "I'm thinking about balancing the new vintage against the house's reserve wines, getting the pinot noir proportions exactly right, how much, if any, meunier and chardonnay to add acidity that extends the shelf life."

"Ah, the formidable Madame Bollinger returns." He leans down and kisses my shoulder.

"Somehow you make formidable sound like a compliment." I lean back into his chest, letting the warmth soak into my skin for a minute.

"It is," his voice soft. "And I love you for it. The woman who runs Bollinger is impressive. The woman who laughs here in Bagnoles is unforgettable. Don't let your label make you forget your laughter. Allow yourself these moments of indulgence."

Warmth washes through me. I turn to face him, my hands settling on the soft wool of his robe. "You always know exactly what to say." I smile, the familiar pang of duty tugging at my heart like a tight corset. "I know. But the blending will not wait."

He nods, his understanding gaze meeting mine. "I know."

The words are tinged with regret. "And I won't ask you to stay."

At the station, the morning air is sharp, smelling of wet slate and coal smoke. The familiar ache of duty settles into my marrow, a heavy, reliable corset. The blending will be a disaster without me, I tell myself. The pinot noir needs my palate, even if it doesn't want my heart. I have to be there.

But as the train pulls in—a great, iron beast hissing steam—the math of my seventy-three years begins to gnaw at me. The conductor, a man with a silver stopwatch and an air of bureaucratic finality, steps onto the platform. "Paris-Montparnasse boarding. Check your tickets, please."

I bolt toward the phone booth, my heels clicking a frantic rhythm on the tiles. My hand fumbles in my purse, a coin clinking against the glass. I dial the Grand Hôtel.

The operator transfers me to Suite 243. My heart is a drum in my ears. He answers, his voice thick with worry. "Lily? Are you alright? Did you miss the train?"

I see the conductor wave his green flag. "Not yet."

"Come back, Lily." His voice turns urgent and low. "They can do the blending without you."

A sudden, jagged breath hitches in my chest. I want to drop the suitcase. I want to run back through the streets of Bagnoles until I'm breathless in his arms. But I look at my hands—hands that have commanded an empire, hands that carry the weight of a name that must never fail.

"I can't." The word tastes like ash. "I am the only Bollinger left to pass this on, James. I've spent my life ensuring the house survives. I can't abandon it now. They aren't ready."

I hear his heavy sigh through the wire. "You're more than a label, Lily."

"Final boarding call!" The engine rumbles to life, steam escaping in a violent hiss.

"I'll call you when I reach Epernay." My voice breaks. "We'll find a way. We'll change the rules. A year is too long, James. I'm done with the starvation."

Silence stretches across the line. Then the train whistle screams, a sudden, violent blast that jolts the phone receiver against my ear.

"You better go."

"I'll call you soon." I hang up and run for the moving steps, my body vibrating with a cold, hollow adrenaline. The conductor grabs my hand to pull me aboard, yanking me back to reality.

I stand on the rear platform until the station is nothing but a grey speck swallowed by the forest. I am the formidable Madame Bollinger, heading home to command the vintage. I have secured the legacy; I have won the world. But as the tracks scream beneath me, the noise only hollows me out. I have never been more utterly alone.

38

DERRIÈRE L'HOMME, LA FEMME

BEHIND THE MAN, THE WOMAN

1968, LONDON. VINTNERS' Hall was a monument to English tradition, heavy with beeswax, old sherry, and expensive cigar smoke. The smells alone told a woman she didn't belong.

Christian was jubilant, his hand on my elbow. "Thanks for agreeing to come with me, Tante Lily. I wouldn't even be in the Wine & Spirits Benevolent Society without you taking a chance on me years ago." He tweaked my arm, his eyes sparking. "Besides, someone needs to make sure I don't make a complete fool of myself after a few glasses."

I was utterly conspicuous in my sapphire-blue Jacques Heim frock—a peacock among black and white penguins. Very expensive, very startled penguins. I'd navigated the hostile corridors of the trade for nearly thirty years, running Bollinger since the war, yet they still see only a widow. The caretaker. I tolerated their antiquated rituals for one reason: the Society's true purpose. Supporting the widows and the broken families was worth the velvet ropes.

LICENSE TO THRILL: LILY BOLLINGER

A flustered gentleman sputtered as we passed. "But ... but you're a ... a lady! We don't allow—"

"I confess to both charges, sir. I am a woman, and I am beyond the threshold. As for what's 'allowed,' it's really not my concern." I cut him off with a dazzling, dangerous smile.

Christian plucked a glass of Bollinger *Spécial Cuvée* off a tray and extended it to me. "Gentlemen, allow me to introduce my aunt, Madame Lily Bollinger. You see, she's quite literally the woman who keeps the champagne flowing."

Leslie Seyd, our sales agent, joined us with a twinkle in his eye. "Quite the spectacle, aren't we?"

"Tell me, Leslie. Is this the wine trade, or the island of lost boys? They look as if they've never seen a female who isn't holding a serving tray."

"Certainly not in these hallowed halls, Madame. I believe you've just caused several heart attacks."

"Leslie, do keep her out of trouble, won't you? I'm summoned for congratulations." Christian gave my arm a quick squeeze and was swept away by the throng.

Cyril Ray swiveled into view, conspicuous in a burgundy velvet jacket and ruffled shirt. My alarm bells clanged. Cyril: the most erudite egotist, infuriating, verbose, and, dammit, most-read wine writer in London. I will never forgive how he eviscerated me in *The Observer* so many years ago.

"Congratulations on your new book about Château Lafite-Rothschild. Most impressive."

"Thank you, Lily." Cyril purred like a starving lynx, already plotting. "Perhaps you'll revisit the idea of letting me write about Bollinger? I could give it the depth it deserves, a true academic dissection. Not that flimsy puff-piece one reads in the trade magazines."

"Bollinger's reputation speaks for itself, Cyril. It does not require cheap ink to sell another bottle."

The dinner bell tolled, a heavy, resounding bronze clang. Leslie guided me away from the scoundrel and up to the head table, but Cyril followed us, pointing at the place cards gleefully. "What wonderful luck! They seated you right next to me. Fate, perhaps, is telling us to collaborate."

The banquet unfolded in a haze of rich food, claret, and, thankfully, plenty of Bollinger. The men ate the inevitable Beef Wellington, that English concoction which prioritized tradition over taste. Cyril regaled me with endless academic anecdotes, blathering on about Dom Pérignon and the perfect curvature of a Sauternes bottle. The purpose of his relentless charm finally revealed: He was determined to write his book about Bollinger. Over my dead body.

"Now, Monsieur Ray." I poured him a glass of Bollinger *Spécial Cuvée*, its golden light catching the chandeliers. "This might just change your mind about the intellectual merits of a fine bubble. And I assure you, it contains far more history than Madame Pommery ever dreamt of."

He drained the glass instantly, his critical gaze softening only momentarily. "It's a magnificent wine, Lily. Robust. Complex. But is it your champagne or your history that made the society honor you tonight?"

My blood ran cold. I set my glass down before I toppled it. "What are you talking about, Cyril? I'm a guest. Christian is being inducted into the society."

"You really don't know?" He glanced at me over his half-spectacles and sighed. "My dear Madame Bollinger, the award isn't for him. It's for you."

My heart vaulted into my throat. I pressed a shaking palm flat against the silk of my dress. "No. That's not possible. But why? Why me?"

"Don't play the coquette, Lily. Leslie Seyd knows the press this will give Bollinger will be epic." He reached for his glass, and a splash of warm claret spread across the white tablecloth like a fresh wound.

Christian bent over me, whispering. "You look pale, Tante. Do you feel alright?"

"You nominated me?"

Christian's brow tangled in a knot. He kneeled beside me. "I admit I nominated you. But certainly not for publicity, Tante. I reminded the society that you helped found the CIVC; that you've funded the educational trusts for the *vignerons's* children for decades; that you guaranteed care for our retired *vignerons* and their widows; all while inventing the revolutionary concept of Recently Disgorged. You don't just lead Bollinger, Tante Lily; you serve as an example to the entire industry."

"The decision was unanimous." Cyril shrugged, wiping his jacket with a napkin. "And they chose me to—"

Confusion and disbelief whirled through my head. No, they wouldn't. But Cyril was already moving.

Cyril approached the podium, his unctuous theatricality amplified under the stage lights. "Gentlemen, and friends of the trade. I have a confession to make. A confession so dark, so profoundly unsuited to the mission of this Benevolent Society, that it may well see me banished from this hallowed hall and forced to drink, dare I say it, German riesling for the rest of my days."

Oh, the drama. He loved this. I steeled myself, ready to bolt, but Christian gestured fiercely for me to remain seated.

"You see, I once committed a cardinal sin. I put pen to paper and penned a—and I shall quote my exact words here—

'disappointingly robust review of Bollinger.' I know, I know. Barbaric! I was operating under the delusion that I was the final arbiter of taste, rather than merely an enthusiast with a typewriter and a slightly over-active liver."

A collective gasp tore through the room, followed by nervous, appreciative laughter. He dared to drag my dirty laundry onto this stage.

"But then, several months later, a second opportunity was granted. And the scales, gentlemen, fell from my eyes. I had judged the wine, but I had failed to see the woman." Cyril's playful demeanor vanished, his voice dropping to a sincere, resonant tone. "Tonight, we are here not just to honor an exquisite house of champagne, but the iron-willed woman who protected the very foundation of our community and craft. She did not just survive the war; she emerged from it with a profound understanding that the greatest asset is not in the cellar, but in the people who work the soil."

I gripped the edge of the table.

"And it is her heart that we honor tonight. This is the Benevolent Society, and Madame Bollinger is the very definition of the term. Long before it was fashionable, she secured the future of our oldest workers by guaranteeing permanent care for retired *vignerons* and their widows. And finally, we honor her for the relentless pursuit of perfection in the cellar. In 1961, she unveiled the revolutionary practice of Recently Disgorged, or R.D., fundamentally altering how we perceive and appreciate aged champagne."

Cyril gestured for me to rise. The spotlight swung, a blinding, theatrical white that turned the bubbles in my glass into shards of gold. I didn't move at first. I let the silence stretch, forcing the room to wait for the woman they had ignored for thirty years.

I rose. The rustle of my sapphire silk was the only sound in the expectant hush. As I walked toward the stage, I passed beneath the looming portraits of past Masters—stiff, powdered men in oil paint who had governed this hall for centuries. I didn't lower my gaze. I climbed the steps.

"Thank you. Thank you all, from the bottom of my heart, for this extraordinary honor. I must confess, when I first entered this hall, I worried I was about to violate every single bylaw written since 1886 and send the founding fathers spinning in their graves. But it's a tremendous relief to discover that some of you are finally ready to listen to the women in the room."

I waited for the ripple of shocked laughter to subside.

"I stand here tonight as the first woman to receive this award, but I am certainly not the first woman to lead a great house of champagne. I follow in the brilliant footsteps of the giants who built this trade—from Veuve Clicquot, who perfected the clarity of our wine, to Madame Pommery, who gave us the elegant taste of brut. They proved that a woman's touch is required in the deepest parts of the cellar. I wasn't the first, and I won't be the last."

My gaze swept across the room of vintners and tradesmen.

"Indeed, no great wine is made alone. The true artists of our craft are our *vignerons* and our brilliant cellarmen. And I share this distinction with the countless women of champagne who stood shoulder to shoulder with our men—and often, stood entirely alone when the men were called to duty. They are the quiet strength of the past and the guardians of the present. They are the ones who ran the ledgers, guarded the cellars, and tended the community when the bombs were falling."

I paused, thinking of the dark, cold cellars and the smell of fermenting hope.

"When I introduced Recently Disgorged in 1961, I was

told it was a gamble. I was told that the English palate wasn't ready for a wine of such intellectual intensity. But I knew the soil, I knew the lees, and I knew the strength of my own conviction. Innovation is not a masculine trait; it is a necessity of the craft. The accommodations provided to our devoted caretaking nuns, the guarantees made to our elderly cellarmen, and the funds for our children's education—these were not merely acts of business; they were acts of survival."

I took a final breath of the tobacco-scented air.

"So tonight, I thank you not just as colleagues, but as companions. This medal is for all of us, especially the women whose work has finally, and publicly, earned its place at this venerable high table."

The applause swelled, a rhythmic, thunderous roar. I stepped down from the stage, having said a thing or two to make them think about women as colleagues. I figured it was too much to ask for real change, but I certainly hoped I'd managed a dent in the wine bucket.

Cyril Ray was waiting for me at the bottom of the steps. He leaned in, his breath warm and smelling of claret. "I'll give you this, Lily, the Recently Disgorged vintage was a risk, a challenge to everything winemakers believe about aged wine. A calculated, arrogant move."

"Like your velvet jacket, Cyril? And like your review of the R.D., it simply proves your standards are too low for my ambitions."

He chuckled, a satisfied sound of two rivals sparring. "Let's just say we're both in the business of proving everyone else wrong. But today, hands down, you won the coup. You always were better at gambling."

"No, Cyril, I'm simply better at recognizing when the winning card has been played. And it's a Bollinger, of course."

Coup de grâce.

39
VIEILLES RACINES, NOUVELLES AILES
OLD ROOTS, NEW WINGS

Oct. 2, 1974, Aÿ. From my dressing table, I hear guests gathering in the courtyard for my birthday party. The joyous sound drifts through the open French doors—boisterous greetings and the rhythmic *smack* of *la bise*. I adjust the Lalique hair ornament, winking at me in the mirror. Seventy-five years is a long time to walk this earth; to have my people gathered to celebrate fills my heart to brimming. Is it a conceit to have planned my own party five years in advance? If so, it is mine, and I'll drink a toast to it.

Tonight marks the unveiling of my crowning vintage: the *Vieilles Vignes Françaises*. The bottles are chilling in ice buckets, reaching the precise temperature for their debut.

I lean over to smell the lilies from my well-wishers—fragrant and intoxicating. Among the blooms, I spy the small, wrapped gift from James. I can't resist; I tear the paper to reveal a brilliant blue box. My fingers tremble as I lift the lid. Resting on a bed of chartreuse moss is a heavy metal key. The leather fob is embossed with a number: 243. The Grand Hôtel des Thermes.

LICENSE TO THRILL: LILY BOLLINGER

Suddenly, the party noise fades. I am back at the Grand Hôtel, suspended in a shimmering lake fringed by deep forest. The air is soft with steam and the scent of damp earth. The only light is the massive, silent moon hanging directly above us. Our laughter echoes off the rock walls. The cool night air rushes over my shoulders, and the rich, mineral warmth envelops the rest of me.

I look up. Moonlight glistens on James's wet skin. We float, suspended between the moon and the water. The struggle, the war, the years of cold fear ... they vanish. The promise of time without end and the depth of his gaze merge into one. "Lead the way, Lily." His voice resonates in my heart, more real than the guests downstairs.

The first notes of the band rise from the courtyard, calling me to the party. It is a spirited swing—a quintet led by a clarinet that mimics the effervescence of a freshly poured glass. I turn back to the bed, the brass key catching a glint of light as I lay it on my pillow.

I drape a sable stole over my shoulders to ward off the autumnal bite. Stepping through the French doors, the October chill nips at my cheeks and raises a tingle across my skin. The air is heady, thick with the fermented perfume of the harvest—a brisk, clean evening that practically demands a crowd and a steady flow of blanc de noirs. I lift the hem of my gown, a floor-length sheath of cobalt silk that shimmers in the fading light. My only jewelry is the pearls Jacques gave me. They rest in a double strand above my heart—a steady, guiding weight that never leaves me.

The Bollinger courtyard below is a living tapestry of gold and cobalt. The sun, dipping low, bleeds into the limestone walls until they glow like honey. Strands of tiny bulbs pulse like captive stars against the deepening sky. Each table is a shimmering island of luxury, set with heirloom silver and heavy, snow-white linens. Thousands of individual rose petals are scattered between the settings, glowing under the light of massive crystal chandeliers hung from the garden oaks. The refraction is blinding—a dizzying, fractured kaleidoscope of light bouncing off a thousand flutes, promising a night that will never be repeated.

I scan the faces of those I chose to share this night with me—the House owners who stood shoulder-to-shoulder with me through the war, and later, shielded the very soul of Champagne from thieves. My sisters and nephews, with their wives and a new generation of children, laugh alongside treasured workers who have spent their lives in the cellars and vineyards. I see the women who helped me sustain the convent and the schools, and the families we sheltered while the bombs fell.

Near the center of the swirl, my niece Claire moves with effortless grace. She is the engine of the evening, just as she is the engine of the office, directing the staff with the same sharp precision she uses to weave the social fabric of the Bollinger name. My loyal sales agents raise glasses with Cyril Ray, keeping their promise to keep him occupied. This is my birthday after all, and I want to enjoy it.

They are all here—everyone who has earned a place in my history.

Except James.

The one person purposely excluded to keep the focus on the Bollinger legacy. It was the right decision, of course. No one knows of him; for all they know, he does not exist. And yet, looking at the joy below, his absence is a loud, echoing silence.

A clarinet soars, casting a joyous melody through the cooling air. I take a breath, feel the silk swirl around my ankles, and descend the stone steps. The sound of conversation swells and then breaks like a wave as heads turn. The courtyard erupts in a symphony of cheers and the rhythmic thunder of palms meeting—a warm surge of celebration that chases away the chill of the evening.

Claire moves toward me, the microphone a silver glint in her hand. I take it, and the courtyard falls into a respectful hush.

"Friends, family, and the colleagues who have become both—welcome. Seventy-five years is a milestone of time, certainly. But standing here, looking at the history gathered in this courtyard, I see that the true milestone is the company I keep."

I nod to Claire. Instantly, her team moves through the crowd, the amber-gold of the vintage catching the light of the torches as they pour.

"You are about to taste the *Vieilles Vignes Françaises*. This wine is the culmination of my lifetime's work, yes—but it is not mine alone." My hand sweeps toward the dark silhouette of the stone-walled vineyards. "These vines are survivors. They endured the Great Plague that ravaged our region when all other vines withered. They are a testament to an indomitable spirit—the same spirit required to weather any storm, be it war, loss, or time itself."

I accept a glass from Claire, the bubbles dancing against the crystal.

"We cultivate these vines using *provignage*—the ancient method of burying the old vine to birth the new. It is the vineyard's most profound lesson: we must honor the deep roots, and the faith Jacques planted decades ago, but we must always reach for new vitality."

My voice warms as I catch the eyes of those at the front. "I see that vitality in our next generation—in Claude, in Christian, and in Claire, who orchestrated the magnificence of this evening."

I raise my glass, the cobalt silk of my sleeve falling back.

"Tonight, we celebrate the roots of Bollinger, born of this very ground, and the enduring strength of the generation that follows. To the *Vieilles Vignes Françaises*! To the past, the present, and the future—rooted forever in the heart of this Maison!"

Cheers erupt, and a fierce, sudden wave of emotion hits me. My life, the struggle, the years of solitary responsibility, all condense into this perfect, glorious moment. The ache of mortality is there, yes, but eclipsed by the deep, quiet satisfaction of a race finished, a torch successfully passed.

I take my seat at the head table. The arrangement is deliberate; I am flanked by the retired hearts of this House: Andre Delage, the cellarman; Paul Lenoir, the vineyard worker; and Yvonne and Marie, who have been with me since the first harvest. These are the deep roots of Bollinger.

As dinner service begins, I lift my glass. The *Vieilles Vignes Françaises* catches the light, a deep, liquid gold. The aroma is immense—warm brioche and baked apple, followed by a profound whisper of smoke and honey. I finally take a sip. The texture is velvet, the mousse fine and silken, before it gives way to a concentrated complexity of citrus and cold mineral.

Beside me, Andre breathes a heavy sigh of contentment. "The depth, Madame. It has the soul of the old roots."

Paul raises his glass in a quiet salute. "Magnificent. It tastes like Aÿ. It tastes like history."

The courtyard air fills with a sudden, electric hum as the first sips are taken. Fragments of discovery drift toward me through the candlelight.

"A concentration you simply cannot find anymore," a prominent vintner exclaims to his party.

Nearby, a renowned collector leans into his neighbor, his voice a fierce, hushed urgency. "A masterpiece. A museum piece in a glass."

LICENSE TO THRILL: LILY BOLLINGER

The wine is already a legend.

Dinner is nearly finished when the music fades to a sudden, expectant silence. Claude walks to the microphone. He stands straighter than I have ever seen him, surveying the crowd with a quiet, burgeoning authority that makes my heart swell.

"Friends, it is my great honor to introduce the Préfet of the Marne, who has journeyed from Paris this evening on behalf of the Republic."

I freeze, my fork hovering over the plate. A préfet? Here? My eyes snap to the figure emerging from the shadows of the stone archway.

He is the very image of the French State: clad in a dark, high-collared ceremonial uniform, the silver oak leaf embroidery on his sleeves and cap glinting under the chandeliers like sparks of ice. He carries a leather-bound folder with the gold-embossed seal of France, moving with a stiff, practiced dignity that makes the festivities feel suddenly, startlingly small.

A new hush descends—a vacuum of sound so absolute I can hear the torches hissing. The préfet steps forward, his boot heels clicking against the limestone in sharp, metered strikes. The sound is an echo of a different time, one that halts the breath in my throat. His voice is resonant and commanding as he begins the formal decree.

"The French Republic recognizes the decades of singular and solitary command demonstrated by Madame Bollinger," he proclaims.

I look down at my hands, feeling the weight of the word *solitary*. He speaks of it as a virtue; I remember it as a burden—

the silence of an empty house at midnight, the crushing gravity of being the final word.

"Her unwavering dedication throughout the Occupation, providing aid to the Allies and standing defiant for France, stands as a testament defining an entire era for our nation."

The words are monumental, fit for a history book, yet they feel strangely disconnected from the cold fear and the sheer grit of the decades spent fighting for this House. He speaks of "defiance" as a noble concept; I remember it as the sour smell of damp cellars and the rhythmic crunch of jackboots on the gravel.

"Furthermore, for her tireless, decades-long fight in courts across Europe and America to secure the protected right to the name Champagne ... and for her crucial efforts in securing the prestige of French commerce abroad."

The préfet pauses, his gaze locking onto mine. He makes a small, sharp gesture with his white-gloved hand, inviting me to rise.

I stand, my spine a rigid line against the weight of the cobalt silk. My breath hitches. A government honor? Now, after all these years? Behind me, Andre's hand grips the back of my chair. That silent, rough-skinned pressure is my anchor, a reminder that I am still the woman who walked the muddy rows with him in the rain.

The courtyard falls into a vacuum of silence. The préfet's voice rings out, carrying across the rows of tables.

"It is for this unparalleled service, for an unflagging spirit that has become a beacon for the Republic, that we honor Madame Bollinger with the *Ordre National du Mérite* and acknowledge the title she has truly earned: The Grand Dame of Champagne."

The courtyard gasps. It's a sharp, sudden catch of breath from hundreds of people that holds for a heartbeat before the sound erupts. Then comes the roar—a wave of cheering from the House owners and the workers so loud that the crystal flute on the table in front of me vibrates.

The préfet leans forward. The crisp white of his gloves blinding as he lifts the heavy medal and drapes it around my neck. The silver-gilt medallion is a sudden, biting chill against my skin—a cold piece of history pressing against the warmth of my dress.

The Grand Dame. The title sounds far too formal and boastfully pretentious, but as I look at the faces of my family, the absurdity of it vanishes. It feels surprisingly light. Claude pulls me into a brief, fierce hug, grinning with the proudest smile I've ever seen on him, then holds out the microphone.

"Thank you."

My voice carries across the stones, and the courtyard falls silent. "I accept these honors, but I do so on behalf of all of you." I stand taller, throwing back my shoulders, and find Cyril Ray's table. I offer the reporter a wide, mischievous smile.

"A certain writer for the *Observer* once asked me when the proper time is to enjoy Champagne. I want to leave you with my answer—a credo I have lived by, and perhaps the secret to a long and beautiful life."

I let the silence hang, catching the eye of every guest.

"I only drink Champagne when I'm happy ... and when I'm sad. Sometimes I drink it when I'm alone. When I have company, I consider it obligatory. I trifle with it if I am not hungry and drink it when I am. Otherwise, I never touch it."

I shrug, a flash of pure mischief in my eyes. "Unless I'm thirsty!"

The response is a riot. Christian and Claude are the first to their feet, cheering. The guests rise in a deafening wave of happiness, the sound of five hundred voices overwhelming and glorious.

The band revs up, their bossa nova swinging into a lively rhythm, and the courtyard is swallowed by dancers, carried away on the effervescent beauty of the starry night.

Cyril Ray begins to move toward me, but I have no need to indulge him. I slip through the press of bodies, making a beeline for the house. I round the corner to the back terrace, where the music becomes a distant, muffled hum.

The air here is still, smelling of cold earth. As I gaze at the moonlit vineyards undulating toward the horizon, they seem to pull me into a farewell embrace. My work is etched into those slopes. The Grande Dame of Champagne has laid her final vintage to rest.

But Lily has more to do.

Upstairs, in the quiet of my room, the party is nothing more than a vibration beneath my feet. I retrieve the brass key from my pillow and tuck it into my handbag. I pack for the Grand Hôtel, Room 243.

The next chapter awaits.

AFTERWORD

The Enduring Legacy of Madame Bollinger
For the next two years after her seventy-fifth birthday, Lily remained the matriarch and moral compass of the house. Though she delegated daily operations, her influence was absolute. She remained the ultimate authority on blending and quality control, ensuring that her rigorous standard that demanded "quality first" was non-negotiable.

But Lily was always more than a guardian; she was a revolutionary. It was during her later years that her boldest visions took flight. In 1967, at the age of sixty-eight, she launched Bollinger R.D. (*Récemment Dégorgé*), a brilliant and innovative concept that transformed the industry by releasing exceptional vintage wines aged for an extended time on the lees, but disgorged just before shipping for peak freshness. Her final, rarest masterpiece, *Vieilles Vignes Françaises* (Old French Vines), followed, launching in 1974—the year of her seventy-fifth birthday celebration. This wine is made from only three tiny, ungrafted plots that remain free of the phylloxera louse. Its

AFTERWORD

profound concentration is a result of ancient, labor-intensive techniques such as planting *en foule* (in crowd) and the layering method of *provignage*, in which a cane from an existing vine is buried to grow new roots. This bottling quickly became one of the world's most sought-after and expensive champagnes, commanding a price of $1,500 per bottle.

When Lily Bollinger was asked on what occasions she drank Champagne, she delivered the immortal reply that perfectly captured her spirit:

"I drink Champagne when I'm happy and when I'm sad. Sometimes I drink it when I'm alone. When I have company, I consider it obligatory. I trifle with it if I'm not hungry and drink it when I am. Otherwise, I never touch it—unless I'm thirsty."

Élisabeth Law de Lauriston-Boubers Bollinger passed away peacefully in 1977, in the residence she cherished, surrounded by the vineyards she had so fiercely protected. Her death marked the end of an era, but the non-negotiable pursuit of excellence continues to define the house of Bollinger.

The Next Vintage

The seamless transition of power she orchestrated was a triumph, ensuring the house would remain fiercely independent and family-owned.

Upon Lily's retirement from management in 1971, the immediate leadership was entrusted to her nephew by marriage, Claude d'Hautefeuille, who served as président until 1978. Claude acted as the steady hand, the uncompromising guardian of the house's signature style. Working alongside him was his wife, Claire d'Hautefeuille, Lily's niece, who, as a direct family descendant, contributed vital technical oversight, ensuring quality control in the vineyards and cellars remained unimpeachable.

AFTERWORD

Claude d'Hautefeuille passed the presidency to Lily's blood nephew, Christian Bizot, who took the helm in 1978. Christian proved to be the visionary successor, serving as the charismatic face of the brand for the next sixteen years and enshrining Lily's philosophy for the future by establishing the Bollinger Charter of Ethics and Quality in 1992.

This trio—Claude, Claire, and Christian—proved that the spirit of Bollinger was not reliant on a single, powerful figure, but was woven into the very fabric of the family's shared stewardship. They collectively inherited the house's mandate: to sustain its independence and its unwavering devotion to terroir. The tradition of family leadership continued seamlessly into the twenty-first century.

The Global Ambassador

Christian Bizot's ascendancy to the presidency of Champagne Bollinger in 1978 marked a dynamic new chapter for the house. Christian became the chief global ambassador of Bollinger. He understood that the house's uncompromising quality needed to be communicated personally and globally, and he traveled tirelessly, evangelizing the brand's unique spirit with a charm and wit reminiscent of his aunt's, yet entirely his own. This highly visible role was instrumental in expanding Bollinger's prestige and market share worldwide.

Bizot's most enduring legacy was cementing the partnership with the James Bond films. The relationship started with a mutual friendship with producer Albert R. "Cubby" Broccoli. Recognizing the perfect alignment between 007's impeccable taste and Bollinger's peerless quality, Bizot ensured the house was the secret agent's exclusive champagne choice, transforming a film prop into an iconic, lasting symbol of luxury and adventure.

In 1992, Bizot formalized his philosophy by publishing the

AFTERWORD

renowned Bollinger Charter of Ethics and Quality. This unprecedented document enshrined the house's non-negotiable standards—from vinification in oak barrels to rigorous aging requirements—confirming that Bollinger's independence and quality were matters of corporate principle.

Christian Bizot retired in 1994, passing the présidential torch to Ghislain de Montgolfier, a trusted professional connected to the family by marriage. This strategic stability ensured that Christian's own son, Étienne Bizot, could rise through the ranks based on merit, eventually succeeding Montgolfier in 2008.

Today, Étienne serves as the chairman and CEO of the entire Société Jacques Bollinger group, a fitting tribute to Jacques Bollinger and the legacy Lily spent her entire life preserving. Étienne stands as the sixth generation of the family to guide the company, balancing fierce quality control with strategic growth, thereby completing the lineage of leadership the Bollinger family has worked so hard to preserve.

Cyril Ray

Cyril Ray's 1971 book, *Bollinger: The Story of a Champagne*, served as a deeply personal tribute that forged a lasting bond with the legendary proprietor, Madame Lily Bollinger. This connection, rooted in mutual respect, survived Ray's characteristically sharp pen. His intimate access allowed him to describe Lily candidly as "dour," "humorless," and deliberately conservative in business, preferring traditional methods due to her cautious approach to decisions. Yet, this unflinching honesty—which highlighted her formidable, unsmiling focus on quality over frivolity—confirmed their relationship transcended a simple author-subject arrangement.

The publication of the Bollinger book became the high watermark of Ray's career as a specialist wine writer. It

AFTERWORD

achieved highly respected commercial success within its niche; its authoritative yet approachable style transformed him from a general journalist into a revered chronicler of luxury houses.

The book's success led to commissions for similar, definitive histories of other elite producers, including the Bordeaux First Growths, Château Lafite, and Château Mouton Rothschild. The work remains a classic of wine literature, cementing Ray's reputation and celebrating his direct, witty style that demystified the world of fine champagne.

Cyril Ray continued his prolific writing career until his death in 1991, with the Bollinger book remaining his most celebrated contribution.

Commodore James McCullough: The Inspiration

Commodore James McCullough is a fictional character, created because every woman deserves her very own "James!" The character was inspired primarily by the history of one extraordinary officer: Commodore Sir James Bisset.

Bisset's fifty-year career defined the history of the sea, spanning from square-rigged sailing ships to the giants of the steam age. His earliest claim to fame was serving as Second Officer aboard the RMS *Carpathia* during the rescue of the *Titanic* survivors in 1912.

His command during the Second World War was nothing short of heroic. As commodore of the Cunard White Star Line (1944–47), he steered the great liners, nicknamed the "Grey Ghosts," on sixty-six wartime voyages. He famously commanded the *Queen Elizabeth* as a troopship, relying on her speed to outrun German U-boats while carrying vast numbers of Allied soldiers. For this indispensable service, he was recognized with a CBE (1942) and a Knighthood (1945).

Sir James then commanded the *Queen Elizabeth* on her maiden commercial voyage in October 1946. He retired in

AFTERWORD

1947 at the mandatory age of sixty-three and spent his final years documenting his extraordinary life in his autobiography, *Commodore*. Sir James died in 1967 in Bournemouth, UK, leaving a legacy as a true hero who safely delivered the Allied victory.

ABOUT THE AUTHOR

Rebecca Rosenberg is a triple-gold award-winning author, lavender farmer, champagne geek, champagne tour guide, and cocktail creator for Breathless Wines. She is the moderator of Breathless Bubbles & Books and American Historical Novels.

Rebecca writes novels about history's real-life women of substance who made an indelible mark on the world. Her novels have garnered many awards, including IBPA, IPPY, and starred Publisher Weekly reviews for her novels, SILVER ECHOES (2025), MADAME POMMERY (2023), *CHAMPAGNE WIDOWS* (2022), *THE SECRET LIFE OF*

MRS. LONDON (Lake Union 2018), and *GOLD DIGGER, The Remarkable Baby Doe Tabor* (Lion Heart 2019).

Sign up for her Bubbles and Backstory Blog at www.rebecca-rosenberg.com